A LIFE IN BOOKS: A SELECTION OF SHORT STORIES, PROSE
PIECES & ESSAYS

By the same author

*What's Been Did (And What's Been Hid) Volume I:*
*Beginnings to the end of the Surf era: 1956-1963*

*What's Been Did (And What's Been Hid): Volume II:*
*Beat boom to blues pop: 1964-1969*

*What's Been Did (And What's Been Hid: Volume III:*
*Album Rock To Glam Rock 1970-1976 (Part 1)*

*What's Been Did (And What's Been Hid: Volume III:*
*Album Rock To Glam Rock 1970-1976 (Part 2)*

# A LIFE IN BOOKS: A SELECTION OF SHORT STORIES, PROSE PIECES & ESSAYS

(an accidental memoir of sorts)

## MICHAEL GEORGE SMITH

The Rupert Press

Body type: Times New Roman
Cover artwork: Mark Alston/Design Heroes
Cover photos: My own, a bit of my library


ISBN:
Paperback: 978-0-6483804-3-6

"And there are stories (it was explained) that consist of such slender means it's a wonder they can be called stories at all." *Eucalyptus*, Murray Bail

"The world as we know it is in the last resort the words through which we imagine and name it." *The Only Speaker of his Tongue*, from David Malouf's short story collection *Antipodes*.

"Only connect" – E.M. Forster

"The poet is a 'rememberer' and it is a part of his business to keep open the lines of communication. One obvious way of doing this is by handing on such fragmented bits of our own inheritance as we have ourselves received." *Epoch and Artists: Selected Writings*, David Jones

This book is dedicated to

My English teacher in 5D, Elizabeth High School, 1969, Mrs Lola Brown (1933-2021)

My UNSW lecturer/tutor for my MA in English Literature, 1980, James Michael Allen

And my most important inspiration, my father, William Oliver Smith (1911-1991)

# CONTENTS

"A birth is not really a beginning. Our lives at the start are not really our own but only the continuation of someone else's story."
*The Thirteenth Tale*, Dianne Setterfield,

# HOW I GOT HERE

There it was. I'd *done* it. I'd written the most complete, the most perfect expression of what I'd been trying to say all this time, exactly what I'd always known had to be said, the defining moment, *my* defining moment. I was breathless, my mind aglow, the smile in my heart endless. Of course I knew it had to be embedded somehow in a longer piece. In a way I knew it was a secret that the reader would have to work at to discover, but that was okay. The story seemed to naturally spread out around it. My excitement knew no bounds. I just had to share it. My tutor was reading it. It was so important that he saw it, that he understood, that in his moment of discovering it, those perfect few lines, the defining moment would be complete and he would see it all, everything, as clearly and powerfully as I had in writing it. The tension within me grew ever more powerful. I'd finally done it and here it was, as long as there were minds and hearts to see it.

That's the power of dreams. For quite a while after I woke, I couldn't be sure that I *hadn't* actually written those few lines of blinding clarity, that surely it was real, lines I'd just left somewhere amidst the tumuli of papers piled around my ever-expanding, over-full library, that perhaps I actually *had* sent it off and somehow it had slipped between the cracks of some editor's indifference. After all, I was sure now that I'd dreamed this exact same dream before. But no, it *was* just a dream and whatever those lines had made so clear remain, like so much else in life and art, shimmeringly intangible, just out of reach; that perfect paragraph towards which I've striven all these years, as elusive, as ephemeral as that dream.

To be honest I suppose that in one way or another I've been trying to explain who I am all my life. Not that I was fully conscious of this fact, or that this has been among the primary driving forces impelling me towards wherever my life has taken me.

There's a nice phrase in the introduction to Douglas

1

Dunn's 1991 book, *Scotland: An Anthology* – "lost to everyday spokenness". Dunn is talking about the suppression of the Scots language but it's a phrase that nonetheless seems to speak to my own experience. My entire writing and reading experience, my understanding of the worlds with which I attempt to engage mentally, spiritually, even emotionally has been steeped in the English language. Yet the first fifteen years of my life were spent in a little Greek village insulated from the *English* reality within which that village existed – initially Islington, London, and then, via Becontree in Dagenham, Elizabeth West in South Australia. We spoke Greek at home – my first language – even my Londoner father, William Oliver Smith, born August 22, 1911. For a man who'd left school at the age of 11, he had a real facility for languages, or at least for those of the lands through which he'd travelled during the Second World War and its immediate aftermath – first Arabic as his regiment of Royal Engineers followed the Allied push across North Africa, then Greek when he was stationed on Rhodes, the largest of the Dodecanesian islands. It was on Rhodes that he met my mother, Eleftheria Lavisianos, born October 30, 1925 and where his basic working Arabic proved very useful. Her mother, my Greek grandmother, had been born in Alexandria in Egypt and understood enough Arabic for my father to work his charms in order to get to know my mum! And he later learned enough Hebrew to read some of the Torah in the original during his post-WWII time in Palestine trying to keep Arabs and Israelis from shooting each other –both sides shot at him instead!

He was a "Teacher without Portfolio" as it were, gave us our letters and numbers, reading and writing, before we got to school. We loved him and we were happy.

Of course outside the home he and we three children, myself and my two sisters, spoke English, lived as other English kids lived, but we were always bound to, constrained by, the reality of that little Greek village to which we returned every day. The power of that village had become irrevocably assured once my father brought my mother's unmarried older sister over from Rhodes on the arrival of my youngest sister to help lighten the load of coping with three children under five. His hope was she'd eventually meet a nice Greek chap, marry him and let his young family get on with it once we children were off to school. Not only did she never marry but my aunt was still there with us when the family migrated to Australia, and she outlived both my father and mother – so the village remained inviolate for the years until my mother's death.

My dad did once invite a Greek chap he'd got to know on the building site home. That was back in London, but he never visited again, and that was that. He merely provided more ammunition to the sisters' gossiping between themselves, gossip filled with the fears and superstitions, the prejudices and enmities of their home village transported into our tiny flat in Islington. Conniving and exacerbating the fear, my mother was riven with shame; shame at abandoning her mother, shame at the fact that she had jumped the "marriage" queue ahead of her older sister. Shame would become her principal sometimes coruscating weapon in trying to control an "ungrateful" son.

In those first few years of course there was no perception of any difference between inside and outside, the village and the actual world in which my sisters and I were growing up. It was all one and seemed as natural as breathing. The dissonance between one and the other only became problematic when we children began to interact with other children at school. It was a slow, subtle process but as we grew into our individual consciousnesses, our mother would detect subtle changes in our behaviour that she inevitably perceived as due to the evil influences outside the "village". As we kids experienced more and more of that "scary" outside world, that *English* world, the dissonances became greater and more traumatic – for our mother and, unconsciously, for us. The only way to deal with those intensifying dissonances was to keep our dual lives as separate as possible. School friends never visited, we never visited school friends, a situation that, of course, became more and more impossible to sustain as we got older, became our own little individual selves and began to flex our increasingly sought after "independence" muscles. The upshot was that we lived double lives – I for one learned to keep my thoughts and experiences in either world more and more to myself. At home I lived more and more inside myself, while outside I got shyer and shyer, unsure how to connect, even though I might seem fairly gregarious, if in an aloof sort of way. I suppose I was clinically two personalities, slipping from one to the other all too easily; a skill that ultimately did not serve me well at all. But that's another story.

The tragedy in all this is that none of it was anyone's fault. Imagine being a young woman who has already lived through war, seen family members killed in the village square, experienced the hunger, the violence, the fear, the trauma of Germany/Italy's war and *then* of civil war, and then leaving all you've ever known to live in a place like post-WWII London, filled with thousands of people none of whom speak your language, and who lived by customs and traditions totally alien to those that had held your community together through all those horrors back in the village. Imagine finally arriving in this alien place to marry a man you love but barely really know and finding yourself in a place that is as war-ravaged and poverty-stricken as the village you left behind, only on a much, much bigger scale. Imagine discovering that this was no imagined "wealthy" England, nothing like the ideal your mother had pushed to embrace. The house next door is a bomb site, those across the road bomb sites. This is a cold, dark, damp land. Within herself, my mother was as fearful as a child, suspicious of the intentions of all around her, torn between loving this man and hating him for taking her away from all she knew and loved.

There was no question about her love for my father, or for we children, but alone in this new world, she also blamed him for all that fear, the stress, the anxiety. Why would the man she loved put her through this? There was no one to talk to about it and so it was internalised. At least when her sister joined us in London she had someone who understood, though the truth was that that sister was just as traumatised by the world into which she had come as her little sister. The easiest way to get through it all was for the sisters to withdraw, to double down and keep the outside world outside and try to recreate as much of the village as they could within the four walls of the home my father worked so hard to provide his little family.

So, as I've suggested, as soon as we began to become little individual human beings, we three children found ourselves having to navigate between these two worlds – though there was also another, beaming out at us from the flickering black and white images on the television – just the one channel, the BBC – which quickly gave us kids another sort of reality that didn't involve parents, though we all shared it with them, father, mother, aunt as well. Again, as we children grew and learned more about the outside *English* world, the disparities and absurdities of our mother and aunt's perceptions of what they thought they saw happening on that TV became more and more apparent. After all, lacking English, the only things by which they could understand what they were watching was to relate the behaviours, mannerisms, looks, to whatever might make sense against their own experiences – usually tinged with all their concomitant fears, suspicions and prejudices, though they *did* laugh too, at the more obvious, accessible slapstick elements of some of whatever we were watching. As we children grew up, it became more and more difficult to explain what was *actually* going on in those shows – our Greek vocabulary, or perhaps it was only mine, wasn't really up to it – so we stopped trying, and watched in silence. As I grew up, when I wasn't trying to over-explain myself, my default mode increasingly became silence. It was just easier that way. It kept the peace. Regardless, we loved our mum, and we were happy.

And it also became more and more difficult to explain ourselves to them. I certainly found it more and more difficult. At least my sisters had each other, and they shared their gender with my mother and aunt. My behaviour gradually grew so far beyond their understanding of what a good little Greek boy should be that it was easier to withdraw into myself at home, which somehow made it harder to "step out" again when I was at school.

Then, in my fourth year of high school, I somehow got an acoustic guitar. Words I didn't have the confidence to use out loud or didn't have anyway were replaced by another language – music. Not that I was particularly articulate in this new language – there was no one to teach me so I just noodled away picking out notes that matched those I could hear in the songs I was hearing on the radio. Nonetheless, I'd found a new voice that gradually gave me confidence, though I still continued to try and explain myself in words, inevitably trying too hard, over-explaining despite not really knowing who I might be and just making the dissonance even worse. Through my guitar, slowly, gradually, I could weep, I could scream, I could shout out my anger and my joy. Or at least that's how it evolved eventually; just not on guitar. Without any real guidance however, my guitar playing got worse and worse, compounding my innate lack of confidence. Finding the bass guitar saved my life – in fact it literally gave me my life. And wouldn't you know it, my innate need to explain myself translated into playing more and more notes! It's funny how it all worked. And there I go over-thinking things again.

My first attempts at "creative" writing, unstintingly supported by my English teacher in the final year of high school, were the usual clumsy efforts at poetry, while my other classes gradually succumbed to my acoustic guitar as it began to dominate, even playing in class, ensuring that every subject but English would suffer. I barely scraped into university. Thank goodness I *did* get to university. Once there, I knew it was where I needed to be. Yet even there, I never really *connected*. There were a couple of friends, just as there had been at school – my dearest friend there Andrew Jones, at university Andrew Cawthorne – but then I was also becoming a musician, wasn't I? Study and band practice – two lives – and then home a third, which became more and more claustrophobic. While I coasted through studies, the bands became home, and with each band break up, I experienced a little more trauma. How I ever managed to keep going from band to band I'll never know but I did; more by accident than design. That's pretty much how my life has worked out, a series of accidents, mostly good, some quietly devastating, small gratifying successes and increasingly less debilitating rejections – like all lives, so I can't complain. I still over-play, still over-explain.

So I was launched into the world without any real idea as to how it worked. Talk about wide-eyed and clueless!

The first short story I ever completed is lost. Written while I was touring with the band Scandal – 1976 through 1978 – that got me out of both the village and Elizabeth, it was prompted by a visit from an old friend from high school, a surprise since we hadn't necessarily been that close but very welcome nonetheless, and the feeling it left in me afterwards. Years later when I was reading the almost impenetrable Henry James novel *The Golden Bowl*, I realised that the way in which I'd written that first, lost story was just as impenetrable – over-thought, over-wrought, hiding as much as it attempted to express. I gave the manuscript to one of our roadies who was leaving us to return to Adelaide, assured that he would get it typed up, and I never saw him or the manuscript again. Which is probably a good thing, but it also might be where that recurring dream began. I'll never know. And I'll probably never write that perfect paragraph that explains everything either, though I suppose I'll continue to try. For me, my writing, at least the "creative" stuff, still all comes back to trying to catch that transitory moment, that perfect distillation of words that will make sense of it all.

There's a nice observation English writer Jonathan Coe makes in an essay/memoir titled *Diary of an Obsession* written about his relationship with the Billy Wilder film, *The Private Life of Sherlock Holmes*, included in a collection of his short stories even slimmer than the one you hold in your hands – just three, along with this essay titled *9th & 13th* – published by

Penguin in 2005: "lost time, lost opportunities, the rapidity with which events recede into the past and can never be recaptured." (p.50) That pretty much sums up the thinking behind what little fiction and prose pieces are contained in this little volume.

These days, I can barely recover more than a handful of phrases in, literally, my mother tongue, the Greek that dominated my first 25 years, oddly about the same as the rudimentary French that occasionally seeps up from three clumsy years of high school. The intent to rediscover it is there but the spines of the half-dozen books on conversational Greek in my library remain uncracked. I had to smile when I read this observation by Robert Dessaix in his 2004 book, *Twilight of Love: Travels with Turgenev*: "According to the Greeks in the fifth century BC, civilisation was first and foremost about speaking Greek, not babbling away in some outlandish foreign tongue, such as Persian." I guess I've long since slipped away into my father's version of "Persian babbling".

As to that other somehow innate language, music, that allowed me to frolic across stages with like minds for five decades and led to parallel careers in writing and music, the opportunities have faded away, it too remains untutored. I also guess I've played my last gig. Yes, there are "jam sessions" in which I could participate, but my other innate attribute, diffidence, has now re-established itself ever more firmly, so instead I sit before my screen quietly chipping at this edifice of my own creation, my histories of Australian rock and pop – somehow I've actually sold a couple of dozen copies across its four volumes to date! – while the occasional idea erupts and coalesces into a piece I think might connect, some of which are included here, and goes on to elicit a brief ripple of rejections from those few journals still courteous enough to acknowledge their receipt.

What follows, then, is those short stories I have managed to finish, some of them published, along with fragments that might have led somewhere, pretty much all previously unpublished, along with a few essays, pieces of

8

literary criticism and reviews, theatrical, cinematic and literary, presented for the most part in some sort of chronological order of "creation", at least within their respective sections, so perhaps it presents a picture of my development as a writer and thinker – or not as the case may be. The way life panned out, the fiction, such as it is, inevitably gave way to the music journalism, in part because my imagination turned out to be fairly limited, and, more to the point, because the music journalism sort of paid regularly though never lucratively – I was never the "cool" guy in that business either – until my accidental ascension into a full-time position as a "Contributing Editor" on a Sydney-based weekly music, arts and entertainment magazine stabilised that income stream for a couple of decades. Thankfully I wasn't expected to actually do any editing! I never really got the hang of "schmoozing", in university, in journalistic or literary circles or even in the music business; more often than not I'd scuttle off home at the first opportunity, much to the detriment of all of the above "careers". At least I can still write. Whether anyone cares to read or publish what I write is a moot point. I've left the music journalism to my Australian rock and pop histories, published under the blanket title *What's Been Did (And What's Been Hid)*. Still I hope there's something of worth within these pages that you might enjoy; that's all any of us can hope for.

There is still so much to read, so much more to learn and to try to understand – so very much already forgotten – and perhaps still a little I can contribute to the conversation. Wish me luck.

Striding, as for some reason I tend to when I'm walking alone, down the High Street the other day heading for the news agents, an old dear – look who's talking! – walking up the other way took a look at me and said, "Well, you look happy."

I guess I am, I really am.

Katoomba, NSW November 2023

# STORIES & PROSE PIECES

# AVENUE OF REMEMBRANCE, BALLARAT

Rising out of the night, stark in headlights, the trees straighten up, swaying slightly, silent sentinels slumbering at attention.

As the dead men who gave these trees purpose.

Heedless, the bright blank-eyed cars skim past, each with its payload of eyes, intent on the rushing, receding black that, just as suddenly, reclaims itself in the wake of their packets of light, fragile as the unseen leaves.

Or perhaps the eyes are merely nodding in drowsy recognition of the flickering, rushing shadows, the trees.

I look out and see the ghosts standing fast, oblivious of the blinding headlights droning past, lit up for one incandescent moment brief as those lives so freely given for a place in these winding wooden rows. But *living* wood. So much more aesthetic than those anonymous white crosses. They make the long flat monotony of road so much more picturesque.

I have seen them in the light, mere trees again, each tagged with an individual green metal plate, like so many exhibits in the Botanical Gardens. Only these names, some now obscured with the patina of time, are not in Latin.

But just as dead.

Some trees have faded, never really fitting into the Scheme of Things. Some have fallen, themselves victim to a later, more ominous conflict. They have joined the unsung road toll of nature. Those that are left no longer seem so very far behind. Survivors huddled silent by the road, each in their allotted trench, parallel snakes, distance-fixed, keeping their ranks as if by some stony obligation. They stand and await the whim of the next highway project to brush them aside, these fading hopes raised against the War To End All Wars.

Now they merely shiver, uncomprehending, with the progress of each lumbering juggernaut. The trees too are preparing for the final going down of the sun.

13

## "THE BLACK"

She sits in the bus shelter squinting along the quivering black ribbon of bitumen, grumpily searching out the bus. A little apart from her along the bench, a woman fretfully pushes a stroller, her baby noisily dribbling back and forth. The old woman looks strange to the young mother. She feels a little uncomfortable near her. She is impatient for the bus. It will ease the tension. Barely noticing the young woman, the old one sits silent, her chubby fingers pushing at a gold band. It is very hot.

The shelter, four slabs of prefabricated concrete spattered haphazardly with stones – the "natural look" – sits precariously functional by the roadside. It does not give much relief. It does not stop the wind. It seems out of place here, in this flat land. There is a hot Northerly coming down from the Centre, funnelled down unimpeded along the Flinders Ranges, blustery and relentless. It whips hot in fitful spasms into their faces as they sit. Overhead an oppressive sun glares down, unremitting in a dazzle of translucent blue sky. There always seems to be more sky here. The air is thick with the weight of it. It seems inescapable.

The hills behind them are low, the land before flat, formless, covered in low red-brick houses mindlessly repeating themselves into the distance. The wheat fields are slipping quietly under fresh outcrops of suburban sprawl. There is a hiss of sprinklers.

From beneath her scarf, a stream of sweat discovers a path among the deep-carved creases of the old woman's face and trickles downward. She is having difficulty breathing in this heat. She is wearing the black; scarf, jumper, blouse, skirt, shoes and stockings, all black, clinging oppressively to her old body. She, resigned, stubbornly clings to them. It is the way. All her days now wear the same cloth; will do so because they must. It has always been so. It is witness to her meaning.

A memory flickers into mind. Seems all now is memory, or simply habit. The days merely pass as background;

15

cluttering trivialities. Costa had always hated the black. He would say of the old women of home who surrendered unquestioning that they were already dead, mere wizened kernels wrapped in funereal mantles of memory. They showed no care for life. They wore their black like stigmata, cocoons of silent faith in eternal bondage. They seemed almost malevolent in the intensity of their self-imposed confines, malicious and gossiping, as if resentful of living; of the living. Costa was for living. The old ways only stifled. He would have a new life far from these calcified shells of blackness that seemed to deny life. He would educate himself and leave behind the old ways. In Australia, he would say, life could be different. There were no old ways and no demands on the living by the dead. There all were for life – new ways and a new start. They could *be* somebody. The world was changing. He would have his family change with it.

There had been many in black after the war. So many. The women, the young with the old, who were left slowly, inevitably, moving towards their dead. So it must be. It had always been so. Change had come and taken away their centres. Now, there were only husks of black.

He had even made a fuss when she had gone into black for her mother, her now long dead, long unseen mother. She had died in the village in which she had been born, had never left, would never leave. Her daughter had not seen her die. She felt cheated. She felt guilty for having let her die so far away, her death unshared. Costa said he was sorry but she was old and must die sometime. He had respected her (had really half feared the old woman, sternly in black even then, when he had first asked for her daughter's hand, so long ago), had cared about the old woman for his wife's sake. But he would not have the black. It made him uncomfortable.

The daughter had wept for months, had wept often since; would suddenly stop doing her chores and sob uncontrollably to herself. Her husband could seem so heartless. She was afraid for him, his disrespect was almost blasphemous.

Her mother had died, unseen, so very far away. She must be mourned properly, as was her right, could he not see? It was always so, had always been so.

But then he was her husband. The wife had taken off the black after a few months, had clung to it long enough for decency, still black inside. For Costa's sake. Now she was in black again. Had been for five years. Would be till death. For Costa. No one, nothing could change that. There could be no more changing now.

The old woman takes her handkerchief and wipes the sweat from her eyes. Everything around is very bright, the glare almost unbearable. Her old eyes blink quickly. Near her, the young mother, grumpy, wipes her fretful child's face. She sees the mother turn her face towards her. The old woman quickly looks away. She does not want to talk. There is no one to talk to now.

The bus appears out of the haze, seeming to float out of a shimmering pool hovering indistinct above the middle distance of the road. Black smoke coughs from its side as it lurches down through gears towards them. The bright blue- and white-painted body gives a deceptive promise of relief. Inside, the heat is just as stifling.

The bus squeals to a halt and concertina-doors slap back mechanically. The driver takes the old woman's fare as he watches the young mother fussily lift her baby from the collapsing stroller. As an afterthought, he steps out of his seat to help. The old woman shuffles along the aisle to a vacant seat a little apart from the other passengers and lowers herself heavily into the faded red vinyl seat. It is burning hot. She squirms about to get comfortable.

\*\*\*

She clambers uncertainly onto the donkey and laughs, animal as she mounts, then leads it forward a few paces. She radiant. She is becoming a woman. Costa holds the head of the

17

sways precariously and giggles nervously at her feat. Costa reaches up a firm, olive-skinned arm and steadies her. They are to be married.

Above them, clinging to the dusty track that climbs quickly into the bare-boned mountains, the village seems to laugh with her. The village is only small, maybe thirty houses all told, with the golden dome of a small white church crouching a little apart, farther up the track. This land is full of churches. It wears its faith conspicuously. The main town of the island is a dozen miles away, just along the coast. The island is not very large.

Some friends stand about, joking with Costa and his betrothed and the old donkey. From dark windows piercing the smooth, bleach-white face of a nearby house, a couple of young women, brown hair falling into soft brown eyes, lean forward to see and to laugh. They laugh at their little sister, so fragile, perched on the donkey. There is no mocking in their laughter. They laugh with her. Below them, an old woman in the doorway looks on, frowning. It is not decent. Costa is laughing. He knows he has the daughter's heart and he is happy with love and youth and confidence. The mother looks on at the couple, resigned and wrapped in black. She knows that she is overshadowed now, but she also knows she is not displaced, can never be replaced. A mother has the right. Still she frowns. Her husband has been dead some months.

All the buildings are white, bleached, as if they are mere natural extensions of the bare white rock that insinuates itself through the thin soil. The bones of this country jut out everywhere. It is an old country, as old as Time. Perhaps Time began with it, a child of the bargain made between Sun and Earth, when Sun and Earth were still gods in this land. Now merely sun and earth. Perhaps. Occasional red-tiled roofs casually break up the mass of white all around, like speckles of blood on chalk. Everything here seems to exist as if by some immortal, immutable habit, instilling it with an inspirent, unconscious ease. There is the comfortability born of timelessness, of having always been.

The sun has known this land long. The great arc of blue overhead, flecked with tissues of white filament as though the air has lightly broken off pieces of some distant mountain top, seems to reach down, protective of its ancient lover. So long have these two caressed, sun and earth, that, like the lazy Cavefish, secure in its cavern darkness, the land has slowly slipped off its mantle of earth to receive the familiar sun. There is no longer need for covering, for the blushing discretion of young lovers, no need for the screen of soil, grass or trees. The cloak of mortal clay slips slowly off, unheeded, into the soft warmth of surrounding sea. Earth lies in supine indifference secure in blue water. She will die with the sun. That is their contract, made before Time. They are in harmony.

The land is poor, trees tenaciously clinging to the thin soil. The people accept its poverty, assured by a consoling Church that that trust will be rewarded, their trust consolation. They will always be poor but there is always just enough to eat. That is all they expect. There is none of the aspiration of the past, when men of this land led the world. The Lord provides and the people are humble.

It is hot; a light, moist heat. There is a breeze mounting from the sea. The sea is never very far away. Islands pierce the sky-blue reflection of sea as silently as clouds. Sky, sea, land and sun have long ago made their peace. They are as one. The doors of the houses seem to heave a sigh of relief as they open to the breeze. Silver fingers ripple through the deep green of olive trees and there is a smell of blossom. The land seems asleep, has slept a thousand years, becoming a single, static frame of light and white. Only the half-forgotten ruins scattered amongst docile flocks of sheep attest to any former interest in the world. The land no longer seems to care, content to slumber in the warm, secure sun, lulled by the soft rolling swish of windmills. Its time has passed.

Far off, on the mainland and beyond, another war is beginning. The face of Europe is changing again, convulsing in reaction to the speed of change. The island is still peaceful. It will not escape the force of change. The signs are already there, come to the island as the Romans had, as the Turks had done after them. The island would survive, as it had always survived. It would be poorer still.

The men are joking with Costa. They are friends or they are relatives. Everyone is a friend or a relative in the village. Except perhaps the old man, Stanopoulos. He is from Kythera, another island further to the east. He is the wealthiest man in the village, perhaps the whole island, and a recluse. He wants no friends. They cost money. He is accepted, butt of cruel jokes about his miserliness. No Greek will have another Greek for his master. Still, he is harmless. He keeps to himself.

There is another newcomer, a schoolmaster from the mainland. He is a Communist and would prepare the island for the fight to come, for the "Liberation". The elders of the village distrust him. They do not like his talk against the King and the Church. Especially the Church. But some, the younger men, they listen, gather in the night in the little classroom and whisper. They would be Patriots, would fight for their land.

In the main town, Italian soldiers have arrived. Not many, but some. To "protect" the island. The teacher must now teach Italian in the school. Mussolini, a would-be Roman Emperor, has ordered it. The old men resent the Italians as they resent all outsiders. Yet they silently put up with them. At least they are not Turks. There are still Turks in Greece, but they are no longer masters. They keep to themselves. The Italians will be thrown out in their turn.

So the young ones are learning from the Italians. They are learning that the world has left them behind. They hear stories of new ways, the new politics and tales of war in a place called Eritrea, rumours of incredible atrocities, of barbarians. They want the Italians out, but they will listen to the stories. And they bring money to the island. Some of the young women find them handsome. The island seems to be awakening from a long, deep sleep. More young men are gathering at night, in secret, with the schoolmaster.

Perched on the donkey, she takes no notice of the world. It is far away and it is near, in this young man, Costa, and in her family. The world may be changing but right now there is love and there is laughter. The donkey is getting grumpy and is refusing to move. The game is over. Costa reaches up and lowers Irini from the animal's back. He is a proud man, proud of his love, of his strength and proud to be Greek. He is ambitious. He would give his bride more than this simple village life. He is a reader, wants perhaps to go one day to the mainland to study. He has seen films of life in America. He dreams of leaving the poverty of the village.

She thinks only of him, the man who will be her husband. As it was meant to be. She had always been his, had been since they were children. Time and God would make them one. He would be somebody in the village and she would be his proud wife. Dust rises around the donkey's grey legs. Small white clouds.

*****

The bus is noisy and uncomfortable. The seats feel clammy with sweat. Even with the windows open, the bus seems stifling, the wind's hot breath pushing into the old woman's face without the slightest indication of any relief. It is almost spiteful in its incessance. Still, she thinks, better open than closed. It is so dry. She looks silently out of the window at the passing houses.

Some dust is being spun up into filmy red fronds in the haze of paddocks that lie behind the houses. The houses here are all red; red bricks, red tiles, as red as the earth, all almost identical as they sit in their segregated little squares. The sun has already burnt away most of last winter's lawns in an apparent wilful denial of fruitfulness – the sun's age-old promise. Instead, the sprinklers slap impotent across red mud as yellowing survivors of lawn tenaciously grip the spreading red dirt by

21

spindly tendrils of drying roots.

The sun has always been here. The land is stark and uncomfortable, burnt a dusty ochre. There has never been any giving, sun to earth, the sun a cruel master to the struggling earth, dust-smothered. Life is merely tolerated. The sun's fire has scourged this land through ten thousand, twenty thousand and more years till even the trees seem more red than green, leaves, a mass of dried-out dun khaki, seem held up in supplication by long, bony, flaking fingers that split out of long, gaunt white arms. The sun disregards the gift and stares on, oblivious, unflinching, unforgiving. It hangs, that sun, in the unblinking eye of sky, fierce and crackling. Even the air seems to jangle with the tension, flicking about in hot rushes away from the light, quivering into melting distances that turn into illusory water. Cicadas, hidden, drone into the night. The wind is shaking the drooping heads of the trees. They seem tired of the effort of rising up. There are little explosions of bright crimson fire splashed through the trees like so many drops of paint, flowers with spine-like petals couched in hard brown nuts, tightly gripping a hopeful future of trees. There is a dust haze hanging on the horizon. Perhaps there will be a dust storm. That might at least break this awful heat. Most probably not.

Some believe that there are no gods in this land. There are old ones who know who are hidden away to die. The young ones deny the tales, vague superstitions… or so they would have you believe. The gods, if they ever existed, were long ago bulldozed under supermarket carparks. The old woman knows nothing of the old ways of this land. She does not want to know. She only knows her own land, only wants to know her own ways. There is nothing here, for her.

The baby has decided it has had enough and erupts in a violent wail of frustration. It rages against a universe it does not comprehend, that will not pay attention and stop this annoying heat. The universe begins to rock the baby jerkily, irritable. Mother Universe herself has also had enough without having to put up with this. The old woman thinks the young one a bad mother.

Two women across the aisle complain to themselves about the heat, droning into each other's faces. It's all these rockets, they upset the atmosphere. The old woman only vaguely comprehends their chatter, suspicious that it might be about her. "You must learn to speak English now, girl," Costa had prodded. "You are in a new land now and you must learn to speak its language."

"I am born Greek and I shall die a Greek," she had said, eyes flashing defiance. Stubborn, she stared into Costa's thick moustache. He still wore it as they did on the island, never really becoming the cosmopolitan he thought he could be. "And so you will be always a Greek, as I am and always will be," he assured her. "But we are in Australia now and so we must live by the ways of these people, become one with them. The old ways are behind us now. We must become Australians and begin again."

He too had learned, from the Italians, then the Germans, and finally from the Allies that Greece had been left behind, that because it had forgotten the world, the world had rushed in and tried to take it for itself – for Italy, for Germany – as the Turks had done centuries before. He was too proud to accept any foreign master, had been in the Resistance. But he was also too proud to be left behind. He wanted a better life for his wife, for his family, than any a poor, worn-out Greece could give. His brother had gone to America and wrote to him of his two cars. He knew nothing of Australia, except that some parts had vineyards and a climate like Greece. He knew a little of vines from his father's piece of land. And it might be easier to get established in Australia. America was so expensive. His brother's letters told him so. In Australia he might start a new life that would be more than a little cottage with a few goats and these old ways, the women in black. He would have more than that for his family. His sons (he would have sons) would have a future, away from the dying and the poverty. There was so much poverty now the war was done. So many had died of hunger, not just bullets and bombs.

23

She *had* tried to learn English, had tried for Costa. She could speak well enough. She could talk to shopkeepers, the baker. Maybe occasionally the neighbour, about their children. No respect, not like Greek children. No need to speak to anyone else. They had no opinions that could interest her. She only half comprehended now, had never grasped the abstractions. There was no more use for her now half-forgotten English. No need to speak at all really since Costa had died. Only now and then, on the special days, when she would make the trek to the City by train to go to the church. And then, to be honest, she only spoke Greek, as she recited the old prayers lighting a candle for Costa. She kept to herself even then. There was no one there of her island. That made a difference.

Truth be told Costa had never really been able to adjust either, though he had worked hard. His English was too heavily accented and though there were none of the old ways of his old land here, there were ways that pushed him aside from the people he had thought would welcome him. There was prejudice in the land as deep as his own against Turks, or Germans, only now *he* was the minority. There were no other Greeks in the factory in which he worked or the suburb in which he lived. With no papers he could never really do much more than factory work and there were the children to feed. They had a small bungalow, just like all the others around the suburb, and he kept a couple of goats in the paddock behind it. Once arrived, he had neither the money nor the knowledge to get to the vineyards. He had a vine in his garden, and a few vegetables and fruit trees which kept him busy. But it wasn't what he had expected. The land was hot and dry. It didn't seem to care at all. There were some friends at work but no one close. His sons – yes, they'd had sons – had English friends, Australian friends. They eventually followed *their* ways. He felt left behind, but could not change. He followed the ways he knew. He never really felt Australian.

She did not really like her neighbours. They did not seem decent. They were not Christians, not Orthodox. She mistrusted them.

They thought her strange; more so now, a little black beetle of a woman.

She still had relatives in Greece. They were poor. They wrote when they had something to say and she would reply, wishing she could find the money to go home. The letters were fewer since her mother had died. She would probably never see her island before she herself died. She would often cry to herself over this. She would die far from home, without a witness, like her mother. And now no Costa. Her sons lived interstate, had lives and wives of their own. They loved her and would visit occasionally, but they resented her in little ways and were glad to get back to their own lives. They had become Australians, their friends outweighing the pressure to be good Greek sons. She was sad that they seemed so ashamed of their origins. Away from her, they were proud of her. She tended to smother them. They would have liked one day to send her back to her island. They knew that it was what she wanted. But they also knew that she would never leave their father. And he was here. He was finally part of Australia. It all seemed a little sad, but that was their mother – a mind of her own.

The sun flashes a hundred little suns around her, piercingly bright in the chrome of bus seats, passing cars and windows. The reflections make her eyes water. The black bitumen seems to grow soft. In the distance it dissolves altogether into the shimmering mirage that hovers above the road. An illusion of cool relief. The sun often plays tricks with this land, taking away by an abundance of giving. There is smoke rising far off in the Ranges. The old woman wishes for the relief of a cool breeze off the sea. The rims of her eyes are red.

\*\*\*

The taverna is full of people. The room is singing and shouting as the men drink mastika. The young men are dancing, intense, concentrating on the subtleties of their steps, their arms outstretched like wings, fingers snapping, feet stamping out the rhythm of the bouzoukia. The old men shout out approval or instructions on the right way to do it. They smoke Turkish tobacco, thick and aromatic, as they sip from their glasses. The village is gathered to celebrate the wedding of Costa to Irini.

The war is still far off. Soon it will overwhelm everything.

The church had seemed bathed in gold, a warm comfortable yellowness of light drifting down from the stained glass portraits of Christ and various saints who clustered into the windows above as if for a better look. The gold and silver inlays of the icons winked reflected suns into the whispers of smoky incense that seemed to carry with them the prayers and songs of generations, mingled with the droning of the small dark man perched in a box to the left of the couple, reading catechisms from a heavily jewelled book before him. Long white candles, held by children, were festooned with white ribbons. The priest was dressed in a heavily embroidered cassock, with a great silver crucifix nestled beneath his full beard. It is all in the traditional manner. Even the smallest church in Greece has treasures. The people give what they can ill afford and the church displays their faith in opulence.

Irini wears the crown of white blossom in her thick, brown hair, tied by a fragile cord of ribbon and flowers to the crown nestled incongruously in Costa's black hair. His face is very serious, his moustache waxed in the old way, his high, stiff collar cutting into the painfully close-shaved pink of his neck. The couple kneel before the altar as the priest chants over them in heavy, luxurious tones. His voice is soothing, lost in his beard. Irini is blissful.

The stern faces of the host admiring in the windows seem to have softened. A trick of the light. She looks at Costa, this stranger she has known all her life. She is giving herself to him now, before God, for life, for love. He seems different, but he is the same. He is ambitious. He is her husband, to love and obey, till death.

Her name is Irini. It means Peace. It is more. She carries his name now. A new beginning. The wife of Costa. He will *be* somebody.

***

Her old brown eyes blink, watery, beneath the black cowl of scarf drawn tight over the old woman's hair. She takes the handkerchief clenched in her hand and wipes the moisture from her eyes. The hair, barely visible beneath the scarf, is steel-grey, not yet white. Her face is deeply creased, with the beginnings of a web of smaller connecting creases that will soon become a permanent veil across the once young face. There is still some resilience in the skin, struggling against inevitable collapse. She is merely a shrivelled kernel of a self, what remains when the substance is removed. Costa had always wanted life to go on after death, hated the denial of life in those left behind. He could never see, could never understand the secret candle, always alight, the old women carried about in their black. Now she bears his death, defiant of the ways around her, proud of the witness she bears so conspicuously in the perpetuity of black. It is her sign that her love is eternal. That Costa lives on. It has always been the way. It is as it should be.

Her eyes lower to scan the hands crossed in her lap. They are chubby and arthritic, covered in the blotches of years in a hot, unyielding sun. Her skin is olive, distinctly Mediterranean. The simple rings of her undying marriage are wedged firmly in the flesh of her fingers. They have never left her hand. They will go with her to dust.

The bus lurches to a halt and she lifts her heavy black form from the sticky seat and shuffles down the aisle. She feels a little nauseous from the diesel fumes and the suffocating heat. She has never got used to buses, any more than to the heat, this different, dry, harsh heat.

The shopping centre is all concrete and glass and plastic.

People mill about in groups or in silence to the overhead piped music. She bustles about her business quite alone. She knows a few faces, but no one to whom she has anything to say. She keeps to herself. Her people are gone from here. Even her sons. As if already dead. As if *she* were already dead.

"Why did we come here, so very far away? It is so hot and dusty. There is no green here, no softness. There are no other Greeks. Who will I have to talk to? Who will be my friend? Why did we have to leave home? I will never see my mother again, never see my home, I know it. I do not like this place Costa. The people, they stare. Why did we come?"

"It will be all right Irini. It is just a little different here, that's all. We can have a new life here without the wars and the superstitions, without the old, dead ways. People like you for what you are here. They give you a new start. We will have a good life here, you'll see. I wanted you to have all I could give. I wanted a new life for us. I brought us so we could be happier. I wanted you to be happy."

A couple of children playing begin a chant, dancing around the old woman in black, meaningless taunts from lips that do not yet comprehend the spite in the words. It's just a game, with words they have heard the grownups use. The old woman looks so odd, absurd. A disgusting old black beetle of a woman. Quickly bored and not a little scared at the old woman's scowling, they run off to new adventures.

The old woman frowns. It is not proper, these children, have they got no homes? They must have bad parents. A good Orthodox Greek boy or girl would never behave like these little ruffians. In Greece, a child has the proper respect. Ain my land, there is…

She forgets the children and carries on with her shopping. She is oblivious to the other shoppers. She carries on as if by habit. There is no resistance. Only the longing, the long withering towards his death. Her sun has gone out. She is faithful to their bargain. The flesh is slowly slipping away from life. Merely the cold, worn-out husk of the black signifying the night Costa has left behind.


## POSTSCRIPT:

Like *The Avenue of Remembrance, Ballarat, "The Black"* was born of those hours of overnight driving between Melbourne and Sydney in the Scandal band station-wagon, the shadows of trees looming out of the darkness for mile after twisting mile in those pre-Highway 1 days.

The genesis of this story was scribbled in pencil on a scrap of paper sometime in 1978. As I dozed in my allotted seat in the back, head against the window, the image of a face floated into my mind... *"Her old eyes blinked in the bright light, a little watery. Hot, white light, familiar but now foreign. Her skin, more wrinkled than not, pale with brown blotches, stretched over fragile knuckles. The sun was hot, but the scene was red, the red dust of Australia, red-tiled roofs of suburbia's desert, not the white of home..."*

As I mentioned in the introductory essay, my mother's name was Eleftheria. It means Freedom. She did eventually learn to speak English.

I was 28 when I wrote this. I'd never been to Greece. I've still never been to Greece.

"The sun had expanded its reach across the entire sky, killing its blue with whiteness." Now *there's* line I wish I could have written. It comes from a distressing essay on the illegal but thriving bird-netting industry in Cyprus, *The Ugly Mediterranean*, in a collection titled *Farther Away* by Jonathan Franzen. I can only hope that things have improved a little for Europe's songbirds since it was published in 2010.

"If the foundation of identity is a shared history, we are all the poorer for forgetting."
Royce Kurmelovs, *They Built This City…*, *SA Weekend*, May 11-12, 2019, p. 10

# WAR GAMES

To the north, some enormous battle must be unfolding; Tobruk or El Alemain or something equally monumental. It's just a feeling, a tightness in the stomach, a nagging awareness of the fighting. How can he know? He's never seen a real battle, never been in a real war. Here, alone in his tiny pocket of sand, crouching low in readiness, it all seems a fantasy; fantastic. He aches to see it, to join in and fight. He stares out across the sand in expectation. There will be a battle.

Tom would have preferred to be with his friends, to be out there meeting the enemy head on with his friends around him, facing the ambushes, the guns, the bullets knowing he wasn't alone. He could be the hero before them, be admired for his bravery and share the glory of his wounds with them, but today he must be alone, far from their noisy companionship. Today he must face it alone.

Tom looks at his motley troops arrayed around him in the sand. Six stiff figures in khaki, each striking some suitably heroic posture in stone-faced readiness. Will they win? They share Tom's hollow waiting for the battle to begin, Tom peering over a small ridge of sand, the only defence. Second-in-command is the Sergeant, standing defiant with his pistol held firm in outstretched hand, cap pulled down on straw-coloured hair. Tom has always felt closest to the Sergeant. There is something of his father in the stern look, the assertive stance. Or perhaps he just imagines it. His father had been a Sergeant too and had fought in the Desert and now it would be Tom's turn. All his faith would rest on the Sergeant. He would know what to do, how to order the men, just as Tom's father must have when *he* had been the Sergeant. This would only be a minor action, one of those unrecorded deeds of heroism that Tom had read made the War a victory and it would be he, Tom, and the Sergeant, who got the men through.

The sand is hot. A breeze blows some sand up to Tom's left but otherwise all is silent. Except for a couple of birds squabbling in a nearby bush, and the vague hum of cicadas. A spiteful gust suddenly slips through the silent defence of Tom's clothing making him shiver. It is time.

Suddenly, the decisive move, so patiently anticipated. In the distance, before the stiff-armed Sergeant, a Panzer tank clinks forward, oddly out of proportion to the waiting soldiers. Behind it, a dozen fierce green figures, infantrymen, are advancing on Tom's position. Never mind that they aren't wearing the khaki of Rommel's Desert Corps, they are still the enemy. Quickly, we must make a move. The Panzer trundles forward relentlessly, pushed on as if by some unseen guiding hand straight for us. The Sergeant must act. He is pushed forward, pistol still resolutely in hand and thrust out at the oncoming enemy. The others silently hold their poses. There is a tension building in Tom. This isn't like the battles with his friends. He is on his own and somewhere in the back of his mind there is a vague feeling of responsibility. He already knows how this will end.

The enemy soldiers move stiffly forward with the tank, each with his own self-conscious pose, curiously imitating Tom's own men. One inconveniently already holds the pose of death, arms splayed out as the figure topples backward, almost like the little figure on the crucifix. There is a minefield. Yes, the hollow Tom is defending has a surrounding minefield. There, that takes care of the dying soldier. So, the Panzer too must blunder into this minefield and, on cue, a plume of sand spurts up against the side of the flimsy rubber tank tracks.

Now for the charge. From the hollow in the sand, Tom's khaki troops surge forward, matching the staccato rush of the green enemy. Each man holds his heroic pose as he faces the other, shuffling across the sand, stiffly advancing. Into battle! Tom's battle. This is his test. The rules for this battle are his rules and Tom feels as Monty must have felt or perhaps even like Churchill. Like the men in the films who dare all and win for King and Country. Today he is John Wayne, or Tyrone Power, Errol Flynn or John Mills. The fate of the battle and all his men rests with Tom. He can send out whomever he pleases and retrieve only his favourites. Just like the comic books he spends so much time reading. Big heroes, big battles, big words he has only a faint sense of but which sound so heroic – actions, medals, blazes of glory, King and Country. Into the fray!

With his friends, Tom must play by their rules, but here he is in command. This time he can be the hero; the Cowboy not the Indian. Out of nowhere, the ominous whistle whine of a Stuka shatters the battlefield tension, flashing from his mind into bullets spitting up handfuls of sand, his lips making the whooshing sounds as it dives and dives again. He would have had to submit long ago if he was playing with his friends, would have had to play dead just because they were bigger than Tom, or because they owned the guns, his calls of "Not fair" drowned out in the noise of machine-gunning mouths chanting their horrid "You're dead, you're dead" down at his prone body. Here Tom is facing "the might of Nazi Germany" alone, sending sand flying as the whim takes him, with "clenched fist and jaw", just like his father must have done. His father had been a Sergeant and perhaps one day *he* would become a Sergeant and fight in the desert, just like his father.

Tom knew what it would be like. From when he was very small, he had loved to look at the photographs his father had of his war years; black, white and brown images held in that musty old album. He'd never seen another like it, with its polished wood cover, a camel and palms carved into it, the black pages holding the wonders of the East and Tom's father's days of glory. Tom knew the strange places – Haifa, Tobruk, Lebanon, Port Said – even if he wasn't quite sure where they were, fantastic places. And he knew the faces of the men, fighting men, not just the comic book heroes of his friends and himself. He had stared at those faces so often, revelled in the musty smell of the album, each photograph with its little packet of vanished sunlight and beaming young faces that would sometimes win a name from his father – Smudger, Sparky, Jonesy – as a curiously detached smile would cross his father's wrinkled face. (Odd, the face of his own father as it too stared out of those photographs, young, unlined, cheerful; the face showing Tom these memories so creased, stubbly and tired.) None of these old friends, comrades in arms, ever visited, but Tom knew them, thought he knew the secret moments that must hold them together through the years, those moments in battle fighting together, just like the games with his friends. Odd though; there were no photographs of those men, or his father, in action. No photos of war. Always the laughing group beneath palms or by camels, in the water or by a ruin, ears painfully jutting out beneath short, spiky mats of hair, all picture-postcard poses. There had been medals too, but Tom never saw them, thrown out long ago by his father. And Tom so wanted to see them, tell his friends of them, tell them his father's stories of battle. There never were any stories.

The battle is over. Before Tom, the tiny sandpit is silent. Fist-prints pockmark the scene, the tin tank tipped ridiculously onto its side, half smothered in sand. Nearby, the arms and torso of the crucified German soldier jut stiffly from the sand. All around, plastic soldiers in green and khaki lie scattered about, their plastic bases pressing against legs held in grotesque poses. Only the Sergeant remains standing, in that familiar pose, pistol in hand, arm outstretched, cap firmly in place. Tom looks at him from his place in the sand, face pressed against the grains, prickling his skin as they cool. The afternoon is drawing cold. His face feels numb. He is playing the role of wounded soldier, just as he would with his friends. But something is wrong. It feels different. The numbness is in his head and in his stomach, the knot of anxiety that anticipated the battle grips even tighter. He feels so alone.

There is the Sergeant and all around is devastation; all his men dead. Even Tom feigning the pain of mortal wounds – the wounds are always mortal. But why doesn't Tom feel triumphant? His side won the day; the enemy lies scattered and destroyed before him. Only the Sergeant survives. He had to

34

survive of course. Because Tom is the Sergeant today. It was his command. And he is the Sergeant staring out at his men and knowing he is hurt and alone and there is nothing around him but sand and the dead. Tom suddenly feels so empty, so alone lying there among his dead men. And he can't understand why it should feel so different, but it is, oh hell it is. Perhaps it's the silence, or the chill that makes him shiver now that the breeze has gone colder with the sinking sun. No, not just that. It's what he has done. An empty, nagging ache inside him makes him feel slightly sick, the cold sand prickling his face, his eyes level with the scattered soldiers in the tiny sandpit; just a jumble of plastic bodies and the lone Sergeant.

He feels that tell-tale gush of tears trying to push up into his eyes. No – I'm a soldier. I can't cry. *But he feels so alone.* His Sergeant falls at the touch of a breeze and Tom's imagined wounds are the Sergeant's. They lie together in the silence of their shared pain, the arm still outstretched, useless plastic gun held firm, face grimly set. But for what? Everyone's dead. Perhaps Tom is too? It feels horrible. But it's not like this at all. When we play together, there is all the noise and we know it's just a game and we always get up again, don't we? Why don't they get up again? Why do I feel like I'm dead now? I feel so empty. I don't understand. War isn't like this is it? Is it?

But then it was Tom who had caused it, wasn't it? He'd been in command, hadn't he? Is this what being in command means? Losing everything? Would this be my friends and me if this was for real? Tom rolls onto his back and stares at the sky.

Perhaps this *is* war? This empty ache. I feel so pointless. All the dreams and nothing in them; just this horrible empty ache. Is this what my father knew as war? Tom's father had always avoided talking about the war, except living in troop ships and seeing all those foreign places. Nothing about the fighting. Was this why? Because, in the end, there was nothing to say? That it was all pointless? Just silly, useless waste? There were his soldiers all scattered about and lifeless and he was alone staring up at the darkening sky…

How could Tom's father explain to a little boy of eleven the churning anger and pain and disgust of seeing friends blown to pieces by mindless bits of steel, or the soggy thud of a bullet as it ripped into a stomach, a shell creating a hole where men had stood seconds before? How could he explain that it was just so, that there was no sense in it but it must happen? Why should it happen at all? What did it gain? Tom's father had simply avoided it. He wouldn't spoil Tom's games. Tom would know soon enough without his saying anything.

But why then? What had been the point of the fighting, of all the dying that was supposed to make Tom's world a better place to live in? He couldn't explain, perhaps would never be able to explain. He didn't really know himself. Oh, there was there was all that stuff about Hitler and that was fair enough, it had to be done. It hadn't been so bad after all, and there were good memories too. It had been a good life. But the senseless deaths. Were there any sensible ones? At least Tom had a chance of perhaps never having to know. No. Better that Tom never has to know. But a boy of eleven asks so many questions, so many, many questions…

That's why he'd dumped the medals. Nothing fancy really, just Good Conduct Medals, but what did they count for? They had seen films of the desert since the War, Tom and he, some still landscaped with twisted sculptures of distorted metal, tank shells – shells of tanks – and gun barrels pushing through the redeeming coat of sand, echoes of forgotten battles and forgotten deaths… or mostly forgotten. Some brought out in private, mourned in private, recalled from anonymity for a moment and then stowed away in the dust of fading memory. Men churned into mud and dust for what? King and Country? Is that ever a good enough reason?

Who knows?

Let the boy have his dreams, for they are only games, just children's games, and he will grow out of them soon enough. Tom's father kept his war to himself and Tom dreamed on and played his games…

36

Lying there in the sandpit, Tom knows more than anyone can imagine a boy of his age can know of war. Or is it Tom that imagines? Just for a moment?

It is getting dark. He feels that numb ache in his stomach changing from emptiness to hunger. Slowly lifting himself from the sand, he gathers up his toy soldiers and places them in a corner of the sandpit. There, enemy and friend united, he leaves them, the tank remaining in the centre of the pit, ignored. The breeze by now is getting very chilly, the cool country wind of evening. The birds have been joined by a hundred others in a noisy twittering in the twilight. Tom walks back to the house.

Inside, his father has returned from work. His mother has the supper ready. Everything is as it should be. Tomorrow he might go and visit one of his friends. Tom looks at his father for a moment. Perhaps tonight he will tell me about the War? Perhaps I know now anyway? Perhaps, perhaps I don't want to know what it's really like? There are other games. No, that's silly. What about my friends? It's just a game. I don't want them to think I'm soft. No. Forget it. I was just getting cold. God I'm hungry. I'll see how I feel with some food inside me. No, it wasn't anything. Where's that comic? I was just starting to find out how the English Captain was going to slip out of the POW camp and single-handedly...

Tom settles down to dinner and his father is as much a stranger as he has ever been.

## POSTSCRIPT:

I have Theresa Wattis to thank for fighting in my corner against the other four editors for this story to be published in the short-lived literary magazine *Brave New Word*.

My father and I never really talked about his experiences in WWII, a fact I will always regret. But then, a lot of men of his vintage didn't talk about their war.

# FOR THE CHILDREN

But of course she never would. How could she? Things just weren't the same anymore. She wasn't really Greek anymore. No, *that* wasn't true! *Of course* she was Greek. She could, would never be anything else, no matter what they said about being naturalised or becoming Australian by marriage, she was Greek and would *always* be Greek. But she'd been away for so very long. She didn't seem to fit anymore. She knew that from the moment she'd met Marigoula again, after so many years. She'd felt so awkward, so foolish as they'd talked, gossiping and reminiscing. After a while she had even felt a little distrust for this woman, Stamatia, still so emphatically Greek standing before her. It would only be worse if they met again. What could they talk about? The old ways back home on the island certainly, the village and their old friends – yes, it would be so good to recall all that she had missed for so many years. Tears prickled her eyes as she remembered; she missed it all so much. How often she had yearned to go home again. But *no*; it was impossible. She had her life here now. What about her children, and her husband? Things had slipped too far. She could never go back now; it was just too late. Seeing Marigoula again would only make things worse, she in all her Greekness, with her Greek husband, it would be too humiliating if she saw just how far Stamatia had slipped. But how could she have done otherwise, alone as she was. She had tried so very hard but it was just impossible alone, and sometimes she felt so very alone.

She *had* tried, was *still* doing all she could. After all it was only that morning that she had brought the boys to church and it was there that the two old friends had met again. Stamatia had got the boys up good and early, at five o'clock, as she always did when they had to prepare for these Special Days. The closest Orthodox church was twenty miles away in Innisfail and since she'd never learned to drive, taking the boys in to attend mass was a major operation, a chilly, early morning train ride to get to the church in time for the beginning of services. For all

39

the complaints, the boys quite enjoyed the "adventure" and the chance at a day off school, since Greek Easter fell on a different weekend to their schoolfriends' Easter. And it meant having breakfast with their father, who would normally eat alone or with their mother since he started on an early shift at the refineries and was usually gone by the time the boys were awake. He of course wasn't Orthodox but had let Stamatia have her own way with the boys' religion. It made her happy. For her part, Stamatia was often afraid that when they died they would be separated because, after all, Church of England wasn't really Christian, not like Orthodox, and though it only ever came out in anger, she felt deep inside that his soul was lost forever, a dissolute pagan, and that she dearly wished there was some way of making him Orthodox. But he hardly ever came to church with them, and even when he did, he would wait outside, grabbing a quick smoke. It was all a bit silly to him. But no harm done.

Stamatia's conscience however demanded that at least the boys grew up Orthodox. It was her duty, so, whenever she could, she would get the boys up and the early morning ritual would commence. Even so, she had never held them to the forms as strictly as she knew she should. With each passing year, the necessary preparations had gradually relaxed, though there were the occasional twinges of guilt. It was just so hard preparing them by herself. She would of course fast herself, as was proper, but the boys were always allowed *their* supper, and then breakfast, even if a slightly lighter one. How could she refuse them, her own boys? She couldn't properly explain to them the necessity for fasting and it was so hard to think of their going hungry. Besides, no one would really mind as long as *she* kept up the forms and did all she could. It was different for the boys. They were growing up Australians, though she spoke Greek around the house, as *they* did, so they would never forget how great was their heritage. Even her husband spoke Greek, though none of them, the boys or her husband, were terribly fluent, only really capable of conversations limited to food, clothing and the other basic needs. As they grew, English was becoming more and more the norm at home. Still, there was enough Greek spoken and that was the important thing. But it made it so much harder to explain things sometimes. She certainly couldn't explain the right Orthodox ways of doing things when they didn't have the words, and her own English didn't stretch that far the other way either. Besides, how could she explain the ways of her church when she herself only understood them by faith and habit? It was just the way things were done. If you were Greek you just knew. One day, when there was more time and the boys were a little older and could understand better, she would teach them better Greek, help them understand and feel more pride in their Greek blood, their heritage. Right now it was just too hard, what with four boisterous boys to cope with and a home to run. As long as she got them to church as often as she could and taught them the proper things at home, that was all she could ask. They had their childhoods to live and she would not force anything upon them. They were *her* boys – *they* came first.

If they were not to fast, she could at least make them presentable. The Archimandriti deserved respect after all. So Stamatia always made sure the boys were properly showered, cleansed of all she could cleanse before they set off for church, and there was only a light breakfast. No going to the toilet after their showers either, so they could enter Christ's house as pure of earthly corruptions as she could make possible. But even this was getting harder lately. Not that the boys would suffer from light breakfasts. And she always made up for it by buying them special treats after the service – baklava, kataifi, loukoumia and their favourite, halva – that was their favourite part of the ritual of going to church – but getting them up so early, and dealing with "I don't want to wash my hair, mummy" and "But why is my hair too long? There are children at school with much longer hair" and "Why is it bad to spit? I've got a cold and I can't *help* sneezing. Why isn't it proper?" Four boys were just getting to be such a handful and the explanations, so obvious, at least to her,

41

were hard. How could she explain? Growing up in Greece, it was how the proper respect was paid and now the boys were just being awkward for the sake of it. No, they must do as they were told. And *then* she'd found that little Phillip – Phillipachi – had lost his filacto, *again*, playing in the nearby fields with the neighbours' children. It was a dreadful sin to loose such a safeguard against the evil eye, but how could she scold him, poor little thing? How could she scold *any* of them? They weren't to know how important these things were. She had hurriedly concocted a makeshift filacto with a few special things she had kept for this sort of emergency and had herded the boys off to the station thinking that she must write to her sisters back in Greece for the necessary sacred herbs and charms to make up a proper filacto as soon as she was home from church. At least she had them to fall back on – her Greek "connection". They had so often been her strength, but so far away, so far…

So there she was, finally leading her boys into the church after the usual rabble and banter of the train ride and she had sent them to stand by the doors next to the usher while she bought the candles for them to place in the trays of sand that sat before the icons of the day, when who should appear as if out of a dream but Marigoula – her own Marigoula from the village back in Hydra – after all these years just the same. A little stouter perhaps, and the lines in her face were beginning to show her years, but her eyes, yes, those old friendly eyes, her face was her Marigoula and, after a moment, *she* recognised Stamatia, and it was tears and embraces and good wishes as the two women remembered what they had both left behind so long ago, while the boys looked on a little lost as they so often were when they came to church, but now wondering who this old woman holding their mother could be – and why they were crying and laughing at the same time.

Of course the two women quickly regained their composures since, after all, they were in God's house and such things were unseemly, such fussing indeed on Kalí Paraskeví, Good Friday. But they chatted a moment longer in hushed voices, Stamatia remembering her boys and quickly introducing them as she hustled them inside to kiss the appropriate images of Christ and the Saints of the day, motioning them to light their candles and place them before each icon, each reflecting an ethereal glow from the blaze of dozens of similar long brown tapers already placed there by the faithful. Stamatia directed the boys to the right hand side of the aisle, though little Phillip followed his mother and Marigoula into seats on the left, only to be pushed back to sit with his brothers as was proper and told to be quiet, face the Ikonostasis and watch the other men as they attended to the Mass. Before them, behind the great table, the Archimandriti and the priests were already intoning the prayers of the faithful for the mass of the Holy Eucharist.

"No, no Yannis (It was Johnny at school), your hands before you, never crossed behind. Make sure you watch your brothers do the same." Stamatia was feeling awkward. Her boys now seemed so ill-mannered, bad enough in church but now in front of her old friend too. She felt they were doing everything wrong, no matter how hard she had tried to make them good, to have the proper respect. Why must they be so badly behaved now? She felt ashamed. "No Mikhali, look up, not at the floor. Keep him still Yannis, and don't forget to cross when I do – and, three fingers and thumb, head to chest, right to heart... Good." All muttered under her breath across the aisle as she kept one eye on the service, the other, self-consciously, taking furtive glances at her boys.

This would not have been tolerated back home. As she sat there next to Marigoula, Stamatia could feel the blood rise into her face. She must seem such a poor mother before her friend, her own children so obviously ill-mannered and unruly right there in church, before Christ Himself and the Archimandriti on this holiest of days. And there sat Marigoula, *so* proper, so attentive to every murmur and gesture from the priests, a pious Greek woman in every way. Stamatia was feeling so conscious of her own shortcomings, her mind constantly wandering away from the seriousness of the Mass, as

43

the Archimandriti worked through the traditional rituals before the Ikonostasis in preparation for their disappearance through the great Holy Door behind them that would signify the entry into the tomb of Christ and the greatest miracle of all, their return to the Ikonostasis, as if the stone before Christ's tomb had once more been rolled away, and His Representatives, the Archimandriti and the other priests could bring the faithful the final Act of Communion and with it their salvation. And here was Stamatia, having instead to attend to her boys in case they misbehaved. It was just *too* bad; really, they made things *so* hard for her. Perhaps if she had brought them more often when they were younger they might understand better, would have learned to follow the forms as they were meant to, as *she* had always tried to… and Marigoula so obviously did. *She* was still Greek, through and through. Stamatia looked on, determined to try harder.

If only her husband had become Orthodox, he could have given her the support and strength she needed so much, but he wasn't even really Christian, and Queensland was so far from the real churches she had known as a young girl, despite all the Archimandriti had done to make his church a truly Greek place of worship. Oh, her husband was good to her and was a good father to the boys, but too soft. He'd never really worried about teaching them the respect she thought was proper. But then, how could she really expect him to if he wasn't even Greek. At least they'd married in an Orthodox church. She'd insisted on that. It was only proper; otherwise it would not be a real marriage. They'd married in Melbourne soon after she'd arrived from Greece and they'd stayed with his family until he'd got this job here in Queensland. They'd met when he'd visited her island after a tour of duty in Cyprus during the troubles and he'd been kind, so strong, even quite handsome. He had been brave to go through a service he couldn't really understand, but he had done it, for her, no matter how awkward he might have felt. No, he wasn't a bad man and yes, he was a good father, but he just didn't understand how important it was for the boys to grow up showing the proper respect. Next time she would make them fast properly, and perhaps have Yannis trim his hair a little instead of trying to hide its length by damping it down. It was already starting to spring up a little and the Archimandriti would comment; she knew he would.

She had the boys in the aisle now, joining the rest of the congregation as they lined up to be presented to the Archimandriti and receive his blessing and the Holy Communion, a piece of bread following the sip of sweet wine – His Body and His Blood. "And his name?" "Yannis Christos," and the golden spoon tipped wine into the boy's mouth as the holy words were intoned and the jewelled mantle was held beneath his chin, his eyes staring into the Archimandriti's beard as the spoon was withdrawn and his lips were dabbed dry. The same for each of the boys, each automatically looking to their mother to confirm what they should do, then for their mother, then Marigoula, and so for those who followed as the ceremony proceeded. The boys watched the two women move past the trays of bread pieces, seeing their mother take five pieces, one for each and one for herself, breaking their fast as she passed out the pieces. She hurried the boys out of the church as, for all her efforts, they now began chattering away loudly to each other, their relief at the ritual having finished, the excitement at the treats they knew were to come building. Stamatia too felt a little more at ease as she returned to the outside world again, free of the pressures of maintaining the proper piety in her boys. The boys slipped out of the gates and began to clamber over a nearby bus seat as they waited while their mother once again stopped to talk to her old friend.

"I can't stay too long," she apologised. "The boys you know. They are so energetic, so full of life, and they need their breakfasts now. I always take them to the markets after church and buy them some good Greek food. You can't buy them where we are you know. But *you*, look at you! You have hardly changed at all!"

"Ah no Stamatia, look at this tummy! And you've put

45

on a little yourself, but then you have good reason – *four* boys!"

"Yes," a little defensively.

"Costas and I never had children. Ah but he is a fine man, from Castellorizon. We have only just moved out here to Innisfail. We lived in Brisbane you know, ten years from Greece. It must be almost twenty with you?"

"Almost. Eighteen. A long time."

"Yes, a long time indeed. We're happy here but it is so different from home. People here are so crude. Even some of the Greeks, second generation and third, they've forgotten the proper ways. Have you heard about Archimandriti Leonidas? And there is talk about sending this young Archimandriti Erotokritos up here as a punishment! Punishment for what? They have even lost respect for the Church here. This sort of thing could never happen in Greece. Ah yes, there there is a proper respect. It's all over the papers – *Neos Cosmos* and the rest."

"No, I had not heard," Stamatia admitted, feeling a little foolish. "The Greek papers don't reach us where we are. Besides, my eyes, they're not so strong anymore. They hurt with too much reading. But forgive me. I must get the boys to the market and fed. It's been so good to see you again Marigoula mou. We must see one another again. Kalí Paraskeví."

The two women embraced once more and shed a few more tears together, quickly recalling old friends each might have heard from, and some who had gone, each declaring that yes, they must see each other again when Stamatia was next in town. And so they parted, Stamatia gathering her boys together and heading off to the markets. Across the road from each other, the two women waved once more, and it was a little death to each, this goodbye. The boys were now rushing off ahead, anticipating the delights of the markets and the sweet cakes they would soon be devouring.

Back home now, with the boys all lying down in their rooms resting, that empty ache inside Stamatia had returned. She wanted so much to see Marigoula again, but she had decided that she could not. Not really. Not anymore. What *was* there to say after all? Stamatia felt ashamed that she only really remembered the old Archimandriti, Athenagoros. He had been there when she'd first arrived in Australia. But all these others she did not know at all. It was another world. And the Greek papers, they had nothing to say to her anymore, all those stories of a Greece she no longer recognised, of people who seemed to live lives that had no connection to her own. Oh it was nice to flick through the odd Greek magazine once in a while when her husband brought one he'd found at work, but she really had nothing to say to the occasional man he might bring home from the refinery just because he was Greek and thought she might like to chat about life back home. So what if her husband wasn't Greek. He was a good man. *He* was her life now – he and the boys, and all the Greek friends in the world didn't matter over them. She could never be anything but Greek, would never *want* to be, but she was no longer Greek like Marigoula. Things had gone too far, and she wasn't going to pretend. Why should she? If her boys were a little unruly, they were still *her* boys and no one else's concern. *They* were her life. No, Marigoula would have to slip by, as all things Greek had gradually slipped by Stamatia, because that was how it must be. She had a duty to her family, as was proper, and that duty must come before all. This ache inside, it would pass. But it would have been nice… perhaps…

**POSTSCRIPT:**

It was a different time. There was a woman, one day long ago, at a different church, an old friend, or at least someone known from the island. No word was ever said of her again.

*"My woes are written in crimson ink; my doubts are inscribed in black.*
*But the love in my heart is traced in gold and the name of my soul is light."*

*The Woman Who Read Too Much*, Bahiyyih Nakhjavani
(Redwood Press, Stanford University Press, 2015, p. 309)

## SELF-DEFENCE

I don't wanna hear – the words
That were supposed to make my life so whole
I don't wanna feel – the pain
That cuts so deep inside my soul

I don't understand – just why
I find myself a victim every time
I'm not gonna play – don't try
To match a motive to this twisted rhyme
I don't wanna know – your name
You turn my world around and upside down
I don't wanna lose – again
And have my heart and head all – spun – round

I don't wanna see – your face
I can pretend I'm just imagining
Any other face – but yours
So I won't give in to what is happening
   'Cause I've been here before
   I was cut to the core
   Thought I could cope, I couldn't take any more
   Didn't make any sense
   Tried to build a pretence
   Keep the world outside, but I'm just
     Practising self-defence

I don't wanna know – your name
You turn my world around and upside down
Thought I was safe – from love
You took my heart, disguises all fall down

I don't wanna see – your face
I can pretend I'm just imagining
Any other face – but yours

So I won't give in to what is happening
        'Cause I've been here before
        I was cut to the core
        Thought I could cope, I couldn't take any more
        Didn't make any sense
        Tried to build a pretence
        Keep the world outside, but I'm just
                Practising self-defence.

        Keep the world outside, outside your door
        'Cause I don't wanna see your face no more
        Repeat, repeat, repeat – END

## POSTSCRIPT:

My one and only complete song, words and music, recorded by the band I was in between 1986 and 1990, Cruise Control, in which, for a little while, I felt confident enough to attempt to write and present my own songs. In the end I only wrote lyrics for three other songs, the music written by the band's very fine guitarist Leigh Perry, one of which, alongside *Self-Defence*, also featured on our independently recorded and released six-song eponymous mini-LP. We pressed 500 copies – it didn't go anywhere, and whatever I'd hoped for the band and, once more, for a little while, my musical future with them faded.

The rhythm came first, inspired by the pace of my walk as I trudged towards the Festival Records offices and studio in Pyrmont to interview someone or other. As the rhythm formed I could hear Jimmy Barnes screaming out the words, so it was written with that voice in mind. My personal life had been going through some pretty seismic changes so I suppose that's what ultimately directed the lyrics, though it wasn't a conscious thing. Make of them what you will.

# SNAPSHOT

Twenty past one in the morning and I am exhausted. Tom Waits leads a raggle-taggle army of musicians up a country lane across the television screen to the tune of *In The Neighbourhood* and she leans forward pointing, I realise, at the coffee table, tugging at my shirt. We must dance. I place her on the table, and she goes into her seesaw dance, skipping across the table, one end to the other, chiding me for not following, clutching all the while my hands and chirruping nonetheless. I look down at my tiny daughter and burst into tears. I am my father, dead six months now, looking down at my daughter, so alive, who must one day look into her dead father's eyes, my eyes, and weep as I weep. Her careening dance gets wilder and my tears choke with laughter and I clutch her to me, tight, sad beyond words that my passing must bring her so much hurt. My mortality has never weighed so heavily. It is not a fear. Merely a sadness… But *what* a sadness. "Daddy, more." Her feet return to the coffee table and another song flickers across her eyes from the television set. I would hold her for all time against that last, final hurt, no fault of mine, that *I* must inevitably inflict.


# POSTSCRIPT:

Written in the very early hours of Sunday May 17, 1992.

We are all of us children, seeking. Some of us think we know the answer and blithely turn our backs on any further seeking, playing a new game we think is real – we pretend we're adults. And then something comes along and pricks the pretence to which we attach so much and we are children again, afraid and alone as we see we have rushed into a shadow we mistook for light. So we start again, the brave ones at least, while the rest hide, shutting their ears and denying the truth in order to preserve crumbling illusions instead of shedding them and standing naked once more, humble and chaste, ready to admit there is still so much to learn. This is what we *must* do, for it is the *wonder* that is important, the seeking, wide-eyed and innocent again as we re-gather wisdom and begin to perceive again the widening horizons that once took us beyond our childhood dreams, beyond the stifling framework set out so rigidly for so many of us. We must never forget the child within us, for, in the end, we are all merely children – seeking.

## FOOTPRINTS

Proud mother
Holds her baby,
Stamping defiant
Footprints
In the water of a pool,
Setting his mark
On his new world.

## SHE

Her hair was longer. That's what threw me at first, long blonde curls cascading around a face that was fuller than I remembered; her figure a little fuller too, sheathed in a long white cotton dress. The darkness didn't help either, all eyes trained on the small stage at one end of the crowded, smoky room. But it was her. She didn't see me, wrapped up as she was in her own world, a small group of men not far from her suddenly eliciting recognition and polite kisses. Yet still she seemed detached, self-contained, barely conscious of their obvious vying for her attention. There was no denying her aura. As the band tilted into their next song I moved closer to the stage, closer to her hoping… for what? That she'd pick me out of the darkness? Remember what we'd once been to one another? That we might pick up where we'd left off? Where she'd left off?

## POSTSCRIPT:

The things you imagine you see from the safe cocoon of the stage… perhaps…

China Doll, Sheila's, North Sydney, August or September 1985, singing, admittedly a little venomously, "Don't look back, you can never look back."

## HOME ALONE

Tonight, walking home from the station, commuter-weary,
I look over my shoulder across the semi-darkness of a valley
swathed in suburbia
to be surprised by a moon just off its fullness,
hanging low and burnt orange just above the horizon.

In the morning the System will once again remind me
in no uncertain terms
that poetry will never satisfy its insatiable demands
for pecuniary pounds of flesh.
For this, I get to see, once a fortnight,
how quickly my girls have grown without me.

And my heart breaks.


## POSTSCRIPT:

It was tough being a disenfranchised dad. It still is. All
part of life's jolly cavalcade of disappointments.

# FRAGMENT, FRAGMENTING

So here I am shredding this poor woman with a torrent of slashing words uncontrollably pouring out of me as I desperately try to explain why I believe I did what I did was right, even as the whole bloody edifice crumbles before my eyes with as much rapacity as my mind tries to shore it up. And yet, for a moment, I seem to step outside of it all and in that moment notice that we're going down this reconstituted alleyway in Sydney's Rocks precinct dubbed, I notice the plaque, The Suez Canal, and my eyes briefly skitter across the words, memories, connections flickering before the harsher words pouring out of me drag me back into *this* Suez Canal, desperately clinging to the wreckage of a love affair I once had with a woman who has tipped me over the edge into a vast sea of depression that now sees me killing one love pleading my case for loving another who chose to walk away. So this twisted logic is pushing me to declare that love, openly, honestly, foolishly too late, pointless as it was dishonest. Ah the sorry desperation of emotional survival...

## POSTSCRIPT:

The plaque at the top of The Suez Canal in The Rocks states that it is "one of the few survivors of the many narrow alleys that acted as thoroughfares in the Rocks... The narrow part of the lane remained unchristened but was known by the locals as 'The Suez Canal', no doubt named after the torrent that poured down its course every time it rained."

The piece itself would, I imagined at the time, be part of a novel exploring the complexities of emotional and psychological disintegration resulting from the collapse of a love affair. As usual I was overthinking it and it obviously went nowhere, so I hope you'll forgive the indulgence of my including it here, a small window into a mind desperately searching for expression, snatching a phrase here, a moment there that might lead me to... who knows where.

# CHRISTMAS PRESENT, CHRISTMAS PAST

"Can you spare any change?" she asks ruefully, face so wasted her age is impossible to determine.

> *Maybe it's because I'm so clearly a Baby Boomer and literally the result of the Second World War that I have so nostalgic a vision of what Christmas should be.*

His eyes bore cavernous vacuums of nullity before him as he marches heedless towards me, raises his foot a disconcerting ninety degrees and kicks hard the parking meter between us.

> *Maybe it's because I'm a Londoner, who still remembers snow in December where today I read the snow often doesn't come to London till February.*

"The November figures indicate a strong consumer optimism despite the flagging Aussie dollar that is likely to make the December trade figures the best in the past three years."

> *Maybe it's because I had a father whose strong Protestant work ethic demanded he do anything in order to give his only son a piece of his own aspirations.*

"Will Daddy be coming home for Christmas," she asks, too young to realise that Daddy isn't merely late from work.

> *Maybe it was the joy of finding those wondrous stacks of annuals at the foot of my bed – Rupert Bear, and Beezer and Topper, Beano and Dandy, Eagle too, as I got older – though it never occurred to me to actually ask Santa for them.*

The shredded wrapping paper lies scattered around, the toys that didn't catch the imagination already lying forgotten amidst the chaos under the sagging plastic branches of the twinkling tree.

> *Maybe it's because I grew up with '50s American
> sitcoms and English kitchen sink dramas –* I Love Lucy
> *and* The George Burns & Gracie Allen Show, Dixon of
> Dock Green *and* Z Cars, Perry Mason *and* Dr Finlay's
> Casebook *– most all but forgotten in today's
> technicolour, computer-enhanced, multi-media, social
> influencer-informed perceptions.*

Horns blare, eyes glare, heat shimmers blankly as he burns
across the pedestrian crossing intent on letting no one impede
his progress.

> *Maybe there's some sort of repressed Peter Pan
> complex at work deep within, denying the pain I've
> grown into with age, or perhaps it's just my desperate
> need to feel useful, wanted, needed... that I belong.*

Jimmy Stewart's *It's A Wonderful Life* is reprised for the
umpteenth time for indifferent Christmas television viewers,
George Bailey's doubts about his life and worth all too real as
his guardian angel tries to show him that yes, he has made a
difference.

> *Maybe, sometimes, I too am Jimmy Stewart, wondering,
> just like George Bailey, if I've made a damned bit of
> difference.*

The heat is unbearable. The hole in the ozone layer is twenty
years away from being detected and the sun is scorching this
brand new house in a brand new suburb in a relatively new
satellite town north of Adelaide, built with the highest of hopes,
suffocates.

> *Maybe I just never came to terms with a hot summer*

*Christmas, though my dislocated father tried his best.*

"No sugar in the tea I said to them," the angry young man bitches to no one in particular as the baggy-trousered homeless shuffle in and out of Our Lady of Snows looking for their free Christmas dinner. "It comes pre-mixed, freeze-dried and vacuum-packed," says a bleary-eyed soak, but angry man goes off to complain nonetheless before regaling the other "patrons" with his angry boast of having cut back to a mere half kilo of hooch a month because it was interfering with his kick-boxing training. A woman of undefinable age surreptitiously scrabbles butts from an ashtray and scampers off without a meal.

*Maybe it's because I want it to mean so much more that it hurts to see Christmas mean so much less.*

The teenager staggers around in the park having filled the void inside his Nike track suit with enough bourbon to kill a grown man. The rites of passage no longer serve as his entrance into adulthood. Now it's about the fastest passage to oblivion. He falls into a bush and vomits.

*Maybe I'm just kidding myself and the love with which I try to infuse Christmas was always illusory.*

Somewhere, someone is drinking death in through the head of a needle, someone else is holding a gun at the head of his former neighbour's child, while another has pulled up momentarily wondering if they should turn back and check on the pedestrian they've splayed across the road. Somewhere, everywhere, the point of Christmas hasn't meant a thing to the killer, the junkie, the loser, the loner. Somewhere, someone has chosen this day to say goodbye forever, not a guardian angel in sight.

*Maybe this will be the Christmas where the message of love delivered so long ago in the tale of a virgin mother and child is finally lost in the dazzle of designer labels and disposable toys.*

"One day I shall choose." Eyes intent yet vacant he stares through me as if searching inside for a sign from me, a stranger. Turning, he stumbles off into the night leaving me to the question and the darkness.

> *Maybe, just maybe, like Jimmy Stewart, I'll come out the other side of Christmas knowing that there is a point, some glimmer of hope, as I pick up my red haired, brown-eyed baby girl and kiss away the sleep in her eyes and, perhaps, pass on another little piece of my own aspirations.*

December 2001


## POSTSCRIPT:

The American "Beat" poet Allen Ginsberg died in April 1997 and his passing heralded my unexpected and brief emergence as a "Spoken Word" performer. This is how it happened. An over-enthusiastic musician and aspiring writer friend was so affected by Ginsberg's passing that he felt compelled to organise an evening of music and words at The Annandale Hotel in inner-city Sydney in tribute to the poet. He convinced three or four bands to perform, he would read a short story based on a recent visit to New York City and he decided I too should write something and read it on the night. While I'd studied Ginsberg's seminal masterpiece *Howl* as part of an extra undergraduate course in American Literature at Adelaide Uni in 1976, he wasn't a writer about whom I really knew very much. I did however have a biography, so I set to work only to find the more I read the less I liked him. There was absolutely nothing about Ginsberg with which I could relate. So I stumped up to the tribute night armed with the one piece of writing that might resonate – my piece, included in this volume, titled *Snapshot*. At least I could talk about loss, about death and their impact as I personally had felt them. I guess it went well enough. I wasn't booed off the stage. For some reason however, my friend's enthusiasm knew no bounds and the decision was made to get us both out there presenting ourselves as Spoken Word artists – and for about a dozen performances over the next couple of years I hit stages armed only with a couple of bits of paper and, where possible, my bass guitar, basing my performance around the odd paragraph from my few short stories that seemed to relate enough to each other present a coherent "story", which, for me, somehow inevitably pondered this curious creation dubbed Identity, as well as the odd piece written for particular nights. This, of course, was one such "particular night" piece. My Spoken Word career faded out ... which was probably for the best...

## SURRY HILLS JUNE 10, 1999

They're dressed just like the guy they've got spreadeagled up against the wire fence, one frisking him, the other... What? Questioning him? I don't see any guns or badges. The darkness is closing in. Somewhere, some snot-nosed kid's torching someone else's car. Across the road, an older man, his arm around a younger one, all bleach-blonde hair and attitude, is saying he'll make him breakfast.

Were they really cops?

## STRANGE FRUIT

There he hangs like some long forgotten child's action toy,
A slave to the whim of any insolent passing breeze that might
skitter by,
His cloak of leathery skin wrapped uselessly close around his
lifeless body betrayed,
Held tight by claws that thought to find refuge in lines draped
between bare, dead trees.
Another plume of diesel smoke chokes skyward from the angry
chatter of traffic towards the softly swaying fruit bat, quietly
rotting away unnoticed.


## POSTSCRIPT:

The things you do notice driving to an interview along
Botany Road on the way to the Iron Duke Hotel in Sydney's
Alexandria. I can't remember who I was going there to
interview.

# IT'S ALL IN THE MIND

Thoughts skitter

Sometimes impudent,
cheekily peering from behind a memory,

sometimes longing,
teary in some afterthought,

sometimes illicit,
hoping to be caught out,

always elusive,
a reminder, inevitably, of my own ephemerality.


## POSTSCRIPT:

I realise that I have a particular fondness for the word "skitter", for which I can only apologise.

## A LITTLE BIT OF HOME

Kneeling, I thrust my fingers into one of the multitude of cracks in the soil of my old family backyard and scoop up a lump of the hard, dry red earth I took so very long to learn to love, and slip it into my pocket. I will place it somewhere in my now briefly family, now just my own backyard, on the other side of the continent, an absurd keepsake only I will know is of a time and place I tried so hard to grow away from and now somehow seem to need in some curious way to keep this small token near me. No, it's more just the knowing that it's there, another secret thing in my secret place among the tumuli of flotsam and jetsam in my mind. Pointless of course, and I know it... utterly futile. To what end can I conceivably justify what I feel so compelled to do? Yet it is enough, to feel the heat of that unknowing clod of earth seeping through my coat pocket, the place for it already imagined, mine alone to know, and forgotten soon enough when I too become a lump of hard, dry earth.

## SIGN OF THE TIMES

Mist shrouds the trees, branches glistening with pregnant
raindrops, the air, even with the highway in the background and
the rail lines a few steps away still vaguely mystical, like an
Antipodean Brigadoon. Above, tucked into a corner of the
platform veranda, a feisty little bird, some sort of Mynah
perhaps, is cheering itself by running through the most
impressive repertoire of trills and coos, reproducing songs it has
collected from other birds in its travels. Directly below, a young
woman stares at her mobile screen, oblivious.

# WHATEVER HAPPENED TO THE REVOLUTION?

"Honestly, I think we can do without this one Max." He's leaning across lifting the mic stand that's fallen on my chest as the drunk reeled past me, bumping the PA stand that now briefly wobbles precariously on his way to the door leading into the poor excuse for a beer garden. Max looks at me with his usual quizzical half smile, half pain look. Poor bugger. He never quite gets it, our Max. Truth be told, it's sometimes seems like it's all too hard for him. He's the band's singer, the band's booker and the band's manager, so he's got more than a full plate on his hands, but the rest of us either can't be bothered or just aren't cut out for it, having to spend all day on the phone trying to get gigs, ringing up pubs and those bastard agents who've managed to lock up practically all the rooms in town between them never returning calls – sod that for a game of soldiers! Max might be the ultimate grouch sometimes – everything seems to be a bloody drama of monumental proportions for him – but he's tenacious and he gets the gigs, at least three, sometimes four a week, and that's the point isn't it, so who are we to complain? Brad was telling me – Brad's over the other side of the stage ripping riffs at the rate of knots out of that Fender Strat of his – God he's good. Oh, and let's not forget Bruce, all enigmatic Cheshire cat, effortlessly counting the beat, not a tousled hair out of place – so cool, so unruffled, so solid. Anyway, Brad had asked Max how his night off had gone – we'd finally had a Saturday night off, first one in ages, always feels odd after so many years spending them playing – the first time I had one I honestly wondered what normal people did on a Saturday night I was so locked into the gigging, and of course if I wasn't playing, the last thing I wanted to do was go and see someone else playing… unless of course it was some big overseas band I'd always been into. Anyway, Max just grumbles to Brad that it was terrible, fell asleep half past nine, complete washout – can't even enjoy his night off. He's a funny bloke. Still, as I say, he gets the gigs. Though you have to wonder what the bloody point of doing this one is, the Minto bloody Inn that is, as you watch the whole room empty into the beer garden to watch a couple of inebriated Islander gorillas set into each other. That's Brad's complaint about most of the gigs we play really – "What's the bloody point?" – so he dresses like a total slob and inevitably gets up Max's nose even more. Brad's invariably late getting to gigs as it is. But he's often right really. What is the point? Invariably you turn up to some godforsaken pub out in some pokey dormitory suburb and discover that, yet again, you have to set up in a corner behind a bunch of pool tables or next to a row of gleaming new poker machines right by the entrance to the toilets and find you're confronted with an increasingly familiar scene of disheartening emptiness broken only by a few desultory lowlifes propping themselves up by sheer inertia, the repressed anger all too palpable in their faces matched only by their indifference as they wait for the next race to start up there on the row of TV screens that flicker relentlessly throughout the night – no switching them off just because there's a band playing. Some nights, if they acknowledge our existence at all, it's often with a mixture of irritation and resentment at the fact we're there at all. Then there's that other band-vibe crusher, when you're doing your best to play a set of songs that you love and have inspired you, even chucking in a few songs of our own, only to have the punters call out for *Khe Sahn*, which, of course, Max will adamantly refuse to sing – we're a blues band! It says so on the poster! Funny, the number of times I've played with a band that *did* play some request persistently shouted out from the audience only to see those shouting loudest for it leave halfway through. That's if they haven't decided that *now* is the time for that all-important game of pool. So when we say to him, "Sod playing the Minto Inn," Max simply replies, "Do you want to work or what?" And like I said, he certainly gets the work – and goes on and on about how much work he gets us too – so yes, who am I to complain? The whole live scene is pretty much on a downward spiral these days. I don't know how a young up and coming band can make any kind of go of it. The fact we're getting so much work makes us the envy of the other blues bands gigging round town. So you go into a room and do your thing, power out the music with the lads as best you can and hope that a few of the punters pick up on it. That's the gig. That and the fact that there's a quid in it at the end of the night of course (Shit, this is a cheque gig, isn't it? Damn. It'll be a month at least before it comes through. Bloody marvellous. Oh well, money in the bank I suppose. Where are we tomorrow? Shit, Ingleburn. At least it's a cash gig.) Of course, I could be home enjoying a comfortable night in front of the telly with my little daughter snuggled up next to me, nodding off but determined to watch *The Bill* with Daddy, myself sliding softly into sweet relief after another week slogging away at the day job. But the pay packet just doesn't do the business these days does it? What with mortgage repayments, council rates, electricity bills, phone bills and even payments on "the encyclopaedias the kids had to have", though I swear I'm the only one's ever bothered even opening one to date. The gigging certainly isn't about trying to recapture my youth, I can promise you. I have to admit I never really took it as far as perhaps I could have. Never ambitious enough I suppose; lacked that necessary killer instinct or fire in the belly, I dunno. Certainly never interested enough to be hanging around the old long-gone Manzil Room until dawn watching the other wannabes and has-beens bitching about that week's heroes or sitting up front holding court to groupies and assorted lesser minions, swapping road tales and dubious chemicals in the hope of that elusive break, the session that would change it all... Sod that. That whole thing, chasing all clichés that have accreted themselves to playing in bands never appealed to me, even when I was a young man new to the game. I just loved playing – I *love* playing! – and I guess I got good enough at it to keep playing long after that "used-by date" that hovers over the heads of anyone working in a "youth-oriented" game passed me by. So instead of living the "rock'n'roll lifestyle", whatever the hell that is (was?), in the hope of scoring the plum gigs, those "breakthrough" sessions, it's always been

69

just steady work in pretty good bands and, if I was lucky, a certain amount of respect – "Man, you're a wicked bass player" – though how much that means when it's coming from some totally pissed-up broken-toothed biker at the end of a night I don't know, but anyway – and, alongside the good to great, the shit gigs like this one, that just pay the rent. Until of course you have a mic stand fall on your chest and the room empties and you're hearing David Bowie in your head singing about cavemen fighting in the dance halls. Bet he never had to play poxy rooms like this one, even back when he was plain David Jones sporting a Mod haircut and only dreaming of Spiders from Mars. I mean, look at this lot will ya? You wanna know what happened to the Revolution? It's all there in your local suburban pub. Kids who weren't even born before Jim Morrison died in some scum-encrusted bath in a flophouse in Paris are shouting for us to play *Roadhouse Blues* and then shuffling into their beers indifferently after you've done it, and you wonder where their heads are at, trapped in some time warp that's not even theirs but their parents' parents who left them at home while they were out "doing their thing, man", pissing off down the pub to get drunk or score – when did drugs become an obligatory part of the rites of passage for Christ's sake? – and now these kids are all grown up, too soon, dropped out of schools that couldn't deal with their deep-down inarticulate anger and disillusion, barely having been affected by what those few teachers who did give a damn tried to instil in them, ending up in the same pubs as their parents, looking to get drunk or score or… Pubs that have long since passed their "glory days", clinging to existence only by the number of gaming machines that can be crammed into them, those that haven't converted themselves into boutique "dining experiences". Welcome to the fag end of the Pub Rock age! This must be how the jazzers felt as they watched their gigs haemorrhage, audiences drifting away seduced by that new-fangled television, the hipper youngsters opting for this new scene, rock'n'roll. And here I am, still plying the trade I thought would keep me alive until I was old, a trade that I once thought was an art form, one I tried so hard to master, and I'm as irrelevant as those old jazzers, myself displaced first by punk, where it was attitude not aptitude that counted, and now left with a dwindling scene that has succumbed to everything from big budget Hollywood blockbusters to "concept" bands, suburban backyard piss-ups to computer games. And why not? Rock'n'roll's what your mum and dad did, right? And who in their right mind would turn up to a gig like this if they were honestly looking for a good night out? Of course, the tragedy in it for us is that here are four good craftsmen who have spent forty-odd years getting their chops, paying their dues, living the life, all that stuff, and the ship's gone out on us. Whatever happened to the revolution indeed.

But there are still a few great gigs out there, where punters congregate to actually *listen* to the bands, or at least participate in the performances, gigs for the up and comers, the Triple J crowd, the proven recording acts, a few "heritage" acts still lionised rather than demonised for being old. Too late for us though, players who never really broke through just trying to carry on being players for as long as we're allowed, even if it means playing crap rooms like this one.

So by now you're probably agreeing with us – What's the point, right? And here it is. Brad's just launching into that blazing solo in *Crossroads* and suddenly we're all locking in behind him and the energy level has gone up exponentially. He's smoking, quietly smiling to himself as the whole band takes off like an F1-11 roaring into the stratosphere. Brad really is a gun guitarist, Bruce's drums powering out like there's no tomorrow punctuating my bass playing with all the power the song needs while still full of his sassy swing, and you remember all over again and know *exactly* why you're doing it, that incredible charge, the energy and the emotion and the passion that was there when you were sixteen and you got hooked into the whole silly business is suddenly right *there* again, just like the first time, that hit no drug can ever replicate. We're improvising madly, each drawing up sounds from deep within us, each

71

surprised at what we're creating together out of thin air, the joy within us limitless, smiles all round. That's it, *that's* the point – you're in the zone, the most extraordinarily *Zen* place... As fleetingly infinitesimal or inconsequential as it might be, it's fantastic, unbelievable. There's nothing like it. It's brilliant... And it's enough. Even when we finish and the palpable indifference is only momentarily punctured by a desultory clap here or begrudging grunt of approval there. It's not like that every night, thank God. I mean, some nights, if the crowd is with you, you come off that stage so charged up it feels like you could light up a small city – just plug me in! It's quite amazing, the power of it, the exhilaration you feel. Every corpuscle in your body sings. It can take hours to come down. I know why some musicians turn to the drink or the drugs or the girls, whatever, just trying to maintain that high. Pity those nights are so few and far between these days but there you go; it's just how it is. At the end of the day it's still all about the playing, getting into a room with a bunch of players and trying create a bit of musical magic and hopefully sharing with anyone who will listen... The sheer *joy* of performance.

"Hey Max, watch that PA column on your side will you?" Three more songs, then one more set and we're out of here. Counting out my life by set lists! Who'd 'ave thought?

***

## POSTSCRIPT:

Obviously pure stream of consciousness, pouring out one quiet afternoon sitting at my window desk in *The Drum Media* office in Surry Hills, the literary nabobs to whom I submitted this piece assured me that the characters were unlikeable and unrealistic. This was at the height of what was a literary romance with what's been described as "heroin chic". If the story being told was couched in the associated (expected?

assumed?) drug culture, it was deemed to be the real deal. Faction? Prose vérité? So a simple tale of drawn from the life of a jobbing musician with no unsavoury habits to speak of other than a certain disappointment was obviously *not* the real deal. Well, I'm sorry to have to disillusion you but...

For me, the point of the story of course was the reason why we musicians bother to put ourselves through nights like this – for those moments when everything locks in and we fly.

Either way this remained unpublished until now, which was probably for the best. There was too much of me, too much angry polemic in the original. So I've edited out a lot of the disillusion I was feeling at the time of its writing. It's obviously very much of a time and place now long gone. Thankfully, these sorts of pubs have pretty much all faded away. Thankfully the passion to play has not.

Back in 1989, while the band was on a US tour, the drummer with The Sunnyboys at that time, Peter Hincenbergs pointed out the realities for the band back home to a journalist for *The Philadelphia City Paper*: "In Australia, you can get a hundred people in a venue and the band will be playing and they'll all be in the back getting pissed and playing pool." (July 24-August 4, 1989, p. 14) Sounds a little too familiar...

I've never had a slew of cracking "sex, drugs and rock'n'roll" stories from my years of playing to impart. For me it was always about the music, the gigs. I'd rehearse, I'd play and I'd go home. Sorry.

At unexpected moments the unsummoned prickle of tears rises more easily these days, hidden of course, but elicited nonetheless by a few words, a moment, an image, a landscape in a movie or documentary, a memory as age and its attendant disappointments tips me deeper into an ever more pronounced awareness of loss. It's all in here one way or another.

## POSTSCRIPT:

I wrote this sometime in my mid- to late 60s. In April 2024, I picked up a slim volume titled *A Farewell to Gabo and Mercedes*, a memoir published in 2021 written by Rodrigo Garcia about the final few years of his father, the celebrated Colombian writer Gabriel García Márquez, best known for his novel, *One Hundred Years of Solitude*, and his wife Mercedes Barcha. On the occasion of Márquez's 80th birthday and all too aware that his life is nearly over, his son asks him if he is afraid.

He answers, "It makes me immensely sad."

## ON BEING 50 (A MODERNIST'S LAMENT)

And the thought suddenly strikes, unsolicited
                                       of course.
I don't fit any more,
Irrelevant before I've even really started
in this post-modern, post-Structural din.
I don't know my Semiotics from my antibiotics,
burdened in this used-by state by some forgotten aesthetic.
Terminal cancer of the literary colon:

I'm now less funny than tinned Duchamp merde, absurd.
Bugger.

Water cascades onto skin
Skittish rivulets chase each other down
Pregnant with the dust of dreams and soapy schemes
And I think of you…

****

Perhaps, after the initial tidal wave of love has subsided, the vestiges of that first efflorescence remain as ripples in the sand, echoes of what could be, and will, with the next wave, quickly or slowly be washed away. Pick up a shell and place it at your ear and you can still hear it. Unlike the sand, the human heart is more like the universe where, if you listen very carefully, in silent wonder, the ripple of *its* first kiss, that inexplicable Big Bang, continues to pulse through us a billion, billion, billion years on. So with human love. It explodes, it fades but its core, within each of us, continues... and sees us reach out to see if, in another heart, that fading echo can again become an explosion.

# JUST KEEP MOVING

**4.15am November 4, 1956. Soviet tanks roll across Hungary's borders, their orders to suppress the spontaneous uprising against Soviet control of the country. December 24, 1956: Australia agrees to provide political asylum for up to 10,000 refugees fleeing Hungary as a consequence of the crushing of the uprising by that Soviet invasion. May 10, 1957: 1300 Hungarian refugees arrive in Melbourne. Now: Not everyone got away.**

An old man, Slavic... perhaps Polish. I dunno. Definitely Eastern European. Big heavy overcoat, looks ex-military, like from one of those army surplus places. Crazy in this heat. Odd sort of hat, perched atop a bald head edged with greasy steel-grey hair, cheeks all grizzled and unshaven. He's pushing an old trolley piled high with bags, crusty-looking like him. There are battered suitcases too, old-fashioned, the sort made out of some sort of heavy cardboard. Obviously homeless. Probably dosses down in some doorway nearby. There are so many of them now. Looks old, *really* old, his face all crevasses and stubble, skin dark, a mix of dirt and sun though who can tell? He's wearing those fingerless gloves, fingernails dirty. And he's mumbling away, off in his own world. He's charging off across the street from the station now, on a mission, head down, mumbling away ten to the dozen. Can't understand a word...

*'Nemszabad hogy túdassam velük hogy, hogy én túdom. Ezek reám mútatnak és rögtön egymás helyre visznek. Tardsd le a fejed ezeknek szemükvan mindenhol az átkozottak. Istenem, én még most is látom a tankokat! Jajj-Jajj...'*\*

*['I must not let them know I know. They point you out and next thing you're 'relocated'. Keep your head down you fool – they have eyes everywhere damn them. Just keep moving. God I still see the tanks! Ah-ee-ya...']*

He's startled. A car has honked him out of its way. He's looking around, all dark, dark eyes, suspicious, retreating even further into that old greatcoat. Probably trying to avoid the cops.

'*Miéret vannak itt a tankok annyú? Nézd mama, most megfordúlt! A vezetö biztos bevan rúgva mint a Miklósbácsi. Nem anyú, én látniakarom. Hova megyünk mi? Miért szaladúnk mi el? Én akarom látni a tankokat! Miért sirsz te? Te olyan bóldogvoltál mikor az ember bemondta a radioba, hogy szabdok vagyúnk. Te nevetél, énekeltél apukával eggyütt... Holvan apú? Miért nemjött haza anyú? Mivolt az?'*

[*'Why are there tanks, Mumma? Ha ha, look Mumma, it's sliding around! The driver must be drunk, like Uncle Milos. No Mumma, I want to watch. Where are we going? Why are we running away? I want to see the tanks. Why are you crying? You were so happy when the man on the radio said we were free. You were laughing and singing and so was Pappa... Where is Pappa? Why hasn't he come home Mumma? What was that?'*]

The old man is ducking, like there was a bang or something. Now he's scuttling off into an alley. Weirdo, mumbling to himself. God knows what he's going on about. Can't understand a word. Bet my taxes are paying to keep him drunk!

'*Miért lövöldöznek a tankok reánk anyú? Mitörtént aval az emberel? A feje anyú, mibajvan a fejével anyú? Oroszok? Rendörség? Hovámegyünk anyú? Mivan apukával? Légy csendben! Igen anyú. Én fáradtvagyok! Miért bújkálúnk eben az erdöbe? Nagyon sötétvan. Én fázom nagyon hidegvan anyú! Én alúdni akarok! Csendben maradok anyú, igérem. Mi most játszúnk? Mikor mehetünk haza? Fogd be a szád, fogd be a szád! Milyen örök anyú? Hovámegyünk? Tards le a fejed; igen anyú, csak mozogj gyere sies... Anyú?'*

[*'Why are the tanks shooting at us Mumma? What's happened to that man? His head Mumma, what's wrong with his head? Russians? Police? Where are we going Mumma? What about Pappa? Keep quiet? Yes Mumma, but I'm tired, so tired.... Why are we hiding in this forest Mumma? It's so dark. I'm cold Mumma, it's so cold... I want to sleep. I'll keep quiet Mumma, I promise. Are we playing a game? When can we go home? Shut up, shut up! What guards Mumma? Where are we going? Keep my head down; yes Mumma, just keep moving, just keep moving... Mumma?']*

*Translations into Hungarian by long-time Mudgee resident Istvan Csuba. May 2016.

## POSTSCRIPT:

The late and much-missed Miklós József "Jackie" Orszáczky, one of the finest bass guitarists to grace Australian stages between 1970 and his death in 2008, lived through the 1956 uprising. As an eight year old in Budapest, he remembered emerging from the family cellar a week after the uprising and seeing "the pancake people", who'd been run over by Russian tanks.

## BITS &...

You wake and suddenly half the year has flown by and you know you lived it but somehow it feels untouched, an idea rather than a reality, fleeting as a thought, subtle as a touch, elusive as a shadow. What remains is the memory, of a smile, a smell and, deeper than time, a love. In the end, nothing else matters.

## PIECES

The humidity is stifling. Every so often the room seems to sigh and gulp in a mouthful of cool air from somewhere, sending chilly ripples skittering across sweaty skin.

## POSTSCRIPT:

Yup, there's that pesky skittering thing again!

# DOWN AT THE OLD BULL & BUSH

I'd wished it so often so many lives ago, but to my undying shame I didn't realise it was her until I got home. My mind was filled with my current relationship, the new band, the repertoire I was about to showcase, the hope that this time it might kick off and I could once more be a viable working musician – her appearance in the "band room" just before I stepped out for the show was so unexpected. After all, it had been thirty years, more loves, more losses and more everything else, since we'd last seen each other. She still looked so young. We exchanged cautious pleasantries, I clumsily, she, perhaps, hopefully, probably soon realising that I hadn't recognised her – and she was gone. Another of life's all too many regrets. In the end, all I have is memories. In the end, it was me that happened, me that failed her – and I paid dearly.

It was some kind of industry do, I suppose, all banquet tables, napkins and so on, as you'd expect at the APRA or Songwriters' Association Awards nights. But it was neither. Somewhere along the line Cliff Richard turns up and is surrounded by well-wishers. I try to keep my moment of conversation, as he moves past me to collect something before leaving, to something hopefully articulate and relevant. I've no idea what it might have been, but it's got to be better than some of the silly things some of the others are doing – the odd Monty Python sketch? As the room clears, I look around and notice a jar or bag of goodies – chocolates and little toys – and I go over and start putting things in my pocket, noticing a woman at another table similarly scavenging. I nod and continue, picking up a little toy only to feel my chest cave in. I realise there's no point. I have no children anymore. They're long gone and all grown up. That doesn't diminish the ache, the hurt I feel. Will I cry? Instead I drift into consciousness, the dream fading even as the hurt softly lingers.

# FOR MY DAUGHTER, ON HER 25th BIRTHDAY

The mystery, the alchemy
The passion, the ecstasy
The hopes, the dreams
Conspire in the darkness
In an instant,
Miraculously,
Transforming the idea of you,
The hope of you, love made manifest,
*Into* you
Our joy
Your life, your adventure,
Your future

# THE RAVEN AND THE COCKATOO

The sacred songs had been sung, the ritual dances, the ceremonies. Long since, the Elders had signed to the one who would be Guardian and the young men had gathered themselves together for the Journey ahead, chattering amongst themselves, filled with the tensions of expectation, of their impatience to finally come of age and embrace their manhood, when they would take their place within the tribe as keepers of the Knowledge. It was as it should be, as it had always been, since beyond time.

The journey had taken them far from the Inland Plains into the Great Hills, the high lands at the edge of the world. The forest was thick and the land steep and everywhere there were deep gullies and shadows. So different from the vast flat interior. Here the sun could hide among the leaves of the tall ghost trees, so thickly grouped together. There was a cool breeze that could surprise a chill through the body and at night a mist sometimes settled and the young men would crowd together around the flame tongues of the campfire, sharing the warmth with their companions. The land seemed stronger here, different somehow. Not just colder but concealing an aching emptiness. It was all eerie greenness.

The journey was near its end. Another day, so the Guardian had said, and they would reach the Men's Place and the final Revelations would be made, the youths would become Men and they would take their place within their families as providers, within the tribe as keepers themselves of the old stories, of the ways of their tribe, guardians themselves of the Land, as it had been the way through time immemorial. Their youthful exuberance was giving way to a strange, unexpected tension. The prospect of finally reaching the Place now seemed somehow forbidding and the cool mist and deep shadows only aggravated their apprehension. There was a yearning quietly building amongst them as they recalled the childish games, the safety of nestling into the arms of mothers now far off, back in the Plains. But they knew, too, that they must follow the path drawn for them since their birth, the inevitable journey into manhood, into responsibility, to their families, to their tribe, to the Land itself. Still, the cool of the night pressing in saw them rock together gently to the rhythm of the songs they knew would calm this place – and themselves – the songs due to this place, and the Place to which their journey was leading, out there just beyond the darkness.

Sounds. Out there in the darkness, sounds such as none the group of young men had heard before, a muffled groaning as if some part of the mountain was slowly crumbling in the knowledge of its own dead weight. The trees whispered amongst themselves overhead. The rocking of the wakeful group was becoming more urgent, the shadows from the fire chasing across eyes fixed firmly on the lips of the Guardian and the sounds they shaped as he intoned the Knowledge. The Moon, such as it was, had left them in deeper shadow. Only the songs and now the words of the Guardian held them against the night. Motioning the group to silence, the Guardian now began the most serious story of all, the one that had led them to this point, that they must know in order to nurture the Land they have inherited, for which they, as Men, must now also become Guardians, stewards and keepers of the Knowledge for all those who would follow. A gust scattered itself among the dark leaves around them.

"In the time of the first Dreaming, the Land, having grown lonely for the sound of life, had called forth all the animals, and chief among them, in the part of the Land in which we now sit, gathered around this fire, was the Raven. We are the People of the Raven, and knowing we had been given life to care for the Land, the Land shared its bounty with us and together, we and the Ravens became fruitful, sharing in the gifts of life in harmony, each grateful for what was given. The Land, the Raven and his people, everything under the Sun prospered.

"But the Sea became jealous. Ever changeable, the Sea seemed unable to know the peace of the Land, the balance that had come generation after generation. Even when it appeared calm, the Sea hid its dangers beneath the foaming waves that in a moment could take away all it had given. Though it would share its own bounties, the fish, the food shells, even its grasses, the Sea seemed to share begrudgingly. But that too was how it had always been and, again, the Land and all its creatures found a balance with the Sea, and there seemed an unspoken respect until, one day, a mighty wind lifted the waves so high that it ripped the crests of the massing waves and threw them into the howling air where they turned into Cockatoo, as brash and noisy as the waves that had given them life.

"The Raven and his children looked on and, since the Land was bountiful, they accepted the Cockatoo and invited its children to share in their plenty. But the Cockatoo couldn't forget the chaos of the storm waves that had given them life. Their songs grew louder, their greed knew no bounds and they soon overwhelmed the balance that had reigned across the Land since the Dreamtime, drowning out the songs of the Raven and his children. Soon the Cockatoo and *his* children were pushing all before them off the Land, cackling that, since *he* was the colour of the Sun – in fact he carried the glare of the Sun in his crest – the Land belonged to the Cockatoo, and that the Raven and his children should fade into their own colour, the Night.

"So the Raven and his children were pushed aside as the Cockatoo and his children reshaped the Land in their own image, using the power from the Sea, which could cover the Land as its mood took it. Even so the Cockatoo wasn't satisfied. As greedy as it was noisy and brash, Cockatoo and his children pushed out beyond the coastal plains, past the Mountain barriers and out into the Inland Plains and beyond, to the Desert Lands, pushing aside all the Land's children, whether Kangaroo or Emu, Eagle or even Crocodile, filling the skies with Cockatoo, all screeching noise and glaring crests, the mechanical beaks of its children gouging into the Land, cutting down its trees, desecrating the Land, even its most sacred places where the children of Kangaroo and Emu, Eagle and Crocodile, and all the rest had kept the sacraments between each and the Land for countless generations. Everything fell before the greed of the Cockatoo, greedier even than the Sea that could take away a whole beach or headland or those who gathered food from its fringes.

"Though driven into the shadows by the Cockatoo, the Raven and his children did not forget the Laws, their covenant with the Land, though with every wave of Cockatoo, its children multiplying faster than the Termite and desecrating all before them, it became harder. Some lost their way in the glare of that false sun flaring from the crest of the Cockatoo. So many died too as the Raven was pushed into the shadows, the bounty of the Land now lost to them in the face of the insatiable Cockatoo.

"Finally the Land and its old companion the Sun decided it had had enough and conspired to teach the Cockatoo and his children that they were as nothing, merely the whim of a jealous Sea. The stolen parts of the Sun that Cockatoo and his children had so brazenly flaunted in their crests were released and filled the sky with the power of a hundred suns, scorching all beneath it in a blinding light. Where once the Raven and all the other children of the Land had balanced the gifts of the Sun, the fires that gave warmth, that held back the shadows of night, that cooked the bounty the children gathered, had brought new life from its ashes after dry winds took up fire as its own – all was lost before the power of those hundred suns. The Land was turned to dust and so were the Cockatoo and his children. The Sea took its revenge and rose and rose, but soon it could rise no further and slowly a balance returned.

"It was an empty Land, but it had not forgotten. It knew that, since the Dreamtime, there had been a covenant between itself and the Raven and his children, and so it brought them out of the shadows once more and renewed their guardianship."

The embers of the fire breathed out the last of their warmth and the group, the story now ended, allowed sleep to take them. Tomorrow they would be taken down to the Flatlands between Mountain and Sea to the crumbling places, long since burned to dust, of the Cockatoo, all flash and noise, who had imagined they would rule this Land forever, forgetting that, without balance, without respect, the Land, the Sun and the Sea would never bow before them.

## POSTSCRIPT:

The first version was originally written back in 1983 as a possible radio play, but I hadn't quite figured out why the Land should turn to dust. I knew it had to be from fire, but from where – an atomic apocalypse? It took forty-odd years of mounting evidence for catastrophic climate change to show me the answer. Now it's a children's parable or fable. Hopefully it isn't anything more prescient. This is obviously *not* based on any traditional Dreamtime story or actual tribe. No disrespect is intended.

# THE GREEK INSIDE

"Greek tears are the ink for the dead t lives," Anne Michaels, *Fugitive Pieces*.

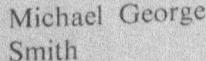

Michael George Smith

Λονδίνο 1952

Γεννήθηκε στο Λονδίνο στις 18 Μαρτίου 1952 από μητέρα Ροδίτισσα και πατέρα Άγγλο. Το 1964 ήρθε με τους γονείς του στην Αυστραλία και όλοι μαζί εγκαταστάθηκαν στην Αδελαΐδα. Μετά το Γυμνάσιο σπούδασε Αγγλική Λογοτεχνία και Γεωγραφία στο Πανεπιστήμιο της Αδελαΐδας (1973, Bachelor of Arts) και Αγγλική Λογοτεχνία στο Πανεπιστήμιο του New South Wales (1981, Master of Arts).

Ζει στο Σύδνεϋ και εκτός από το επάγγελμά του (μουσικού «ροκ»), συνεργάζεται ως ελεύθερος δημοσιογράφος σε διάφορα αυστραλιανά περιοδικά με άρθρα, βιβλιοκριτικές κ.ά. Παράλληλα τον ενδιαφέρει και η λογοτεχνία. Γράφει πεζογραφήματα στα αγγλικά. Ενώ οι πρώτες του προσπάθειες έγιναν το 1978, το πρώτο του διήγημα δημοσιεύθηκε δύο χρόνια αργότερα στο περ. «inprint». Επίσης, λογοτεχνικές του συνεργασίες έχουν δημοσιευθεί στο περ. «Access».

Διήγημά του έχει περιληφθεί στην ανθολογία *The Strength of Tradition: Stories of the Immigrant Presence in Australia* (επιμ. R.F. Holt, St. Lucia: University of Queensland Press, 1983, σ. 240-252).

**«The black»**

She sits in the bus shelter squinting along the quivering black ribbon of bitumen, grumpily searching out the bus. A little apart from her along the bench, a woman fretfully pushes a stroller, her baby noisily dribbling back and forth. The old woman looks strange to the young mother. She feels a little uncomfortable near her. She is impatient for the bus. It will

650

This is the biographical note written by Dr George Kanarakis introducing *"The Black"* in the Greek editions of his book *Greek Voices in Australia: A Tradition of Prose, Poetry and Drama.*
The photo was taken in 1980 by UNSW friend John Nagle.

92

# HELLENISING TERRA AUSTRALIA: THE GREEK FACTOR IN REDEFINING THE AUSTRALIAN CHARACTER

*"In a strange land the stranger finds a grave, far from his home, beyond the rolling wave."* Andreas Papageorgepoulos, *The Greeks in Australia – A Home Away From Home*, Alpha Books, Sydney, 1981, p. 40.

This is the inscription on the gravestone of one Antonios Manolis, born in Athens, Greece, in 1804, who died in Picton, New South Wales, Australia, on the 22nd of September 1880. It is virtually all that remains of the life and times of one of the first Greeks, a sailor, known to have made his home in the then still relatively recently colonised island continent of Australia. Of his fellow seaman Gikas Voulgaris, who, like Manolis, had chosen to remain in the colony of New South Wales after their sentences of transportation for life, which had been pronounced upon them, had been revoked, is buried in Nimmitabel, in the NSW Monaro, having passed away in 1874. Manolis and Voulgaris had apparently been convicted of piracy, as had five other Greeks seamen, all Ionians – the Ionian islands, the largest of them Corfu, were at the time under British jurisdiction and were therefore bound by British law – who had been transported to Sydney aboard the Norfolk, arriving August 27, 1829 – the other five choosing to return to Greece after Greek diplomatic intervention. There is evidence of an even earlier Greek presence. An article in the *Sydney Gazette* of 1818 noted the dangers presented to the good people of Sydney's free settler children by "Irish, English and Greek riffraff". The first record of a Greek woman in the colony seems to be one Aikaterini Plessas, who came to Sydney in 1836 as Catherine Crummer, wife of a Battle of Waterloo veteran, Major James Crummer. Her grave can still be seen at Waverley cemetery, where she was buried, passing away at the age of 98. Such were the humble beginnings of an Hellenic presence in the Great Southern Land that was called Terra Australis.

Australia inevitably saw comparatively few Greeks arriving on its shores in the early years of white settlement, when it was, first, a penal colony for Great Britain, and then a free territory within the British Empire. The bulk of its present Greek population (as of 1988), estimated to number upwards of 700,000, arrived as part of the great wave of government-initiated immigration set in motion after the Second World War. Even so, at the beginning of that war, there were approximately 15,000 people registered as having been born in Greece who were residing permanently in Australia, according to figures quoted by Josef Vondra in *Hellas Australis* (Widescope Publishers, Melbourne, 1979). It is difficult to get really accurate figures since there would have been second and third generation Greeks born here whom the census would not have counted as being of Greek descent, as well as the added complication of those places of birth that were outside what was officially considered Greek territory at various times – Greek Cypriots for instance, or Dodecanesian Greeks, who were under Italian rule between the two World Wars; or Alexandrian Greeks, who would have been registered as Egyptians. There were certainly Greeks and Greek blood present in the local population by 1939 – the census of 1891 had counted 4582 Greek-born nationals residing in Australia, yet just thirty years later the number stood at 3654. Whatever the actual figures, the Greeks have come to be the third largest ethnic group represented in the Australian population, second only to the Italians in what had previously been a predominantly Anglo-Celtic society, a significant enough population to justify the publication in Melbourne in 1913 of the first Greek-Australian newspaper, *Afstralis*. The following year saw the publication of *The National Tribune* (*To Ethniko Vima*) Inevitably those Greeks, like the Greeks who took passage to the United States, Canada and Latin America, have made a significant impact on the land they have helped colonise, on its history, society and culture.

That impact, just as inevitably, has taken a little longer to gain recognition in this new homeland than it did in the

United States. And fair enough. As of the early 1980s, America counted over three million people who could claim Greek descent and identify as Greek-Americans. In the nine years between 1891 and 1900 alone, 15,979 Greeks entered the United States. By the end of the decade ending in 1920, that figure had risen to 184,201, according to the 1980 edition of *The Harvard Encyclopaedia of American Ethnic Groups*. Again, these figures are seen as an underestimation of the actual incoming migration by Greeks to America. The overworked officials of Ellis Island, who were faced with the onerous task of processing the millions of people entering the country during these years could not hope to understand the unique characteristics of the people who were making up the Hellenic sector of this human flood, the deeply embedded knowledge that regardless of place of birth, a Greek is a Greek no matter what. So, many of those Greek-Americans have had a significant impact on America's fortunes for at least half a century longer than those in Australia.

The emphasis on the place of birth for those officials was merely as a tool to qualify those who were entering and allow them to be officially differentiated from the dominant ethnic stock that was then seen as having primary rights to the land. From these attempts at qualification came the uniquely American concept of ethnicity. Since I want to consider some aspects of this concept, I will use what I consider one of the clearest definitions of that concept, as presented in an article by the American sociologist, journalist, novelist and, as it happens, Catholic priest Andrew Greeley, who says that an ethnic group is "a collectivity based on presumed common origin which shapes to some extent the attitudes and behaviour of those who share that origin, and with which certain people may freely choose to identify at certain times in their lives." In the essay from which this definition comes, *The Future of the 'Ethnic' Revival* (*Quadrant*, Nov/Dec 1972), he describes the concept of ethnicity as having been important to Americans in the way that it allowed them to determine their own "Americanness". However, he goes on to describe how this also led to the

95

misguided concept of the "melting pot", the phenomenon by which immigrants were supposed to experience some sort of catharsis on entering the United States that would "transform" them into Americans. The redundancy of this concept has of course been shown up by a number of commentators apart from Greeley, most notably by former US Ambassador to the United Nations, Daniel Patrick Moynihan and his writer colleague Nathan Glaser, in their book *Beyond The Melting Pot*, published in 1963. What they found was that the so-called "melted" immigrants were producing children who were remaining loyal to the mores and customs of the countries they had ostensibly left behind. In fact, second and third generation immigrant children were often turning out to be more Greek or Lithuanian or Polish than their forebears as they rediscovered their roots and would "wear" their respective "ethnic" backgrounds proudly, giving rise to a whole new concept, the *hyphenated* American. Today, apart from Americans, you'll meet Greek-Americans, Polish-Americans, Norwegian-Americans and so on.

The consequences of this revival of ethnic pride has been, among other things, the proliferation of what should properly be termed "Hyphenated American Social Histories", so that today you can read in considerable detail the impact of Greeks or Poles or what have you on various parts of America, and this is a good thing. It has allowed Americans to take pride in, not only the high profile events of the dominant ethnic group of colonists, the Anglo-Germanic group, but also to accept the contributions of all the other cultures that have inevitably contributed to creating the mosaic that is the American ethos. It has also allowed the best (and sometimes not so good) aspects of those other cultures to filter through American society in general. Of course, none of this takes into account the stories of the Native American tribes who were displaced by these colonists and immigrants.

What has all this to do with the half-forgotten grave of a Greek "pirate" in a small town some 80 kilometres outside Sydney in far-off Australia? It has to do with the awakening of the Australian consciousness to its multicultural past and the growing concomitant recognition it is affording to those Australians who, like those "hyphenated" Americans, do not share the benefits of belonging to the predominant ethnic group, which, till now, has proffered *its* history and culture as the only one worth serious consideration – the "tyranny" of the First Fleet if you will. It has to do with the revival of ethnic pride and the consequent desire to redefine the concept of Australianness taking into account the contributions of those various ethnic groups to whatever it is that has made up what Australia is today. Just as in America, there had been something of a "melting pot" mentality at work in Australia, and it was not until the early nineteen seventies that officialdom finally began to recognise that there existed people whose needs were specific to the ethnic group to which they had belonged before arrival and who therefore were necessarily being discriminated against while the system remained as it did. Concomitant to this was a similar revival of ethnic pride, again among second and third generations as had happened in the US. As Australia began to perceive itself as a "multicultural society", there arose to some extent the "hyphenated" Australian.

Again, similar to the American experience, among the consequences of this reawakening in ethnic pride has been a desire to discover a place of honour within the history of the making of this country. This has seen some curious historical facts come to light, such as the discovery of a Pole having been in the fleet led by Captain James Cook that discovered the continent – point one to the Poles. Beneath the predictable dash for legitimacy that this sort of fact is striving to attain is a sincere desire to retrieve whatever actual contributions the overlooked members of these various ethnic groups may have made towards forging the Australia character and the country's growth towards nationhood. By so doing they also seek to enhance the quality of understanding between the ethnic groups that makes this country their home.

The last twenty years or so have seen a number of

excellent histories concerning specific ethnic groups published, especially on the Italian experience, and though there appears to have been a number of books on the Greeks and their experiences of Australia, most have been short on history and, in typically Greek fashion, long on polemics and politics. The best have been the books of Charles Price, but even he looked predominantly at the post-war migrations. The last couple of years, however, have seen some vigorous research by a number of individuals, the most eminent of whom is Hugh Gilchrist, who has published an exhaustive three-volume history, *Australians and Greeks* (Halstead). An equally remarkable piece of scholarship is the work of Dr George Kanarakis, (then) lecturer in the School of Communications and Liberal Studies at Mitchell College, Bathurst, about 200 kilometres west of Sydney in regional New South Wales. His book, *The Literary Presence of Greeks in Australia*, surveys some seventy years of writings by Greeks and the children of Greeks in response to life in Australia, a work not only of cultural significance but also a remarkable piece of recovery, much from probable obscurity, of a rich literary heritage. With the rise in recent years of an increasingly significant contingent of Greek-Australian writers affecting all aspects of Australian literature – writers like Antigone Kefala, Angelo Loukakis, Spiro Zavos and the enigmatic poet and commentator π.O., this study has gained even greater significance. Originally published in Athens in 1985 under the title *I logotechniki parousia ton Ellinon stin Afstralia*, the English edition was published by the Australian National University (ANU) Press in 1987.

The importance of the "rediscovery" (recovery?) of an Hellenic or any other ethnic group's heritage in the land in which it has chosen to make its home is manifold and should be obvious. Having overcome the crippling imposition of "second-class" citizenship imposed in an earlier period, these people can not only take pride in both their country of origin and their country of adoption, once no choice at all, but also take pride in the experiences and achievements of those of their fellow expatriates who came before them. So the "Greek Factor" in the creation of the Australian character can take pride of place, however small or large that contribution may have been, alongside those of the dominant ethnic group. There is also the comfort, for those newly arrived, in knowing the stories of those previous "Odysseys", a useful means of coming to terms with the traumas of migration and connecting with their new home.

Australia's celebration of the bi-centenary of its colonisation by Europeans inevitably proved an enormous spur to the increasing awareness of the country's colonial and post-colonial history, and one of the major projects that was funded by the Bicentennial Authority for those celebrations was the gathering of the stories of two hundred ordinary people and their experiences in the period between 1900 and 1920 with regards to conditions, education and, for those who migrated here during that time, the experience of dislocation, especially among groups not part of the Anglo-Celtic majority. This sort of thing will boost the already proliferating local historical societies that can be found around the country, but more importantly, it will enhance the reputations of the small groups of ethnically-oriented historical societies that have emerged. One of the earliest has been the Australian Hellenic Historical Society (AHHS), comprised of a handful of very enthusiastic amateurs, which was asked by the Bicentennial Authority to lend its burgeoning collection of Greek-Australian artefacts for an exhibition hosted by Sydney's Powerhouse Museum in 1988. The AHHS has specialised in gathering oral histories from the oldest members of at least Sydney's Greek-Australian community.

By the by, the man who designed the Federation Pavilion erected to mark the centenary of Sydney's Centennial Park is one Alex Tzannes.

For me, one of the most significant contributions to this research in which the AHHS has been involved is in the area of redefining the concept of "Australianness" or the development, if such there has been, of a distinctly recognisable Australian character. There are the more obviously historical discoveries such as the "rediscovery" of a section of a once thriving township called Tambaroora, which was called Greektown, in which more than a dozen names of Greek families have been uncovered. There was the recovery of a treasure trove of photographs from the gold-mining period that spawned Tambaroora and other towns in regional New South Wales, photographs of stern Greek faces like that of the Karkoe family, residents of Yerranderie. These faces are obviously an important element in the early life of the colony, but then the goldfields, like those of America during the same period, attracted people from all over the world, many of them only for a transitory stay, till the gold petered out, before returning home. The Greeks were no different, though there is evidence now that Orthodox churches were being established on the goldfields, important at least among the women of the communities, a fact that might have hinted at a desire for some more permanent residence.

Australia, through the medium of film, has, over the past few years, been seen outside Australia as presenting a number of stereotypical character traits that are predominantly Anglo-Celtic. Does the typical Australian male behave like a Crocodile Dundee, or a Mel "Mad Max" Gibson, or are they all like the Barry Humphries caricatures Bazza McKenzie and Les Paterson? Though these images seem disparate, there is a common thread running through them, a sense of rugged individualism, albeit subverted by a propensity for self-effacing self-mockery; a determination to battle and win against the odds. Is this necessarily the distinction that defines the Australian character? There is a phrase often used in Australia, particularly within the political classes – "the little Aussie battler".

A good example of the little Aussie battler might be the life of Jack Lewis who, in his day, was one of the most respected and well known all-round endurance athletes in Australia. At twenty-one he won the third Victorian Marathon, held in 1911, coming in at the record time of two hours, 59 minutes and 30 seconds. He was a contender for the Olympics in

Stockholm in 1912, and again in 1920, though it seems he ultimately failed to be selected. Beginning as a member of the South Sydney Harriers, Lewis made his name and his home in Warburton, a small town in rural Victoria, now as a member of the East Melbourne Harriers. In 1922, Lewis gained the record for the 25-mile event, and then in 1926, at the age of 33, he won the 50-mile walk in a then record nine hours, 20 minutes and 24 seconds. Many of the records he set were his for some thirty years. He worked as a ranger for the Victorian Government Tourist Bureau and in that capacity was something of a local hero after walking up into the Victorian Alps to rescue a lost picnicker on Mount Donna Buang. He also led the expedition that attempted to recover the crashed Southern Cross, the plane flown by pioneer aviator Kingsford-Smith from Britain to Australia in record time.

This typical Australian, AHHS research uncovered, was born Ioannis Gerakitys in Kythera in Greece in 1890. Ioannis became the Anglicised Jack, while his nickname, "Glou", became Lou and finally Lewis. Migrating to Australia sometime in 1903 or 1904, he initially settled in Queensland, where he started racing in 1906. Lewis/Gerakitys died in June 1956, a tiny fragment of history, but an Hellenic fragment having lived as Australian a life, of its kind, as any.

The single most important event in the creation of the Australian identity as a nation that had come of age wasn't, unfortunately, the establishment of the Federation of Australian states in 1901, but the experience of the First World War. In that war, Australia sent some 300,000 men to fight a cause that was far from the interests of the local population, and they were sent off proudly. The experiences of those soldiers in the trenches of France and on the cliffs of Gallipoli have become the stuff of legend for all Australians. By the 1980s no less than four feature-length films had been made celebrating the battle of Gallipoli, which was a military disaster, recognised even by Constantine I, the King of Greece at the time, 1915, as an exercise in futility. Instead it has become the baptism of fire that "forged the nation" and those soldiers have become the near-legendary ANZACs, the Australian and New Zealand Army Corps (and yes, let's not forget the equally heroic New Zealanders). In its first two years of research, the AHHS uncovered no less than fifteen Greeks who joined up and fought alongside their fellow ANZACs involved in that most Australian of historical moments. It may seem a small number, but it is a contribution nonetheless, and those Greeks fought as *Australians*. Even if the idea of killing a few Turks might have been attractive to some, those Greeks also brought honour to Australia.

Aged 25, George Pappas volunteered in September 1914, just one month after the declaration of war. He was assigned to 13th Battalion and was part of the second day of landings on the beaches of Gallipoli. He was evacuated in December 1915. Before that, in August, his battalion had been ordered to reinforce an attack on a prominent position designated Hill 60. For this action, Pappas was awarded the Distinguished Conduct Medal, second only to the Victoria Cross as a medal for heroism, the highest award given non-commissioned officers or privates during World War One.

Nikolas Rodakis, born in Athens in 1876, came to Australia in 1900, moving to a town called Warrnambool on the southern Victorian coast. He volunteered in 1917, aged 41, and in September that same year received the Military Medal, an Imperial award, for an action in which he was wounded five times. In September the following year, Rodakis was awarded the Distinguished Service Cross, this time an American decoration, which he seems to have gained when, as a machine gunner with the 4th Machinegun Battalion, his battalion was seconded to an American division on the Western Front. This was the first American DSC to be awarded to a non-American soldier in World War One.

Dean Casos joined the Australian Imperial Forces (AIF) in October 1916 at the tender age of seventeen years two months, despite the fact, obviously all too often ignored, that recruits were meant to have had previous military experience and to be physically mature. Casos saw action in France. Born Dionysios Vatholamaius, which would probably best translate to Bartholmew, the family changed it to the name of the island from which they had to come to Australia, Kasos. He joined up again in the Second World War, serving as a Lieutenant in the Intelligence Corps. His son James, born in Australia in 1922 after Casos married an Australian girl named Violet Taylor, served with the Royal Australian Air Force, training in Canada and flying as a navigator with 460th Squadron, Bomber Command, in some thirty-three missions over Germany.

The youngest Greek ANZAC the AHHS had uncovered to that point was Minas Aslanis. Born in Australia and more commonly known as Mina Ashton, he joined up in 1916 at the age of sixteen years and two months. Like Casos, he saw action in France, where he was gassed in 1918. The two young men evidently met on the front line, as in letters sent home from hospital in England while recovering, each mentions the other. Mina Ashton returned to Australia in 1919 and also appears to have served in the Second World War.

Four Castellorizian boys from Western Australia enlisted in 1916 – Agapitos Michael, Stavros Kakulis, Con Passaris and Michael Gunellas. Agapitos Michael's son, Michael, served as Lord Mayor of Perth between 1982 and 1988. He too had enlisted in the Royal Australian Air Force in 1940 and was posted to Darwin as a member of 77 Squadron. Gunellas, meanwhile, received a Distinguished Service Medal for his efforts in the First World War.

As it happens, Greeks also appear to have served with Australian forces during the Boar War. One Michael Manousou, who came to Australia in 1853, had married an English girl and produced twelve children, two of whom, Alfred Aristides and Frank Homer, served with cavalry units in South Africa between 1899 and 1902.

## POSTSCRIPT:

For a second attempt at an "academic" essay, hopefully this isn't too clumsy or naïve. By the time I wrote it I was well into my second year of an MA in Studies of 20th Century American Civilisation at UNSW – hence the American references. I've tidied it up a little and added a few lines from another less academic essay I got published in a free weekly magazine in Sydney titled *Nine To Five* (7/11/88, pp. 8-10 – I've chosen not to include it in full here). My membership of the Australian Hellenic Historical Society lasted a mere four years and, sadly, the group fell apart a year or two after my departure, though the archives are still being held by its president. Obviously the Greek presence in Australia continues to make itself an invaluable part of Australia's identity, whether through sportsmen like Nick Kyrios and Thanasi Kokkinakis, writers like Christos Tsiolkas and Nick Giannopoulos, journalist and political historian George Megalogenis, actors Alex Dimitriades, *Home And Away*'s Ada Nicodemou, Andrea Demetriades and sisters Zoe and Gia Carides, film director George Miller of *Mad Max* fame, the son of Kythira-born father Dimitrios Miliotis, or comedienne Mary Coustas aka Effie Stephanidis and the *Wogs Out of Work* crew. Then of course there's ABC-TV *Gardening Australia*'s Costa Georgiadis. And I should also mention my former colleague in Australia's most successful surf guitar band of the 1960s The Atlantics, the band that gave us the classic *Bombora*, guitarist Jim Skiathitis and their original second guitarist and keyboards player Theo Penglis.

# REDISCOVERING THE GREEK SURREAL

A review of *The Mule's Foal*, by Fotini Epanomitis (Allen & Unwin, 1993)

The first thing that struck me about this first novel by young Perth-born academic, Fotini Epanomitis, the winner of the 1992 *Australian*/Vogal Literary Award, was how consummately *Greek* it is. Ms Epanomitis may have grown up in Perth, spending only her twelfth year in the tiny Greek village of her grandparents, but every word of *The Mule's Foal* shouts out "I am Greek", which speaks volumes for just how far Australia has come in accommodating not only its multicultural population but that population's intellectual potential. It also shows just how much more cosmopolitan is the judging panel behind the *Australian*/Vogel Literary Award these days. The last Greek Australian manuscript to win, *Ilias*, by Jim Sakkas, a mere six years before in 1986, seems almost parochial by comparison to the surrealistic landscapes conjured up by Epanomitis.

The "surreal" element is the second thing that struck me about *The Mule's Foal*. The bulk of the more widely known literature published by Greek Australian writers – and my own too – has tended to be in the "migrant experience" genre, or xenetia, as Dr George Kanarakis defines it in his seminal compendium, *Greek Voices in Australia: A Tradition of Prose, Poetry and Drama*: "the difficulties of immigrant life in Australia and the Odyssean dream of return to the homeland." (Australian National University Press, 1987, p. 5) *The Mule's Foal*, on the other hand, never moves more than a few miles from a dilapidated little village somewhere in the mountainous north east of Greece, without a hint of nostalgia for some longed-for lost homeland or dreams of life in a new land far away, such as Australia. In fact, rather than sentimental, *The Mule's Foal* is filled with grotesque people who live lives filled with grinding poverty, brutality and ugliness, and yet command a very real respect for their ability to not merely survive but to somehow do it with an honesty and dignity.

Where the "surreal" tag came as something of a surprise to me, personally, was in the suggestion, courtesy of the accompanying press release, written by Barry Oakley, that the publisher very kindly sent with my review copy, that here is a book of "Magical magic-realism; [Ms Epanomitis is] the Gabriel Marquez of the Greeks." Why that struck me as surprising is, quite simply, that, while I was reading the book, no matter how bizarre the tales of the inhabitants might have seemed, it all seemed perfectly *natural*. This is because the element of the fantastic that readers who are not Greek might see in these characters and events is just the way Greeks, especially the less literate, peasant Greeks of whom Ms Epanomitis writes, actually perceive the world. *The Mule's Foal* is an extraordinary insight into the mind of that simple Greek peasant.

Perhaps, in fact, what we have here is a book that helps us recall how *all* our ancestors once perceived their usually circumscribed world, in small country villages that Thomas Hardy would have recognised through to the more nomadic lives of the world's indigenous peoples. For what you have in *The Mule's Foal* is the collective memory, over some three generations, with all the distortions that inevitably imbue oral histories, of families in this obscure little village, memories of slights, of ancient battles, of superstitions, coincidences, paradoxes and plagues, where an event that might have taken place a hundred years before is still as vivid in the lives of the book's present as that afternoon's coffee down at Manolio's place. It is a world in which, despite nearly two thousand years of Orthodox Christianity, the ancient occult beliefs are still very much alive, where the concept that an individual or a whole community can be plagued by bad luck because of the "Evil Eye" (*matias*), is not only believed virulently by that community but is endorsed by that community's Orthodox priest.

*The Mule's Foal* is ostensibly told by the village whore, Mirella, and focuses on the fortunes of three generations of the families of Yiorgos and his wife Stella, whose daughter Vaia is thought to bring the *matias* to the village for allowing her child, who seems to have been born looking like a gorilla, to live, rather than follow the age-old tradition for disfigured babies of being left at the foot of the bridge to be eaten by the village pigs; and also of Meta and Agape of the Glowing Face. Meta turns out to be the grandmother of that gorilla child, who had been sent to gaol many years before for perhaps murdering a tinker who had tried to buy her favours with gold coins he had found in a part of the valley the village avoids because of its connections with the deaths of many Greeks at the hands of Turks a century or so earlier, which gave the village the enigmatic and dubious St Vaia. Meta turns up later in the novel as a man – of course. Stella, meanwhile, routinely pulls out the bones of her grandparents and fondles them for comfort and good luck.

There are stories like this throughout the gloriously chaotic book, told with an unembroidered, matter-of-fact simplicity, like that of the woman who ate her mother-in-law – "but this was out of desperation" we're assured. The woman had been sent to complete an impossible chore and the story suggests that some kindly spirit has turned into a big brown bear so she would not have to do it, and she ate the mother-in-law instead. Fairy tale stuff and, as I've noted, to the sophisticated, city-dwelling Anglo-Celtic Australian, pure fantasy – indeed magic realism. But let me assure you once again that this is how many an unsophisticated, village-dwelling Greek *still* thinks. Or at least the older generations, whose world has not yet been completely swamped by Western consumer culture and its more disposable iconography.

## POSTSCRIPT:

It seems *The Mule's Foal*, which also won her the 1994 Commonwealth Writers' Prize for best first book, South East Asia and South Pacific region, turned out to be Fotini's only novel, her only other publications a drama titled *When Coloured Gonads Meet* and a short story titled *All That Was Needed*.

Just by the by, in October 2022, a Melbourne-based publicist sent me an album released by former White Stripes singer, songwriter and guitarist Jack White's independent label, Third Man Records that, to my ears at least, could easily be the soundtrack for *The Mule's Foal*. Titled *Cry With Tears: Greek-Albanian Songs of Many Voices*, it was the debut album from an eight-piece all-female Greek-Albanian vocal ensemble called Isokratisses. Of course, the traditional songs of Isokratisses are from villages in the mountainous region of Albania that borders Greece's west, while *The Mule's Foal* is set in the mountainous north of Greece's east, but nonetheless I think that, if you seek out both the novel and the recording, you'll find they'll complement each other beautifully. Isokratisses is Greek for women who sing the iso or drone, an a cappella musical tradition that stretches back to the ancient sounds of Epirus in northern Greece and southern Albania, so you can't get more authentically traditional than that. *Cry With Tears* isn't the sort of record that was ever likely to storm even world music charts, despite having been produced by Grammy Award-winning producer, musicologist, archivist and author Christopher C. King, but it's an important audio documentation of a kind of music that will inevitably disappear as the world hurtles relentlessly into its uncertain future, as relevant as Maltese Australian singer-songwriter Kavisha Mazella's 1993 *Joys Of The Women* album, which documented Fremantle's traditional Italian community choir, Le Goie Delle Donne. Haunting, *Cry With Tears* is a collection of simple songs about everyday life in the village, from *The Ballad of the Handkerchief* to *Last Night's Dream*, *Little Apple Tree* to *My Basil*, all deeply imbued with the landscape from which it sprang, a remarkable recording that will truly transport you to another time and place.

I reviewed it for *Rhythms* magazine. Inevitably, the review was never published.

# THE ROAD TO SMITHFIELD HOSTEL

A review of *Alien to Citizen: Settling Migrants in Australia, 1945-75*, Anna-Mari Jordans (Allen & Unwin)

The heat was still oppressive, even at nine or ten o'clock at night, as we stood with the rest of the group waiting for the bus that would take us out to Smithfield Hostel. The only other things I can remember from that night are a lot of flatness, probably the Port Adelaide Docks area where we'd disembarked; a big ghostly-looking gum tree and the tatty-looking bus that eventually collected us. Why didn't these people have big red buses like the ones I knew from London? My first impression of Australia was definitely one of disappointment, though once we settled in, mercifully for a mere two weeks or so, the hostel recalled a little of the holiday atmosphere I'd felt on the boat trip out, and even to some extent the family holidays on the south coast of England.

But I was still very disappointed, and I was English, born and bred. Imagine how disappointed my mother must have been, having already experienced fourteen years or so of dislocation in an alien London, having left her village home on the island of Rhodes in the Greek Dodecanese to marry my father – they'd met during WWII when he, a Royal Engineer, found himself stationed there. Even my father, I could tell, was disappointed, but the stoic family man that he was, he got out there, found himself a job and a house and got us out of the hostel and into the then still youthfully hopeful satellite suburb of Elizabeth West, twenty kilometres north of Adelaide. This was 1964. The Beatles had just toured Australia, Johnny O'Keefe and *Bandstand* were Australian television's idea of rock'n'roll and, as a "sophisticated" pop music lover of twelve years old with a couple of years of *Top Of The Pops* under my belt, musical disillusion settled in solidly for at least the next two or three years.

Much as the move to Australia was ultimately good for me – I'd never have got to university back in England – it broke

109

my father. Without the familiar landmarks of London to take us to every Sunday, without a decent bus service to get us to and from such places as might exist of interest – he never learned to drive, chose not to learn – his world became increasingly circumscribed by dull work routine and the flat, featureless landscape and culture that surrounded us. His lack of formal education compounded by his lack of qualifications suitable for employment beyond unskilled labourer here, despite years of self-education and papers to attest his skills as a high-rise building site foreman back in London, meant limited work options.

But, as I say, it must have been far, far worse for my mother, who had still not really come to terms with English, the English and England, let alone this new country, Australia. At least my father, my sisters and I spoke the language.

There was for me, therefore, more than a passing interest in this latest book to be published based on research into social policy facilitated by the opening up of the Australian government archives, of which Ann-Mari Jordens' book, *Alien to Citizen*, is a part. The book focuses on the response to and intervention on behalf of the migrants who arrived in Australia between 1945 and 1975 by the Department of Immigration, the book itself a response, as Jordens suggests, to the call by demographer W.D. Borrie, chairman of the National Population Inquiry of 1972 to "attempt an overview of the response of Australian institutions to changes in the population brought about by the immigration programme pursued since the end of the Second World War.

Ultimately, the heroes of Ann-Marie Jordens' book on those efforts to help the approximately 3.3 million migrants who came to Australia between 1945 and 1971 are that small determined band of social workers the Department hesitantly took on board – and never with more than some vaguely tacit commitment – but wouldn't have been able to help my mother. She'd chosen long ago "not to leave the island" as it were, having managed to get her unmarried older sister first to

England and then to Australia with us. With my aunt as insulation, the outside world could be kept at a safe distance. With the arrival of sons- and daughters-in-law and then Australian-born grandchildren, that all changed to an extent, though the mindset never wavered, but those first dozen or so years of life in pre-multicultural Australia were hard even without my mother allowing the real world into our little suburban home sitting in a dusty paddock of red dirt. For thousands and thousands of migrants who didn't have the advantage of an English husband or wife to help bridge the gap, as the story extrapolated in Jordens' book makes clear, life in Australia could be a nightmare.

Still, *Alien to Citizen* presents a far more optimistic story than that previous paragraph might suggest. There were a lot of committed people within and outside the Department of Immigration determined to help those hundreds of thousands of non-English migrants settle into their new country, and the resulting successes helped change this country into the vibrant and for the most part tolerant multicultural society we enjoy today.

The decision to initiate a program of mass migration to Australia was announced in August 1945 by Australia's first Minister for Immigration, Arthur Calwell, and was taken partly to bolster a shrinking and ageing population and partly to support the international commitment to the relief of the refugee crisis that had been created by the Second World War. Until 1964, the Department saw its job as one of assisting migrants to "assimilate" into Australian society, a discredited term we know all too well today as one that assumes that everyone must dismiss their own cultural mores in favour of the traits and customs of the dominant culture, particularly in the context of the Stolen Children report with respect to Australia's Aboriginal and Torres Strait Islander population.

There was still, though never made explicit in post-war migration policy on which Australian society was based, the "White Australia Policy", introduced soon after Federation,

111

which had been designed to limit non-British migration to Australia. It was an endemic racism that continued to affect the choice of migrants Australia was prepared to accept. One of the earliest ethnic groups to feel that racism was the Greeks. What made the restrictions imposed on the eligibility of many hopeful Greek migrants doubly galling at the time was the fact that other ethnic groups were accepted far more willingly despite the fact that, unlike the Greeks, they had in fact been "the enemy" in the Second World War – Germans and Italians were welcomed where Greeks were not. This was, to some extent, due to a perception not only that southern Europeans in general were a less desirable "type" than northern Europeans, but that there was some question as to the "whiteness" of many potential Greek migrants! Admittedly, as Jordans points out, "darker" southern Italians faced the same prejudices – "selection officers in Mediterranean regions were given the task of picking the difference between 'colour' and suntan. One, selecting Greeks, used to refer doubtful cases to the medical officer, who had them strip to see if they were dark all over."

Restrictions on potential Greek immigration had been implanted by Australian governments as far back as the 1920s, with a blanket policy discriminating against all "aliens" finally being officially introduced in 1930. Considering the fact that Melbourne today is the biggest "Greek" city outside Greece itself, early migration under these restrictions was, not surprisingly, small. Only 8,963 permanent settlers came to Australia between 1946 and 1954, despite the fact that in 1948, a significant contingent of Greek ex-servicemen led a protest against that undisclosed discrimination. The Greek Consul-General at the time argued unsuccessfully for the inclusion of Greeks in the assisted passage agreements for ex-servicemen Australia was entering into with various countries at the time. The argument became even more heated when, in 1951, the Greek Consul-General in Melbourne informed the Department of Immigration that "there is a strong undercurrent of resentment among the Greek community that 20,000 Italians should be brought out here free of charge while no similar scheme operates in respect of Greeks."

Migration officers were eventually appointed to Athens and the Australian government relented to some extent under the pressure of that perceived favouring of former "enemy" aliens over former allies in its migrant selection process. Still, the country into which these Greeks were coming didn't understand the culture within which those Greeks had grown up any more than those Greeks understood the society into which they were entering, a fact not exactly helped by at least one Greek envoy, Dimitri Lambros, who in 1953 suggested that young married Greeks were displaying "a lack of discipline and stamina" by opting to desert work they'd been designated in Mildura in order to return to their wives in the hostel at Bonegilla.

As I've suggested, my mother was lucky in another respect in her initial migrant experience. Unlike the rest of the non-English migrants, as a British migrant by marriage, she was housed in a hostel that was under the jurisdiction of the Department of Labour and National Service. These hostels were far better serviced in terms of social workers and the infrastructure necessary to facilitate assimilation into the wider community than those hostels administered by the Department of Immigration for non-British migrants.

Nonetheless, those non-English hostels became the testing ground for the questioning of a lot of assumptions about both the migrant and host culture's experience and ultimately became instrumental in changing Australian society in general. As Jordens points out in her ominously-titled chapter on "Non-Compliant Women in Holding Centres": "the plight of alien women for the first time drew the attention of administrators to the unresponsiveness of Australian culture and administrative structures to the needs of working women in general, and in particular of women in the community attempting to provide for children without male support ... By the end of 1975 there were child-minding facilities and after-school care in all hostels for working women. The demands placed on the bureaucracy by migrant women contributed significantly to the cultural change that was taking place in Australian attitudes towards the participation of women in the workforce."

Obviously Jordens' book explores far more than the Greek migrant experience but I hope you'll forgive my concentrating on that one aspect in a book full to bursting with information on the full spectrum of non-English-speaking migrant experience if only for the fact that it allows an accessible snapshot of the whole of which I have some small insight. I will however just pick up on the English side of the equation for a moment if I may. The general perception on post-war immigration has always been that it primarily targeted British migrants, and that these did of course constitute the biggest segment of the overall migrant figures by far – around 1,086,500 or so arriving between July 1947 and June 1970 according to figures published by Charles A. Price in *Australian Immigration, A Bibliography and Digest*, N. 2 (ANU, 1970). Jordens reminds us however that British migrants actually formed the minority of the intake until 1958, and that there seems to have been a reticence on the part of British rural workers, a group the Department of Immigration was particularly interested in attracting to Australia immediately after the War to take up the opportunity, since their skills in post-war Britain were similarly in demand and therefore attracted far better wages and conditions there than Australia seemed able to offer.

It's also amusing to note too that, true to the stereotype, Department of Immigration social workers tended to prefer their non-English-speaking clients because they found British migrants "full of complaints, much harder to relate to, and reluctant to seek help from the same people who were helping aliens".

The impact of those 3.3 million immigrants, approximately 200,000 of whom were Greek, inevitably changed the makeup of Australian society and its perception of itself *as* a society, making the change from a predominantly

114

British (Anglo-Celtic) to a multicultural society inevitable and thereby ultimately enriching the lives of all Australians. The part the Department of Immigration played in ensuring that these changes would come smoothly wasn't always right but as Jordens shows in this thoroughly researched book, that part was far greater than we realise. Many of the innovations that it implemented, from education to telephone interpreting services, were never publicly announced and therefore never credited to the Department, making *Alien to Citizen* an important contribution to not only migration studies but to redressing the balance in the public perception of the Department.

It's not an easy read by any means, bound as it must be to the exploits of bureaucrats and welfare workers as expounded by the archives, in the form of reports and recommendations. But *Alien to Citizen* is an essential addition to the body of sources available for anyone interested in the way only the migrants who came to Australia (British, Greek, Dutch, Italian or whoever, and the people who tried to help them adjust to this disconcertingly distant land), but also those who were here already came to understand what it is to be Australian.

## POSTSCRIPT:

Early in 1912, Italy decided to occupy the Dodecanese, the 12 islands (except Kastellorizo) braced hard by the south-western coast of Turkey, as part of their efforts to gain a foothold closer to the country with which it was then at war. Italy remained in the Dodecanese at the end of that war and remained there until the end of the Second World War, when the islands were designated a British military protectorate before finally becoming part of Greece in 1947. Rhodes is the largest of the Dodecanese.

In one of those unlikely quirks of history, when a young drummer named Aldo Civitico completed the lineup of the band that consumed my life between 1976 and 1978, Scandal, it turned out that his father had been a soldier stationed on Rhodes during the Second World War. During one of the band's return trips to Adelaide once we were touring, we contrived to bring my parents and his together at their home in Croydon, just north of Adelaide. Aldo's father had a wonderful time, my dad was his usual convivial self and my mum got to chat, albeit cautiously, in the Italian she'd learned under the Occupation. Sadly, it was a gathering that was never repeated.

## *THE WOUND*, ENMORE THEATRE, 18/3/99

*The Review, written in the cold light of day:*

Don't go expecting a *Wogs Out Of Work*! Despite the subtitle, which is meant of course to be ironic, and the fact that there are plenty of laughs throughout the evening, *The Wound* is ultimately a far more substantial look at the business of identity, nostalgia, guilt and memory than any of the *Wog* productions. Then add to the brilliant ensemble cast the multimedia elements of photo-montage, video and vox pop interviews, a subtle, bare yet immensely effective (and moveable) stage set, music by Tom Kazas (of The Moffs) and Themos Mexis, choreography by one of the ensemble of actors, Helen Dallas, and text by six of our finest Greek-Australian writers – Jon Conimos, Fotini Epanomatis, Frida Kitas, Angelo Loukakis, Peter Lyssiotis and the man who devised, narrated and directed it all, Lex Marinos, and you have an extraordinary theatre experience.

And don't imagine that this is an "ethnic-specific" theatre experience either. Yes, it's as Greek as you're going to get in all the references, but as I watched Zoe Carides as the nine year old Tammy battling her harridan of a mother, played with terrifying gusto by Helen Dallas, in the hilariously black piece by Frida Kitas, I could see the archetypal Jewish "mom" so often presented in American theatre, and all overblown mothers who use guilt and fear as a method of controlling those around them.

That's the point. Like all great theatre, and literature in general, these pieces have a universality that reaches far beyond their genesis as the experience of first, second and third generation Greek-Australians, in the best tradition of classical Greek tragedy and comedy. They all shone too, these vibrant, dynamic young actors – Jen Apostolou, Arthur Angel, Zoe Carides, Helen Dallas, Adam Hatzimanolis and Nicholas Mitsakis. Just go and see it, with an open mind and heart.

*The Response*, written on the night, in the heat of the moment, wasn't published:

"Wherever I go, Greece wounds me." George Seferis.

If there is a wound that Greeks must carry throughout their lives wherever they may roam it is one inflicted not by the loss of homeland but by the wrath of the mother, who demands to be paid in kind for the pain of being rent asunder to give birth to a Greek. It is the wound of which you will be reminded until either you bury her or she buries you. If she buries you, she will live out her days regaling all who will listen of the wound you, ungrateful son/daughter, inflicted on her, and if you bury her, the deep and eternal sense of guilt with which she has imbued every fibre of your body will continue to resonate with the knowledge of that wound until you too are buried. This is the wound, the stigmata only another Greek will know, will see in you but will never acknowledge, because to do so is to open that wound, to reveal it to the light, and the shame, and the guilt. Better then to turn away, to lie, to tend that wound in silence – and pray. And so, a Greek man must be more than a man, all bluster and machismo, because a Greek woman must inevitably conspire with her mother, and hers before her, and so on for generations back, to inflict that wound, that mortal wound which will mark that man out for all time, a Greek.

## POSTSCRIPT:

From what I remember of the reception of *The Wound* on the night, it pretty much outraged everyone, and particularly all those who saw it as an unconscionable slight against all Greek mothers. I don't think it had much of a run. Pity.

Older readers may remember Lex Marinos, who was born in Wagga Wagga to a Greek father and Greek-Australian mother, as the Italian son-in-law in 1980s Australian TV comedy series *Kingswood Country*, a show I never saw – I was gigging. Turns out he was a presenter on Double Jay back in the day. Again, I never heard him on air. September 13, 2024, at the age of 74, "at a moment of his choosing," a post on his Facebook page announced, "surrounded by family and the sounds of Bob Dylan accompanying our vigil," Marinos left the stage for the last time. He was 75.

I was lucky enough to interview Zoe Carides the week before *The Wound* hit the stage. "I feel that being half Greek certainly marked me," she admitted. "When I was a kid I actually did feel it was such a handicap. My mother's English and we certainly didn't have a typical Greek upbringing, that's for sure, though we attended a lot of christenings and weddings and that sort of thing. So I had a lot of contact with Greeks growing up and my cousins are still in my life... I spent much of my life racing away from my heritage and there was a time when I left home, had rock'n'roll band, became an actress and was just a wild rager and didn't want to have anything to do with my heritage at all – not the Greek side anyway! Now I don't feel like that."

*The Wound* was subtitled *Anyone Can Be Normal; It Takes A Very Special Person To Be Greek.*

# THE ENGLISHMAN OUTSIDE

## PROLOGUE

At the end of 1983, my world as I'd managed to construct it to that point essentially began to fall apart. The main band I was playing in and was actually earning a few dollars with closed shop, while my more "arty" side band also folded. Bad enough but I'd found other bands so I could assume I'd bounce back soon enough. But then the half dozen music magazines to which I'd been contributing also either folded or changed editors for whom whatever I might have to say on the artists and acts doing the rounds at the time was seen as, well, irrelevant. So my other income stream disappeared. Fragile at the best of times, my confidence took a big hit. My personal life was also in a precarious state, which I couldn't really understand, but knew was undermining whatever confidence I still had even more. As it turned out, I was a year away from tipping into the most debilitating case of reactive depression I would ever experience, which cost me that personal life and has since become, unfortunately, the basis for a myth that has justified all manner of behavioural assumptions about me, at least within the familial unit I later created – and went on to lose – decades after I managed to dig myself out of that particular rabbit hole.

This seems to be the way it works – or at least in my experience. The centre of the universe is deeply unhappy and nothing you do seems to make any difference. It's a scenario that is obviously distressing but perhaps, given time, an answer will appear and you eventually *can* make a difference and your efforts alleviate that unhappiness. It all seems pretty straightforward. Now, imagine you're a baby. The centre of the universe is mum and she is *profoundly* unhappy. As she is all there is – other family members are all very well but the core relationship is between mother and child, and the child is yet to negotiate relationships beyond mum. So, again, if the centre of the universe is unhappy, it must be your fault. None of this is consciously articulated – the world of words is yet to evolve so the baby's mind is a soup of inarticulate feelings negotiating for its needs – food, security and so on. All the baby is aware of is mum is unhappy and since there's only you, she's unhappy with *you*. There are a variety of behavioural options available to try to redirect that unhappiness as your mind begins to make its connections – you learn that crying for instance gets attention – but what do you do when the unhappiness at the centre doesn't seem to diminish, and in fact gradually amplifies. The baby becomes more and more anxious, more agitated, more distressed, more fretful, reflecting the anxiety in the mother, the closed circuit constantly feeding back into itself. Since it cannot *articulate* these feelings, baby cries or screams, has a tantrum, whatever it takes to get the universe to pay attention. It seems that my strategy was to withdraw; recognising that nothing I did seemed to make any difference. It was as if I was invisible – the centre of the universe saw me but couldn't see me. As I say, none of this was conscious; it was all nebulous feelings of uncertainty, those funny fluttery tummy moments. They pass, fade into the background as the wider world comes into focus and baby becomes child, autonomy evolves and the centre of the universe slowly ceases to be all-important. The problem arises when all those numinous feelings are triggered by the re-emergence of situations, emotional circumstances that replicate those periods in life where one felt powerless. Once again, the centre of the universe – mother, lover, wife – seems profoundly unhappy and nothing you do seems to make any difference. If it coincides with the collapse of whatever other support systems you've constructed to get you through, then withdrawal becomes implosion – Reactive Depression.

I'm over-thinking it all of course, desperately trying to explain myself, but that's how it seems to work. When I tipped into depression I would swing between uncontrollable chattering trying to justify my actions, my existence, to an almost catatonic retreat from everyone and everything. For a few months it felt like a brick had been grafted inside my skull. Yet if I was obliged to do something, the 12-week course in contemporary music I was moderating for Epping CYSS for instance, I could somehow get myself together, head from my place in Enmore in inner-city Sydney to Epping, present that day's discussion, and return home only to dissolve back into silence and welcome sleep – and much desperately explanatory scribbling. It took three or four months of two-hour weekly sessions with a psychologist to be guided through the likely trigger points that tipped me over the edge for the "brick" to dissolve and my torpor to fade enough to get back into both bands and relationships.

Thankfully, it seems that, at least in my case, once you recognise and understand the triggers that tip you into depression – reactive, rather than endogenous, which has its roots in biochemical deficiencies and requires a regimen of pills and so on in order to maintain a viable psychological balance – those triggers lose their potency. From there on, it was just dealing with life's inevitable heartaches and disappointments as they came, like everyone else. Reactive depression is *not* genetic, it's environmental – no one inherits a *reactive* depression gene. And I was *never* suicidal.

Anyway, all this is by way of explaining this first piece of political observation, very much of its time but still, I hope, of interest for shining a light on a particular period of British social history. Rather than allow circumstances to overwhelm me, in January 1984, I set myself a task by way of focusing my energies of a bit of research based on some of the things I was reading and seeing on current affairs programs at the time. After all, I'd learned that the best way to "get myself together" after the band that had brought me to Sydney so unceremoniously dismissed me – another reactive trigger if ever there was one! – was to take myself back to university and do that MA in English Literature I'd attempted to start before the band had "saved" me and sent me off touring and recording for three years. So, I did the reading, made notes and one night I set myself up in my little library/study and literally wrote till dawn…

## NATIONAL FRONT – FARCE OR FORCE:
**Some observations on the impact of Right Wing political movements in Great Britain in the early Eighties**

"I have no doubt that British Nazis see armed violence as quite necessary to their coming to power. The question is, when they intend to use their arms. They have the desire to do it, they have the means to do it, they have the potential to do it. They are waiting for the right opportunity."

Strong words indeed from one Dr Jacob Gerwitz of the Board of Deputies of British Jews, a statement he made to Joanna Mack when she spoke to him for an episode titled *Anti-Semitic Terror* of London Weekend Television's religious programme *Credo*, which screened early in 1981 in its regular Sunday evening timeslot. Certainly the article of that title published in *The Listener* April 30, 1981[1], from which I take this quote, created something of a sensation, if the nine-week run of claims, counter-claims and denunciations that followed in *The Listener*'s "Letters to the Editor" pages is any indication. Curiously enough however, little of the debate in these letters actually had anything to do with the British Nazi threat which had been the topic under discussion. Apart from a reiteration of that threat from Dr Gerwitz in his first response to enter the ensuing debate[2], the only other letter that bore any relevance to the topic came from Mr Ernest Pendrous, the Honorary Press Secretary of the National Front (NF)[3], who stressed the point that there was no "Nazi" ideology in the National Front policy documentation or its election manifesto, nor was it in any way affiliated with the actual villain of the piece, the League of St George.

The implication seems to be that everyone sees the extreme Right Wing factions, parties and splinter groups as a potential threat, but at the same time no one seems able to take any of them seriously. More than once the correspondents in the "Anti-Semitic Terrorism" debate in *The Listener*'s Letters pages dismissed to these groups as "lunatic fringe", though Dr Gerwitz obviously took the potential threat from these groups rather more seriously. The question is how much of a joke is the National Front in Britain today? And is it time to take the threat these people present a little more seriously?

The problem is that it is difficult to separate much of the blustering and violence that is tagged as National Front from what is just pure hooliganism. The most common media portrait of National Front supporters is the skin-headed football hooligan who spends as much time abusing his home team for its shortcomings as he might the "Blacks" and "Pakis" he vehemently espouses should be "forcibly repatriated". There is no way of knowing how much of this is simply that testosterone-fuelled "adolescent phase" out of which one would hope the lout will grow once a job and responsibilities inevitably rein him in. Unfortunately, in Britain right now, the chances of getting that job and its potential consequent sense of responsibility are diminishing at an alarming rate. With three million people out of work, many of the youths that become involved in this kind of behaviour may never get a job. The immediate consequence is that these people are despondent, bored and angry. Worse, as they see it, all too often all they face is rejection in whatever attempt they might make to get ahead, reinforcing feelings of pointlessness. The result has been a higher degree of early school leavers and an accompanying rise of illiteracy; all fertile ground for the extreme Right (and for that matter, the extreme Left). After all, it's got to be *somebody's* fault.

In Mack's original *Listener* article, she listed as British Nazi-motivated actions eight separate attacks on synagogues, the defacing daubing of a Jewish cemetery, four incidents of serious individual harassment of Jews and damage to three Jewish schools amounting to more than £20,000 in one case, all accompanied with the regulation fascist and racist slogans, in the single month preceding publication of her article, fair indication indeed of an upsurge in anti-Semitic activity. Mack certainly felt that these violations were instigated by the extreme Right wing and they are certainly no joke to those upon whom they were inflicted. "Lunatic fringe" or not, there seems some justification for Dr Gerwitz's fears. But how organised is this vandalism and hooliganism and how far are these Right wing factions from escalating this into terrorism or armed insurrection?

The National Front maintains that it seeks power by purely parliamentary means, as various spokesmen are at pains to point out in the British press at every opportunity. The "threat" seems remote enough, with not one National Front candidate having ever gained a seat for which he or she has contested, but the support *is* there if they could get 191,000 votes in the 1979 General Election.[4] The official NF membership is only between 14 and 15 thousand, though NF leaders refuse to indicate just what the membership figure is precisely. The majority of voters quite simply ignore or reject them as a party of any consequence. So how, with such a dismal election record, can the National Front and the various Right wing splinter group ever hope to gain that "legitimate" parliamentary foothold?

Joanna Mack points out that the more extreme League of St George doesn't intend to wait and is actively provocative in the hope of sparking off some form of insurrection. For all the denials, the National Front has a well-documented record of provocation and harassment, all too clearly designed to create disorder. There have been attacks on Members of Parliament who have openly been sympathetic to Britain's burgeoning coloured population over the years, such as two on the home of Labour MP Mr Sidney Bidwell, as well as Mr Mark Bonham-Carter, an uncle of actor Helena Bonham-Carter and Chairman of the Community Relations Commission, and others involved in improving race relations.[5] The National Front is, of course, extremely pro-British in the sense that anyone who is not obviously of white Anglo-Saxon stock should be forcibly "repatriated", a doctrine that runs uncomfortably close to Hitler's Nazis' own advocating the preservation of an imagined Aryan racial purity.

More disturbing than this kind of harassment, however,

is the very real violence inflicted on individuals in the name of the National Front. On the political level, there was the attempt to assault President Kenyatta of Kenya on his visit to England in 1964 by the Front's National Activities Organiser, Martin Webster. On the individual level, to cite just one example, there was the horrific case documented in the September 1981 number of Feminist journal *Spare Rib*. [6] Apparently, an Indian youth named Satwinder Sondh was attacked by three skinhead youths as he was going to college and had his wrists lashed and the initials "NF" carved on his stomach. Whether the attackers were actual Front members or not, there must be a modicum of blame on the organisation simply because it has, over the years, gone out of its way to signify that the ills of Southall can be lain firmly at the doors of the "immigrants", and have helped spark or escalate every racial riot to have taken place there, as well as in Brixton, south London, and other inner London suburbs.

The real menace of an organisation like the National Front becomes apparent when it is revealed that it was instrumental in fomenting a situation that led to flashpoints all over Britain igniting in the 1981 summer riots. The riot in Southall, a suburb of west London, centred on a small pub called the Hamborough Arms. On July 3, three skinhead bands were booked to play there – The 4 Skins, The Last Resort and The Business – all associated with the National Front through an ostensible musical movement/genre called Oi. Considering Southall has had a relatively stable population of Indian and Afro-Caribbean people since it first developed in the early 1950s, and that the bands were guaranteed to attract a hostile audience, the ensuing riot was inevitable. To ensure that this would be the case, however, the National Front actually organised buses to ferry in skinhead fans, who then proceeded to harass the locals with slogans and insults. Once the youths had put a shopping trolley through a nearby Asian restaurant it was all on. The *Spare Rib* article makes a few interesting claims about the police response during the initial stages of this first riot that bears more than passing consideration. It seems the landlord of the Hamborough Arms realised there could be trouble and let shopkeepers in the district know in advance to take the necessary precautions. Then, when the police were finally called, they apparently took 45 minutes to arrive, their excuse that they'd been told that the skinheads were in nearby Greenford, 11 minutes' drive from Southall, and had gone there instead.

The further riots around Britain that followed do not seem to have been so obviously "nudged along" as was the case with Southall, but it's interesting to note that in Pendrous' aforementioned "rebuttal" letter in *The Listener*, he quotes from the organisation's *Bulletin* of July 1980, that "we must appreciate that the 'image' that we have been given by the media, and which may well lose us some potential support *today* (his own emphasis), will be a positive asset when the streets are beset by riots, when unemployment soars and when inflation gets beyond the present minimal control." (ibid). This was quoted in a letter published May 14, 1981, *two months* before the full-blown rioting of that summer kicked off.

The "Oi" movement in pop music is an interesting one. Initially a small cult off-shoot of the punk movement that had emerged in 1976, the most infamous purveyors of which had been The Sex Pistols, Oi was strictly aimed at the skinheads. When punk music was perceived as having become just another commercially viable commodity that, with the correct packaging and marketing, could make record companies money, many of the kids in the music's original audience felt cheated. While the "punks" became "stars" and worse, wealthy, *they*, their audience, remained jobless and honestly felt they had no future. The skinheads resented this punk success even more, being for the most part less literate than the general punk audience and therefore felt more alienated when the punks started getting "political" or sang about more abstract things as "pretentiously" as the bands punk had ostensibly reviled and had emerged to "overthrow". So "Oi" became a sort of "street" punk, more truly the very thing that punk had proclaimed itself to be when it had first emerged.

Oi was certainly not the first rock genre to pick up National Front attention. The rise of ska/reggae-influenced bands that would form the 2-Tone recording label collective that sprang up in Birmingham, which for the most part featured both white *and* black musicians in their lineups, also inevitably attracted what BBC Radio One disc jockey John Peel described as "ruffians professing allegiance to extreme Right-wing organisations"[7]. All these bands, among them The Specials, Bad Manners, The Selecter and The Beat, suffered disruptions at their performances by Front members and were openly disparaged by them in the music press. Oi however was marketed from its beginnings as solidly National Front supportive. A compilation LP of some of these bands titled *Strength Thru Oi!*, featured one Nick Crane, who had been the singer of a band called The Afflicted and was a member of the openly fascist British Movement, on its cover. At the time of writing, Crane was serving four years on charges of conspiracy to assault as well as incitement of racial hatred.

The backlash came when *The Daily Mail* ran an exposé on the Oi movement and what it described as its "mouthpiece", the weekly music newspaper *Sounds*. According to *The Observer*, the singer of a band called The 4-Skins, Gary Hodges, and their manager, Gary Hitchcock, both claimed to be British Movement members in an interview they gave the paper in November 1980[8]. Britain's most influential music weekly, *New Musical Express* pointed out that Hitchcock had claimed he was in the Movement's "leader guard" but had "announced that he was leaving the Movement, disillusioned by its shift towards 'respectability' – standing in elections instead of 'fighting in the streets'."

The majority of the bands that had been lumped together under the Oi banner were quick to disassociate themselves from both the National Front and British Movement. In fact, shortly after the riots, several of them took part in "Oi Against Racism" concerts in a very public rejection of the Front's political stand.

The shows were billed as not only Oi against racism, but also "against political extremism, but still against the system". In interviews with the music press promoting the concerts, the bands involved continually emphasised that the fans had never really cared one way or another about politics and that it was the media that had jumped on the fact that the audience was predominantly skinhead because as a group, they invariably attracted "newsworthy" action. The 19 year old singer of London group Infa-Riot, who were on the bill for one of these concerts, was adamant: "How can they be Right-wing and hate the police and the Army? They've got it completely confused. I haven't met one genuine person yet who says they're Right-wing and knows what they're talking about. That's honestly true. I really can't understand what's going on in their brains."[9]

Of course, it's just this confusion on the part of so many youngsters that makes them a prime target for National Front propaganda. By presenting them with issues that seem patently black and white, with an emphasis on rebellion (since the Front is, as they, the disillusioned youth, are, so obviously repressed by the System in all its manifestations), the Front and other extreme Right-wing movements remake themselves as causes célèbre and joining their membership allies those youngsters with others disillusioned with the status quo, providing them with a sense of both belonging and purpose. Other fringe movements, including those of the Left, offer similar promises of "tribal" connection and security, but the rampant nationalism with its concomitant commitment to violence in delineating the "enemy" as blacks, coloureds and Jews seems to particularly resonate with the more inarticulate and angry young white youth.

Whether Oi was truly a potential threat by way of providing a rallying point through which Right-wing organisations could actually direct their agenda is a moot point (thankfully, in the years since writing this, it has proven to be nothing of the sort), but major-label record companies have taken the possibility seriously enough to shy away from even allying with them let alone signing any of the bands involved. *New Statesman* was informed by the Centre for Contemporary Studies that "it's been known for some time that there has been an organised effort by certain extremist groups to break into the pop world, but it took Southall and the ensuing publicity to make us do something about it. In future all bands will be screened; we're not imposing censorship but we don't want to give contracts and money to fascists." [10]

The National Front's interest in Oi and rock/pop music in general might seem pretty trite in the greater scheme of things, but they have themselves pointed out in their journal *Spearhead* that (apart from the potential "enlisting" aspect, which they obviously prefer not to publicise), as "shocking, disgusting and nauseating as punk rock is, it is totally white in origin" and, as well, "electronic music combines many of the strains of classical and traditional Aryan music in a modern package ... popular amongst the thinking white youth who represent the better type of Briton in this decadent country today." (quoted in *New Statesman*, ibid) I hardly think many ordinary Britons, even then, would have accepted that particular kind of character reference for the boys that carved up Satwinder Sondh or stoked the 1981 summer riots.

The comment of one Southern regional organiser for the National Front on the actions of the record companies, which included the withdrawal from all stores of copies of the *Strength Thru Oi!* LP says it all: "They won't do anything because they know we will only go to more concerts and get more members. They are scared of us, and they don't want to lose any profits, do they?" (*New Statesman*, ibid)

The record companies weren't the only people to express concern about the activities of the National Front, and nor were Britain's immigrant and Jewish communities. When the Front's first chairman, A.K. Chesterton, the cousin of celebrated author G.K. Chesterton, and a confederate of Sir Oswald Mosley, the notorious leader of Britain's pre-War fascist movement, the British Union of Fascists, resigned his post in

1971, he wrote: "I had had more than enough, after four years of stamping out nonsense such as plots to set fire to synagogues. Two per cent of the members of the National Front are really evil men – so evil that I placed intelligence agents to work exploring their backgrounds, with results so appalling that I felt obliged to entrust the documents to the vaults of a bank. Some of those men are at present placed close to the centre of things." [11]

Chesterton, by the way, was the man who had originally steered the National Front away from anti-Semitic activity. As Sidney Bidwell points out in his book, *Red, White and Black*, "He knew that, to stand any chance of success, the National Front would have to keep quiet about its anti-Semitic origins and stick to 'the blacks', but only in the gentlest way." It is this position that Joanna Mack asserts has been abandoned since the Front's failure at achieving any semblance of "respectability" or parliamentary electoral success.

Another man who could see danger in the rising profile of the National Front was Lord Sydney Jacobson, who had edited *The Daily Herald* and *The Sun* newspapers. In his review of Nigel Fielding's study, *The National Front*, for *The Listener* Jacobson concluded with these observations on the two main figures then in charge of the organisation: "Tyndall himself is depicted as articulate, intelligent and an effective speaker, Webster as a good organiser. Intellectually not of the calibre of Mosley, but dangerous men with dangerous ambitions, riding on a current of hatred, fear and violence." [12]

Bidwell presents a litany of offences perpetrated by those affiliated with the National Front that give a clear indication of just what these two men are promoting with their particular views. Both Webster and Tyndall had previously been openly "Nazi" in their orientation, though both later claimed this as "youthful waywardness". Among other instances of violence, in October 1969 Webster had attacked an Indian with an ashtray because he had had the "audacity" to marry a German woman, who was accompanying her husband when the attack occurred.

Bidwell quotes the *South London Press*, October 10, 1969, as reporting Webster saying to the woman that "she should not be married to an Indian" and that she should "think of the glorious past which could have been Germany's and which was Germany's." Bidwell also notes Webster's aforementioned assault of Kenya's first President, Jomo Kenyatta, while the African leader had been in London attending the July 1964 Commonwealth Conference.

For Tyndall, Bidwell's list of offences is more thorough: "Convicted for threatening behaviour (London, 1959); imprisoned for organising and controlling a para-military organisation (case tried at the Old Bailey, 1962); convicted for insulting behaviour (London, 1964); convicted for possessing offensive weapons (Marylebone Court, London, 1966); and imprisoned for possessing a gun and ammunition (London, 1967)." [13] It's those last couple of items that made suggestions of the National Front or any other extremist Right-wing group posing more than a passing potential threat beyond mere thuggery or hooliganism seem feasible. Again, as Dr Gerwitz pointed out in his letter to *The Listener*, "The neo-Nazis convicted by a Birmingham court earlier this year were revealed to have accumulated a formidable collection of sophisticated weapons. There is every possibility that similar arms caches exist elsewhere in Britain. Our monitoring of neo-Nazi activities confirms that a considerable number of racialists arrested for an assortment of crimes of violence kept arms at home." (ibid) This certainly makes the potential threat far more ominous than, say, the sale of anti-Semitic records outside the grounds of First Division football team Tottenham Hotspurs, an obvious insult to more than just the team's Jewish supporters, as Glenn Cook noted in another piece for *The Listener* titled *Soccer and Racialism*, published March 12, 1981, p. 337. Thankfully, to quote Dr Gerwitz again, "In any event, anti-Semitism is not a vote-getter in Britain, as the National Front has learnt to its cost in recent elections."

More blatant among these Right-wing organisations is

the targeting of black supporters and players at various football fields across the country, and the violence directed at the carnivals celebrating black traditions, the black clubs where they share their cultures, musical, culinary and so on, and, of course in the suburbs in which they live. Sadly, the anti-blacks ticket *does* win votes. As the "self-styled rebel and committed racist" John Merritt, then aged 19, asserted in a study of Europe's growing unrest among young people reported in *Newsweek* in April that year, "No government ever asked the people if they wanted a multi-racial society." [14]

Then again, classical scholar turned politician, Enoch Powell, who served as Minister of Health in Prime Minister Harold MacMillan's Conservative government between 1960 and 1963, became something of a hero to many otherwise fair-minded Britons who, by then, were feeling less and less secure in the face of the influx of immigrants from various parts of the British Commonwealth, particularly the West Indies and India, seeking a better life in Great Britain. Powell guaranteed his place in the pantheon of the far Right in April 1968 when he delivered a speech in Birmingham in which he predicted "rivers of blood" if these mass immigrations continued unchecked. It was a speech that "spoke" directly to the fears and prejudices of an increasingly insecure British working-class.

While the thinking of youngsters like Merritt wouldn't have been swayed by some old fogey politician, he certainly would have subscribed to the notion that by "repatriating" all these West Indians and south Asians from India and Pakistan "back where they came from", there would be more work for Britain's white population.

An uncredited piece titled *Pomp and Desperation* published in *The Weekend Australian* in the 12-13 November 1981 edition (p. 11-2) pointed to the sorry irony of a Royal Wedding, that of Prince Charles and Lady Diana Spencer, happening so soon after the worst rioting on English soil in fifty years. "What made Brixton so different," the author suggested of the youngsters who had rioted, "was that these people knew they lived in a country that had no place, and held no future, for them." And this was just over four years after The Sex Pistols had released their own indictment on the Monarchy – the original title of their May 1977 single *God Save The Queen* had been *No Future*. Ironically, by 1981, it was an attitude increasingly held not only among white but also many young coloured Britons, and not only working-class *youth*. David Henshaw, again in the pages of *The Listener*, had this to say: "We are again becoming two nations; not Disraeli's over-quoted division between 'the privileged and the people', but the much more disparate gulf between those who have a job – and those who don't. The ratio is still seven to one." And a little further his essay, he notes that "the character of the unemployed is changing. You can't have three million out of work without a lot of good men and women going to the wall." [15]

Thankfully, the majority of those "good men and women" eventually managed to go on to live fulfilling lives employed as tradespeople, shop-keepers, teachers and even police officers among other things. Another commentator, David Graham, again writing in *The Listener*, in pondering this supposed "lost tribe" of unemployed Britons, suggested that "the fear of immigrants did seem to me more closely connected with the workplace than with the home, more a fear of someone doing your job for less money than someone moving next door." [16]

The chilling result of this "fear" however he makes plain: "There is some evidence that higher Conservative swings [in elections] were experienced in areas where the National Front is strong. This is held to explain the exceptionally high swings in a crescent of constituencies east of London. We certainly found concern about immigration to be widespread in the four areas we visited. The conviction that the Conservatives had been committed to 'doing something about it' was equally common." (ibid)

Whether the National Front actually pressed members to endorse likeminded Conservative candidates or not, the marked swing to the Right has been blatantly obvious. What is also common knowledge is that ten years before, this kind of activity, of National Front endorsement of Conservative candidates and reciprocal endorsement for Front candidates, was blatant and very much National Front policy. In 1972, for instance, members of the blue-ribbon political pressure group the Conservative Monday Club (thankfully no longer endorsed by the actual Conservative Party) openly and enthusiastically canvassed for that year's National Front candidate, John Clifton, who was contesting the western Greater London suburb of Uxbridge by-election. In the event, he only secured 8.2 per cent of the votes, but his total of 2,820 votes was within fifty of the Labour vote on the same day in the Sutton and Cheam constituency in southern Greater London. Denis Healey commented at the time that much of Clifton's vote came from disillusioned Labour supporters. [17] In 1977, the National Front outpointed the Liberals by 108 votes in the Greater London Council (GLC) elections, winning five per cent of the vote. John Tilley, Labour candidate for Brixton at the time, claimed that any racial conflict in his constituency would have to be imported. [18] As we've seen, in 1981, the National Front did just that for the Southall election.

The National Front's platform is quite simple, and it is this simplicity, aiming directly at society's most vulnerable, least informed, politically naïve and insecure, that makes their platform seem so logical an alternative to mainstream politics to this cohort. Their stand is blatantly anti-immigrant, anti-Common Market (the predecessor to the European Union) and pro-British. It reaches out to all the subconscious fears and prejudices against anything remotely different and, particularly, foreign – fear of the Xenos – xenophobia – that may lie buried in the psyche of the common Englishman. By their very nature, coloured people of any stripe or nationality are of course the easiest and most visible targets for those members of society who feel most disenfranchised to vent their frustrations with the direction in which they perceive society is heading. As Stuart

Hall, in another *Listener* article, *The Racist Within*, reminds us however, the actual "race" of a person or group doesn't particularly matter: "Blacks have become the bearers, the signifiers, of the crisis of British society in the Seventies. This is not a crisis of race. But race is the lens through which people come to perceive that a crisis is developing." [19]

So, as I've noted, Enoch Powell becomes a "national spokesman" for this ostensible "silent majority", and someone the National Front could even consider worthy of Premiership. In fact Powell had actually once been offered the Chairmanship of the Front.

As for the Conservative Monday Club, a leading member of the West Middlesex branch had declared without any qualms that, "Of course we have policy disagreements over the Asians with the National Front – about whether to send them back by boat or in boxes!" And there's a nasty little man by the name of Robert Relf, who advertised his house as only for sale to an "English" family and was rightfully prosecuted and jailed under the Race Relations Act for failing to remove the sign only to get released after a forty-five day hunger strike and thereby become an instant National Front "star speaker" and hero. John Tyndall said of Relf, "I am very proud to have him with us!"

Tyndall was the total Nazi until around 1967 when it seemed more logical for him to drop the stance if he was ever to gain the parliamentary foothold he was seeking. Initially in Chesterton's League of Empire Loyalists, Tyndall had left to form his own "National Labour Party", and had been active during the first of Britain's race riots in August-September 1958, where white working-class youths clashed with recent immigrants from the West Indies in Notting Hill. In 1962, his splinter group joined with Colin Jordan's White Defence League to become the British National Party, which utilised Nazi-style propaganda, anti-Semitic and pro-Colour Bar. To emphasise "good, clean, British living", the party even held military-style training camps and wore military-style uniforms to emphasise their unity.

In then becoming the National Socialist Movement, Tyndall pressed a party line that "the only basis for Britain's future greatness is Aryan, predominantly Nordic blood. It is the first duty of the state to protect and improve this blood." When Tyndall and Martin Webster split from Jordan to form the Greater Britain Movement, Tyndall was proposing a policy calling for "racial laws forbidding marriage between Britons and non-Aryans; and medical measures to prevent procreation by those with hereditary defects – racial, mental or physical'! He and Jordan had both recently been imprisoned for training and controlling a paramilitary organisation called Spearhead. Today, both again strenuously dismiss all this as "youthful high spirits", denying it all at every opportunity, as a cursory look at the number of complaints against misrepresentation as a Nazi-style party the National Front regularly brings against the BBC and other television and radio broadcasters makes abundantly clear.

The more blatant anti-Semitism may have been dropped, as I've mentioned, at Chesterton's instigation on his assuming of the leadership of the National Front in 1967, when the League of Empire Loyalists and Greater Britain Movement amalgamated, along with members of the Racial Preservation Society, but this turnabout was essentially a recognition of its being an impediment in terms of the Front's electionability. Since then however, the full force of the Front's efforts has been firmly based on racism, from the Kenyatta incident, through organising the Smithfield porters' strike in 1972, to stoking the rioting in Brixton and Southall.

"There is a small caucus working within the National Front attracted by the trappings and ideologies of foreign nationalisms from the past," wrote John O'Brien, Chesterton's successor as Chairman of the Front, on his resignation in 1968. "These persons see Britain's future best served by her becoming a rigidly authoritarian police state. They sought to use me as a docile puppet behind whose respectability they could operate from the shadows." [20] For twenty years O'Brien had been a pillar of the Shrewsbury Conservative Association. After this, Tyndall and Webster stepped out of the shadows to assume the leadership. But they haven't been able to take the next step and follow through with their cherished beliefs. Rather, they have continued to fail dismally, electorally. The question is, why don't they come out and try taking over as so many people obviously feel they are capable of doing?

I suppose the answer is that, when I was writing this, the safer bet was to bide their time. The numbers seemed to be moving towards them as inexorably as was 1984. I don't for a moment believe that Britain would ever allow itself to elect a National Front leadership, but then, the Social Democrat-Liberal alliance looks less and less like a real threat to either of the major parties, Labour or Conservative. Edward Pearce, in a piece he published in *Encounter* dismissed the SDP-Liberals as disintegrating – "the Liberals can muff anything" [21] – while former Liberal Party leader Jo Grimond could write that "the Liberal Party is not going to win in the long run as a party of compromise, however attractive compromise may look in the short term." [22]

After the 1981 riots, the public reacted as they always react, calling for law and order, greater police powers and a tougher stance against rioters. They weren't calling for Liberalism. The people may want jobs, but one young woman's comments to London's *Financial Times* was sadly all too typical of the general malaise – "Violence is the only way we can show people what is wrong – but violence against property, that's what counts." [23] To which the natural response is, again, a call for law and order, greater police powers and round and round we go.

Of course, this wasn't only happening in London, and truth be told, the police often proved part of the problem rather than the solution, as Olivia Wyatt points out in an essay in *History Today*, looking at the 1975 Bonfire Night clashes between Caribbean youth and police in Chapeltown, the multicultural working-class suburb of Leeds: "West Yorkshire Police was known for its aggression towards Black communities in Leeds – a city with a reputation as a hotbed for racism due to its connections to the National Front." [24]

Just as they'd hoped, the rioting nudged along by the National Front prompted calls for a more authoritarian approach from government. And why rush to get into government when one Margaret Thatcher is reflecting the National Front line without the attendant ideology, whether she is aware of it or not? In that moment in British history, as the British fleet steamed off to the South Atlantic to regain the Falkland Islands from the invading Argentines "for Queen and Country", The National Front's whole "John Bull" attitude and its racial denigrations of those perceived as "not really British" seemed amply justified. It's just that, for a brief moment, "the Argies" were the target of the nation's vilification.

Worse, in their biography of Thatcher, Nicholas Wapshott and George Brock made it clear that far from basing her economic theories of the conservative monetarist public policy theories of America's Milton Friedman, she had been profoundly influenced by the speeches of Enoch Powell, who had pressed for a free-market economy as far back as the 1950s and saw money supply as having a vital role in reviving Britain's flagging economy. [25]

Just how popular Thatcher's more authoritarian approach to government was became clear when she was re-elected in June 1983, handing the Conservative Party its most decisive win in decades, gaining a majority of 144 seats in the Parliament to bring them up to 362 seats in the 523-seat House of Commons. Thatcher's approval rating had fallen to 25 per cent in December 1981 and shot up to 59 per cent after the Argentinian surrender in the Falklands in June 1982. Labour not only lost 45 seats but secured the lowest share of the overall vote since 1918. The leader of the Labour Party, Michael Foot, was obliged to step down while Tony Benn, the Party's firebrand "bad boy" and seen as Foot's natural successor despite his more extreme Socialist platform, lost his seat. Thankfully, The National Front again failed to secure a single seat. In fact, their total vote count dropped from what would turn out to be their best showing, 191,719 votes in 1979, to a mere 27,065. But then again, as I've suggested, Margaret Thatcher was delivering much of their platform for them, ably assisted by conservative thinkers like Cambridge academics John Casey and Roger Scruton, who created a series of dinner-club meetings under the banner of the Conservative Philosophy Group, which itself emerged from the equally conservative Salisbury Group, of which both Thatcher and Enoch Powell had been members. A transcript of one of the speeches Casey gave at one of these dinner-club meetings was published in the Salisbury Group magazine, *Salisbury Review*, presenting his thoughts on the legal status of Britain's immigrant population. He felt that that status should be altered *retrospectively*, "so that its members became guest-workers... who would eventually, over a period of years, return to their countries of origin." [26]

"Where there is high unemployment and economic decay," Rosalyn Higgins observed, again in the pages of *The Listener*, "populism coated with resentment against a visible minority will always find a ready audience... In England, which faces massive economic problems and a wide distribution of unemployment, it is the whole country that is the National Front's playfield." [27]

**FOOTNOTES:**

[1] Joanna Mack, *Anti-Semitic Terrorism*, *The Listener*, 30 April 1981, p. 561.
[2] Dr Jacob Gerwitz, *Anti-Semitic Terrorism*, Letters to the Editor, *The Listener*, 18 June 1981, p. 775.
[3] Ernest Pendrous, *Anti-Semitic Terrorism*, Letters to the Editor, *The Listener*, 14 May 1981, p. 645.
[4] Joanna Mack, ibid
[5] Sidney Bidwell, *Red, White and Black*, Gordon & Cremonesi, London, 1976, p. 95.
[6] *Southall Black Sisters*, Southall section in *A Revolutionary*

*Anger, Spare Rib* #110, September 1981, p. 16.

[7] John Peel, *Making Tracks, The Listener*, 20 and 27 December 1979, p. 879.

[8] Paul Du Noyer, *Oi Against Racism, New Musical Express*, 18 July 1981, p. 3-4.

[9] Lynne Hanna, *Oi Against Racism, New Musical Express*, 31 October 1981, p. 15-7.

[10] Michael Coren, *Steps to Stop the Right Rocking, New Statesman*, 11 September 1981, p. 4.

[11] Quoted by Michael Cockerell, *Inside the National Front, The Listener*, 28 December 1972, p.877-9.

[12] Sydney Jacobson's review of Nigel Fielding's *The National Front, The Listener*, 22 January 1981, p. 116-7.

[13] *Red, White and Black*, p. 91.

[14] Bruning, Nater, Kempe, Donosky; *Europe's Dead-End Kids: The Young and the Restless*, a special report in *Newsweek*, 20 April 1981, p. 36-40.

[15] *Preston Isn't Working, The Listener*, 28 January 1982, p. 2-4.

[16] *Mrs Thatcher's Lost Tribe, The Listener*, 15 October 1981, p. 422-4

[17] Cockerell, ibid

[18] Mervyn Jones, *Going Head-On at the National Front, New Statesman*, 14 April 1978, p. 489-90

[19] *The Racist Within, The Listener*, 20 July 1978, p. 66-8

[20] Cockerell, ibid

[21] *The Perth-Llandudno Special, Encounter*, October 1981, p. 39-42

[22] Jo Grimond, *Liberals Must Not Compromise, Illustrated London News*, September 1980, p. 26

[23] Quoted in Bruning, Nater, Kempe, Donosky, *Newsweek*.

[24] A new addition to this essay, but its relevance should be obvious, *Is Violence the Answer?, History Today*, March 2023, p. 16.

[25] *Thatcher*, Macdonald, 1983.

[26] Quoted by David Edgar in his essay *Bitter Harvest, New Socialist*, Sept/Oct 1983, p. 19-24.

[27] Rosalyn Higgins, *Rights Can Be Wrong, The Listener*, 9 March 1978, p. 293-4

## POSTSCRIPT:

Thankfully, the National Front's electoral record remains untarnished by any parliamentary wins. Through the Noughties, the NF seemed to become a spent force. While Margaret Thatcher won yet another term as Prime Minister in the 1987 elections, the National Front's vote plummeted to a mere 286 that year. Through the '90s, their voting figures fluctuated between about 2500 and nearly 5000, but they began to gain momentum again, reaching 8029 votes in 2005 and 10,784 votes in 2010. By 2015 however, that had fallen again to just 1114 votes shared between the seven candidates they had fielded. Regardless, the National Front is no longer perceived as a viable political alternative.

Unfortunately however, neither racism, anti-Semitism nor neo-Nazism has faded from the underbelly of the British political landscape, despite the efforts of White supremacist Nick Griffin, who replaced Tyndall in 1999 and tried to make the British National Party (BNP) more electable by moderating some of its policies, such as making the repatriation of "undesirable" ethnic minorities voluntary – how considerate! The move at least won them a few local council seats. Depressingly for me personally, since I spent the years between 1961 and 1964 as a schoolboy in the suburb, the BNP won a dozen seats in the 2006 Barking & Dagenham Council elections. Griffin was chucked out of the BNP in 2014 and the party has since headed off in the same direction as the National Front.

Sadly, there has been a plethora of even more extreme Right-Wing parties ready to fill the breach. There's the anti-Islamist English Defence League for a start, and then there's the party that helped tip Britain out of the European Union, the UK Independence Party, formerly fronted by the reprehensible Nigel Farage. Regardless of what has been said publicly, the whole

Brexit movement was fuelled by xenophobia – it was all about keeping "the rising tide of foreigners" out of Britain. The fact that desperate refugees, both economic and political, continue to risk drowning in the English Channel in order to get to the United Kingdom, proved that breaking with the European Union hasn't solved *that* "problem". So the UK Conservative government has embraced discredited Australian Liberal policies from the 1990s and somehow imagine that "turning back the boats" and "sending illegal immigrants to a third country somewhere in darkest Africa" will change that.

Tragically, on June 16, 2016, White supremacist ideology saw a 53 year old adherent stab British Labour Party politician Jo Cox to death. As recently as February 2023, far Right activists clashed with police as they were demonstrating outside a hotel in Liverpool housing asylum seekers. I'll bet they're over the moon about having a Prime Minister, British born and bred, whose parents are expat South Africans from Indian Punjabi stock!

Of course this "tilt to the Right" isn't an exclusively British malaise, as authoritarian regimes abound across the planet, and there's at least one US Presidential hopeful who would love to scrap that pesky Constitution and declare himself Emperor. Then he can carry on "building that Wall" to keep those pesky immigrants out. Sound familiar?

Okay, that's my rant for this book – sorry. I'm afraid I turned out to be the "Socialist layabout son" to my Conservative dad's Alf Garnett – though he was far smarter and better informed than the Johnny Speight caricature portrayed by Warren Mitchell in the classic BBC TV series *Til Death Do Us Part*, though my dad really did think Margaret Thatcher had saved Britain.

I did have a shot at publishing the original version of this piece. I sent it off to a socio-political journal called *Arena*, published by the Phillip Institute of Technology in Bundoora, Victoria. Wouldn't you know it – "Whilst there was positive support for the merits of the piece, *Arena* is trying to focus substantially on Australian issues and themes, and your UK focus is a bit at odds." (July 11, 1984) Fair enough. The editor did suggest I try putting together "a comparative piece examining UK and Australian racist groups" and also, if there were any books I'd like to review... Sadly, as I've explained, 1985 turned into my Annus Horribilis and it took another couple of years to get the old brain back into this kind of work.

## CONLON IN THE NAME OF JUSTICE
**An interview with Gerry Conlon**

Imagine being woken in the middle of the night by armed soldiers who bundle you into a car and then find yourself in a room confronted by plain-clothed police officers who proceed to accuse you of being a terrorist before they beat a confession out of you.

In 1974, Belfast-born Gerry Conlon was 19, a petty thief warned to pack in the thieving by the local branch of the Irish Republican Army (IRA), which had, a couple of years before, recommenced a terror campaign against Britain with the stated aim of wresting the independence of Northern Ireland in order to reunify it with the rest of Ireland. Conlon headed off to London, checked into his aunt's place and, with another Belfast pal, Paul Hill, knocked about in the squats and local hippie scene till one night, penniless, the pair broke into a hooker's house, stole some money and headed back to Belfast.

That same night, October 5, massive bombs went off in two pubs in London suburb Guildford. Five people were killed, 70 were injured and an already nervous British government decided to get tough with the IRA. That's when Conlon found himself in custody, along with Hill, another Belfast pal Paddy Armstrong and a young Londoner named Carole Richardson – four young people who were soon dubbed the Guildford Four, picked out by the British authorities and charged as the bombers responsible. They were held in custody under a hastily passed Prevention of Terrorism Act that permitted arrest without access to legal advice for seven days, which thus suspended the civil liberties of anyone picked up by the Police. The Four were soon charged, having each signed a "confession" of their guilt.

Much as with Sydney's "Hilton Bombers" or Lindy Chamberlain in Australia, the Guildford Four were convicted not only by the Authorities but by a media baying for blood, ostensibly on behalf of its consumers, the ordinary Britons outraged by the horrors inflicted on them by the IRA. Each of the Four was sentenced to life imprisonment with a minimum of 30 years to be served before any possibility of parole. The judge, one Lord John Donaldson, in sentencing, stated that his only regret was that he was unable to apply the death penalty.

A month after the Guildford Four were arrested, two IRA terrorists were picked up and confessed to, among other things, the Guildford bombings. Yet they were never charged with those bombings. A witness to Conlon's actual whereabouts on the night of the bombings also gave a statement to police, but it was never given to his defence attorney. In the event, it would take 15 years, the death in prison of Conlon's father, Giuseppe, who had gone to London on Gerry's arrest to try to do whatever he could to help only to find himself arrested too, and one tiny piece of sheer luck that got the judgement against the Four overturned.

Gerry Conlon was released in October 1989 and went on to write and publish his story and that of his father in a book titled *Proved Innocent*, published by Penguin. That book became the basis of a major feature film, *In The Name Of The Father*, directed by Jim Sheridan. Over the four years leading up to our interview, Conlon has also been trying to clear his father's name, and while the judgement against him was overturned, no admission of guilt or complicity to obstruct justice has been made by the British authorities. As he explained to me, that piece of luck which led to the overturning of his conviction was down his defence lawyer finding one particular file.

"I'm still amazed that they never shredded or burned or destroyed it," he admits, "that it was still lying about. I remember Gareth [Pierce, his defence lawyer] came to the prison one weekend to see me and she was very, very excited. Gareth is a very calm, gentle, serene woman, but I could just see the excitement in her face as she said to me, 'I've found your alibi's statement.' And on the front of the statement was attached this sticker which said 'Not To Be Revealed To The Defence'.

"I can't believe that the British had become so

complacent as to leave that about. It was frightening to see how arrogant they'd become. The fact that Gareth went down on a day she was not supposed to to review material; that the policeman that was assigned to be there to give Gareth the documentation was off sick. If he had been on duty that day, we'd never have seen that document. That's Lady Luck; she can either be so cruel or so kind, and she'd been so cruel for such a long time. We just got very, very lucky. Gareth removed that document, had it photocopied, had it placed back and went to the police and told them what she'd found, and then the police came forward with more evidence that substantiated our innocence."

In his film adaptation of Conlon's story, director Jim Sheridan has chosen to focus on the relationship between Conlon and his father, presenting the pair locked up in the same cell right up to Giuseppe's death, which wasn't strictly true – they were held in cells next to each other.

"It was a *hell* of a way to get to know your father – prison!" Conlon admits ruefully. "It's the one place you can't escape from him and therefore you have to know him, to understand, and you have to fight him in order to get to see what's beyond the exterior and see the interior. In many ways I feel very privileged that I got to know my father beyond just my Dad. I got to know him as a human being, as a man, and he was kind enough to open himself up and show his inner spirituality and strength.

"I remember going into his cell one day – we'd been in prison four and a half years – and we're sitting having a cup of tea and he just said to me, 'D'you know I'm going to die real soon?' And it was like being slapped in the face with a wet towel. I said, 'What are you talking about?' And he said, 'I'm going to die. I can just feel it.' And he wasn't frightened in any way. It was almost as if he was embracing death as a release, to come to terms with it. And I think it was then that my whole psyche changed in relationship to the imprisonment, the way I'd been conducting my one-man war against the system *within* the

151

prison. He let me dip from the Well of Knowledge that he had. He said, 'Don't be worrying. My death is going to be the type of thing that's needed to rekindle interest in this case, for people to come to understand that innocent people *are* in prison and it's going to take *another* victim, just like those people who died in the pubs, before people start to realise it.' And everything he said came true."

Pierce was in the law firm that had defended Conlon's father when he had been convicted as part of the so-called Maguire Seven, the Maguires being Giuseppe's sister's family, inadvertently caught up in the hysteria and accused of having provided a "safe house" and making the bombs used by the Guildford Four.

"Gareth met my father in 1978, two years before he died," Conlon explains, "and although Gareth hadn't been the councillor involved, she had always been upset that not enough had been done to prepare a proper defence for my father. She came to the prison to see another Irish prisoner, and through him she met my father. It was at a time when I was going through a real distrust and dislike of lawyers and when I met her I didn't want to know. It was only when our case started to make headline news in Britain that I realised that I really did need a lawyer. This is four years before I was released. Lots of lawyers came and I rejected them and Gareth came and she was just so remarkably honest and open that within twenty minutes I knew that here was a person I could trust, that I could believe in and would eventually lead to my freedom. I think without Gareth becoming involved I would still be in prison."

Throughout his time in prison, Giuseppe Conlon carried on a letter-writing campaign to bring the injustice of their case to the attention of influential people, something Gerry took some time to come around to seeing as other than another futile exercise.

"Probably because I'd been brutalised by the police and the State, and then when I went to prison I was given the same treatment not only from the guards, whom everyone has to confront and deal with, but also the inmate population, who were really hostile towards us. I remember our first day of imprisonment after being sentenced, we were walking round the exercise yard and English prisoners were throwing jars of excreta at us, and batteries and glass bottles and stones, anything they could get their hands upon, and I became very, very angry and wanted to fight back, and prison's one of these worlds where the only thing that people really appreciate and respect is violence. Kindness is taken for weakness, compassion is taken for weakness. Any sort of normal, basic human trait that you have has to be disregarded. The only thing they understand is your capacity for violence."

Even before the film went into production, Sheridan and its stars Daniel Day-Lewis, who plays Gerry Conlon, and Emma Thompson, who plays Gareth Pierce, found themselves being harassed by the British press for distorting the story and making pro-IRA overtures. So I asked Conlon if he felt anything had changed since the framing of the Guildford Four had been exposed.

"No it hasn't changed a single thing. We've never had an apology for the fifteen years we were in prison, either from the police, the judiciary or the government. We've been campaigning for the last four years for an independent body to be set up with powers to subpoena witnesses and evidence in cases that are causing controversy and where there's a possible miscarriage of justice. I think we're close. They're actually having that body legalised and sanctioned by the government, and I think that will be the first step in reforming the judiciary."

## POSTSCRIPT:

The irony in interviewing Conlon in a palatial suite in the upper reaches of the Sheraton Grand Sydney Hotel next to Sydney's Hyde Park, all million-dollar views and expensive furniture, all laid on by the film company and his publisher – me a kid from a London slum, him an Irish "ex-con" – wasn't lost

153

on either of us.

Conlon hadn't had the best of times after his release, experiencing depression, nervous breakdowns and slipping in and out of addictions, but by the time we spoke he seemed together, determined and, as he explained, committed to campaigning against the kinds of miscarriages of justice that he had endured. He lost his battle with lung cancer in June 2014 aged 60.

It took another 11 years after my interview before Conlon and the surviving members of his family received an apology from the British government when, February 9, 2005, they were invited to a private meeting with the then Labour Prime Minister Tony Blair. "There was a miscarriage of justice in the case of Gerard Conlon and all the Guildford Four, as well as Giuseppe Conlon and the Maguire families and all the Maguire Seven. And, as with the others, I recognise the trauma that the conviction caused the Conlon and Maguire families and the stigma wrongly attached to them to this day. I am very sorry that they were subject to such an ordeal and such an injustice. That is why I am making this apology today. They deserve to be publicly and completely exonerated."

*In The Name Of The Father* remains one of the most powerful and moving films I've ever seen. Nominated for seven Academy Awards, it won none. For me, Pete Postlethwaite, portraying Giuseppe Conlon, was transfixing. It's a film that deserves to be revisited whenever we feel a little too comfortable about just how truly democratic and incorruptible we think our justice system might be.

## *LIVING BY THE BOOK: Ramblings Of A Bibliophile*

"If the pages are brown, then out it goes," said the old
hippie – I can talk! – Op shop volunteer, as he tossed a
yellowing, slightly stained hardcover copy of Bryce Courtney's
*Whitethorn* into the rubbish bins. I met the late Courtney many
years ago and liked him, so I've gathered pretty much his entire
oeuvre, though I have to admit I've yet to read any of it,
probably anticipating disappointment. Nonetheless, the near-
fanatical bibliophile in me still found it hard to walk away from
that copy, if only to pass it onto a friend who might appreciate it.
Too late now, sadly.

I have that "brown pages" policy to thank for my copy
of Russian Nobel Prize winner Mark Aldanov's short story
collection, *Tenth Symphony and Other Stories* (Jonathan Cape,
1950). Hardcover of course – I've been trying to control my
obsession as best I can since I've already filled the double-
garage-sized room – as it was on the original plans – turned
library well beyond capacity with several thousand books as
well as journals, magazines and newspapers, the bulk of my
vinyl singles, LPs, CDs and DVDs consigned as a consequence
to the bedrooms of my long-since-moved-out children.

My Aldanov is a first edition, which might prove
important to my youngest daughter when she finally inherits all
this, but it's only the content that interests me. The writing is
wonderful. He's not a writer I'd previously known, but there are
so many writers I'm yet to discover that I'm just grateful for the
local op shop's decision to toss out whatever doesn't seem
immediately sellable – you know the sort of thing – Dan Brown,
Ken Follett (though I have to own up to possessing a copy of
*The Pillars of the Earth*, also unread to date, having been
impressed by the television mini-series), Jane Cornwall, Wilbur
Smith, John Grisham (I'm reminded of John Cleese's character
Basil Fawlty *railing* against the horror that is the books of
Harold Robbins!), you know who I mean… – because though I
also regular buy books from it, I've recovered, free, some

remarkable volumes as a consequence, like a lovely old book titled *Bonnie Scotland*, featuring prints of paintings by Sutton Palmer and descriptions by A.R. Hope Moncrieff. No idea whether it's worth anything, but it was first published in 1904 by A & C Black, my edition the third impression, published in 1912, the year after my father was born – a delightful object, beautifully illustrated, the text gloriously Edwardian.

It's on the "to read next" pile by my desk. I'm currently reading Sydney R Jones' *Thames Triumphant*, a leisurely jaunt from the source to the estuary of England's most famous river, illustrated by the author and originally published by The Studio Press in 1943, though my edition is a fourth printing from 1949 and was, according to the note to the original recipient on the inner flyleaf, bought at Harrod's in November 1950, a mere 15 months before I was born, just over three miles from that self-same Thames, on the Holloway Road, Islington, London. Copiously illustrated with sketches by the author, the book is even more poignant for the fact that the bulk of it combines impressions of places along the Thames and something of their story as Jones had experienced them in the early decades of the 20th century with an epilogue that revisits those places after the Battle of Britain had been won, noting what had been lost to Hitler's bombs as his journey brought him closer to the centre of London, "with Wapping church almost gone." It reminded me of the bombed out building next to the one in which I spent most of my first ten years of life, the one on the other side of the road long since erased from the map of London evolving from bomb site to open space where the community built huge bonfires for Guy Fawkes night to scrap metal yard before redevelopment sent us to Becontree in Dagenham and finally to Australia.

It also reminded me a little of Jerome K Jerome's delightful though now largely forgotten little book, *Three Men in a Boat*, my edition published by J.M. Dent in 1956, which, on reading, proved to be nothing like I imagined it having seen the film version, also from 1956, starring Laurence Harvey, David Tomlinson and Jimmy Edwards, countless times on the telly through my childhood. Ah, the beauty of books, but that of course is a whole other story.

Now, don't get me wrong – I'm not "stuck in the past" with my reading. I recently reviewed a book by Australian singer, songwriter and diplomat Fred Smith, *The Dust of Uruzgan* (Allen & Unwin, 2016), based on his experiences as "diplomat on the ground" at Australia's base in Afghanistan, Taren Kowt, which also spawned two CDs of songs. Then there was Jimmy Barnes' first volume of autobiography, *Working Class Boy* (Harper Collins, 2016), though that was as much because he's an old friend – I'm in there, on page 305 if you're interested – as wanting particularly to read it. More recently I've read a nice little book for older teens by John Marsden titled *Winter* (Macmillan, 2000) and a fantastic, deeply moving novel with a touch of magic realism, *Snow On The Moon* (Headline Review, 1996), by American writer Keith Heller, another writer I'd not previously come across but bought in the aforementioned op shop. Just by the by the heroine of Marsden's book is named Winter, that of Heller's Evelyn Winter. Between other delights, I dip in and out of Isadore Brodsky's quirky reflections on *The Streets of Sydney* (Old Sydney Free Press, 1962, rescued), discovering a little something more of the town that's been my home and workplace now for more than 30 years. That was preceded by a joyous bathe in Delia Falconer's *Sydney* (New South Press, 2010).

I also try to keep up with as many contemporary journals – musical, literary and socio-political – as I can afford as a freelance writer (a pursuit these days of vastly diminishing returns), but, well, with anything up to two dozen titles a week either bought or rescued, I'm hard-pressed just getting through whatever's closest to hand after I've finished my paltry quota of features or reviews for my currently only outlet as a freelancer. I just can't afford to buy new books!

The bottom line is I can't bear the thought of all these books ending up at the local tip to rot back into dust. Sure I could "feed my habit" far more efficiently via eBooks and all that but, as is obvious, I'm "old school" – I like the feel, the smell, of the actual artefact. And there's a certain sadness, for me, in seeing something that was once a treasured object, read, pondered and perhaps shared with family and friends being so wilfully discarded. My decision to try and keep my collecting only to hardcovers, purely on aesthetic as well as practical (space) grounds probably saw me overlook several other volumes that might also have come from the library of fellow Australian writer, poet and critic R.F. Brissenden. I'm so pleased, nonetheless, that I've saved Barry Hill's short story collection, *A Rim of Blue*, and his novel, *Near the Refinery*, both McPhee Gribble, published in 1978 and 1980 respectively, both rescued, not only for themselves but also perhaps for some future bibliophile who, on seeing the finely-wrought signature of Brissenden written on the inner flyleaf of each, might then wonder who this might be and, after reading the Hills, seek out his own very fine work.

## POSTSCRIPT:

A personal library on the scale of mine is as much an exercise in optimism – a hope that you live long enough to read your way through it – as it is, at least for me – an attempt to preserve these curious repositories of hopes and dreams, knowledge and possibilities, histories true and imagined, beauty and laughter, wisdom and frivolity. My rescue missions continue, my chances of reading all I've "saved" decreasing with every passing day – wish me luck!

This is, of course, the piece that gave this humble collection its title. At least it got published. The next piece, obviously something of a companion piece, had no such luck.

# SAVING *BONNIE SCOTLAND*

It had come a long way, not just in distance – roughly 10,553 miles, 16,983 kilometres (at least from London to Sydney, though I actually live in Katoomba in the New South Wales Blue Mountains, some 100 kilometres west of Sydney, so it's give or take) – but also in time – more than a century. Donated to a local charity opportunity shop, it had been discarded by one of the volunteer sorters as obviously too old and uninteresting to put on the shelves and so unceremoniously dumped outside. How, then, could I allow it to end up in the local tip, forgotten, unwanted, left to rot away? As soon as I saw it, I knew that wasn't going to happen. And what a beautiful gift I have saved, not just for me but also, I hope, for the more academic of my daughters when she finally inherits my higgledy-piggledy, bursting at the seams library. *Bonnie Scotland* is a collection of superb full-colour prints of watercolour paintings by Sutton Palmer and words, mostly wildly unrelated to the paintings, by A.R. Hope Moncrieff. First published in 1904, my edition is the third impression, printed in 1912 by A & C Black – a delightful object in its own right, beautifully illustrated, the text gloriously – and elegantly – Edwardian.

Born in Edinburgh February 26, 1846, Ascott Robert Hope Moncrieff's mother died only a couple of years after he was born, his father following in 1855 when Ascott was nine, "leaving me," as he noted in his "summary autobiography" in *A Book About Authors*, written in 1914, "precociously independent", despite the fact of his father having remarried – twice! By the time he was 26, a graduate now of Edinburgh University, Moncrieff was living in Wales, and over the following decades he would live all over England and Scotland, from Perth to the Isle of Wight, and travel widely – "in fact I have proved immune to the mosquitoes of four continents" – before settling in London, about which of course he naturally wrote a book, *Victorian And Edwardian London*, published in

1910, as well as another, simply titled *London*, published in 1923 as part of the Black's Guide Books series. It was in London that Moncrieff passed away, at the age of 81, while living in the suburb of Lewisham in the autumn of 1927.

It's funny to read his opening sentence to that "summary autobiography" in light of the contemporary obsession with social media: "There is a fashion in our day for authors, like other persons dependent on the favour of the public, to court its interest by posing before the cameras of its curiosity." I wonder what he would have made of a world dominated by the need to accumulate as many "Likes" for a snap of your breakfast/lunch/dinner/naughty bits in order to feel validated as a human being! He goes on, "The catalogues of their works are headed by simpering or studiously reflective portraits; their addresses, clubs, recreations are communicated in works of reference…" Perhaps Moncrieff wouldn't have been quite so surprised by contemporary society's desperation to achieve "digital" celebrity. Yet here he is, writing this over a century ago. Who, however, within all this contemporary clamour, would so elegantly suggest that he feels obliged, in justification of his decision in the face of his own natural reticence, to play out his life in the public's eye, this "humblest (of) craftsmen" and to say something of himself in writing this piece of autobiography, so as "to speak of other authors"? And who among us, we "happy band of scribblers" has not felt that the potential "profit to the author… (has) proved rather a mirage in the cold light of publishing accounts." Ah, the Internet, the great leveller, hungry for content, loath to pay for it!

It's funny, on another personal note, to read in that same "summary", that, like that of my own, Moncrieff's father's "outlook on the world of books was bounded by the adventures of Mr Pickwick and Mr Jorrocks," Dickens his, my father's, favourite author, his novels read and re-read right up to his death a few months after his 80th birthday, a Londoner born and bred, so far from home in Elizabeth, South Australia.

Moncrieff initially made his name writing about his

schooldays, though he later disavowed his early and it seems successful books, even buying back his copyright in order to suppress further publication, only to step back into that same arena, writing of school life for, essentially, young readers after working some years as a schoolmaster and thereby gaining the perspective he felt had been missing in *Book About Dominies* and *Book About Boys*, though, he admits, "the public that buys such books has not agreed with me." He also wrote travel "guide" books of which, of course, *Bonnie Scotland* is one, travel books popular even then, back when no one could have conceived of the Lonely Planet phenomenon, and he also published books on various aspects of geography that became standard school texts not only in the United Kingdom, but also in Germany and the Netherlands. Moncrieff even translated books across half a dozen languages into English, "which I learned for myself, largely in steamboats, trains and omnibuses". There were books on mythology, on medieval chivalry, on various English counties as well as Scotland and its Isles, even on Kew Gardens. In fact, over the course of some 50 years of writing, he published nearly 200 books, though often under pseudonyms, even occasionally anonymously, as well as editing a similar number of other writers' books.

   *Bonnie Scotland* was, as I've said, published under his own name, and is as much a celebration of the timeless artistry of his "illustrator" Sutton Palmer, as the landscape and people of a Scotland that was already receding into history when the book was published. Born in Plymouth, Devon, on December 28, 1854, Harold Sutton Palmer was as prolific a water-colourist as Moncrieff was a writer, and, it turns out, illustrated several books based on travels to various places published by the same publisher, A&C Black, including volumes on his own county and The Lake District. Marrying a Californian in San Jose in 1889, he even painted a series of landscapes of the state during his stay there. He passed away five years after Moncrieff, in May 1933, aged 79.

   My copy of *Bonnie Scotland*, one side of its spine

sticky-taped to its back cover but on the whole in surprisingly good shape, with its epigram from Burns:

*That I for poor auld Scotland's sake,*
*Some usefu' plan, or book could make,*

has no dedication to a forgotten beloved father, wife, uncle or niece, scribbled on the flyleaf, but for all its years and that odd bit of sticky-tape, it's obviously been cherished, the heather sketched below the title and its creators names, and the thistle weaving up either side on its front cover still retaining something of its original colours against the dark blue cloth.

Opening it, the first of Sutton's paintings to delight the eye presents a view "Beneath the Crags of Ben Venue, Perthshire", a frontispiece that immediately makes one wonder what that same view would present today. After the title page, Moncrieff then makes the point that "The author does not attempt elaborate word-pictures, that would seem pale beside the artist's colouring." Instead, he hopes to accompany Palmer's paintings with "an outline of Scotland's salient features, with glimpses at its history, national character, and customs, and at the literature that illustrates this country for the English-speaking world ... a fireside tour". I hold in my hand, literally, a time capsule of the Scotland as it was perceived a century and more ago. The Internet can't replicate the visceral pleasure a body can take in that!

That "fireside tour", for of course *Bonnie Scotland* is essentially one of those travel books mentioned earlier, though with far greater literary worth than any copy of Michael Portillo's much-touted *Bradshaw's*, then takes the reader through a dozen chapters, 255 pages, 75 illustrations, across the Borders, through Auld Reekie – Edinburgh of course – the Trossachs, the Kingdom of Fife, the Fair City (Perth), the Highland Line (to Inverness and beyond), Aberdeen, up to John O' Groats and into the Great Glen, down to Glasgow and the Clyde, into the Whig Country and finally out through Galloway.

Right from the beginning there are as many questions as observations – would a "Southron" be able to tell they'd entered

Scotland, as they crossed north over the Tweed and the Liddel Water, if they stopped "a brawny corduroyed lad tramping along the furrows to his early job," and, hearing him speak, know if he was Scot or Sassenach? "Though," he remarks, "a fine local ear would not fail to catch some difference of burr and broad vowels, marked off rather by separating ridges than by any legal border, as the lilting twang of Liddesdale from the Teviot drawl"? Not today, surely. Even then, a century ago, Moncrieff could say, a little sadly, that "healthily barefooted children, more's the pity, are not so often seen nowadays on this side of the Border, nor the other, unless at Brightons and Margates." Another world, another place – wonderful stuff.

The questions aren't all steeped in times past or simple, cloying Edwardian nostalgia. The biggest one of all is right there on page 2 – "What makes a nation?" Moncrieff gently ponders on our behalf. People, politicians, thinkers the world over are still asking it. "Is it race?" Many a fine mind, historians, ethnologists and archaeologists alike, the canny Neil Oliver among the more contemporary, has been turned to that question with regards to Scotland. "Or is it a common speech?" Pity the poor linguist or philologist trying to untangle that one after so disruptive a century as the one that has intervened between the publication of *Bonnie Scotland* and today. Ah, but, as Moncrieff reminds us, it was a Scot, Dr James Murray – who would befriend the "mad Surgeon of Crowthorne" – born February 7, 1837 in Denholm, there on the Borders, who became the most eminent of the editors of the *Oxford English Dictionary*, so perhaps Scottish linguists might have the jump on the rest on that question.

In the end, it's just the beautiful use of language, of history, anecdote, poetry or reminiscence, that makes *Bonnie Scotland*, and so many books from the period, such a pleasure to read... "Its stony fields and lochans lying between hummocks are horizoned by grand mountains...". It's a style sadly long out of fashion, but one that, when rediscovered is always a joy to experience, as with another book I read recently, one I bought

163

from the same charity shop, Sydney R. Jones' *Thames Triumphant*, a leisurely jaunt from the source to the estuary of England's most famous river, illustrated by the author and originally published by The Studio Press back in 1943. Both books come from more innocent times, Moncrieff's before the horrors of the Great War, Jones' in 1943, though for the most part written sometime in the 1920s. At least I can claim, it seems, a great, great aunt on my father's side born in Edinburgh as some qualification, perhaps, to ponder the idea of Scotland.

There are battles aplenty recalled in *Bonnie Scotland*, of course, another inevitable aspect of nations "defining" themselves, ancient slaughter now the stuff of folk song and battle hymn, their sites meccas for tourists seeking the Scot within them. No Scot or Sassenach could fail to wonder at the reference to "the triple Eildon Hills, in whose caverns Arthur and his knights lie sleeping," and then not want to see them for themselves. But then, imagine a time, too, "when the average income of the Scottish Bar is perhaps five pounds Scots per annum"!

And interspersed, of course, throughout the delightful prose are those remarkable scenes, of the landscapes in all their "aweful majestie" or gently rolling rivers meandering through pastures, captured by the brush of Palmer – tiny gulls, for instance, caught mid-flight over limpid waves breaking beneath the monumental cliffs of Bass Rock off the coast of Haddingtonshire, some puffins, perhaps, crowding diminutively along rocks a little closer to the viewer, equally in wonder perhaps – or, more often, gently rolling rivers meandering through pastures, a farm, village, castle, cathedral, ruin or a Ben rising or "lowering" in the background. A sentimental style, picturesque, pastoral yes, certainly now long out of fashion; but the light! If nothing else, Palmer knows how to capture the magic of the light, as he does, for instance in "Golden Autumn, The Trossachs, Perthshire". One can only wonder what he might have made of Australia's light. He might have ranked comfortably beside Tom Roberts, a master in capturing that "terrible" continent's light.

Inevitably there are people – real and fictional – referenced in these pages that would have been well-known to the readers of Moncrieff's day but who are now for the most part obscure or long forgotten, but there are many more, commoners and kings – and king-makers – whose names and stories have been inextricably woven into the rich tapestry of Scottish history and myth, names that still resonate far beyond its borders, from Malcolm to the Bonnie Prince, Sir Walter Scott, Stevenson and Burns – naturally – Rob Roy, Wallace and the Bruce and more, Moncrieff breathlessly noting their various connections to places as he looks out of the train carriages of a rail network that had opened the country up in a way unprecedented before late Victorian times, most of which, as contemporary train enthusiast Michael Portillo laments on our behalf, is now long gone.

Place names too – Aberfoyle, the "disgraced" Mentieth, "Inversnaid, near Rob Roy's home", Loch Katrine, Stronachlacher, the Vale of Leven, the Carse of Gowrie and far too many more to mention – Moncrieff knew the poetry of place and, again, like most of the educated of his generation, could casually enlist all manner of poets and philosophers, novelists and historians, even earlier travel book writers to add their lustre to his own descriptions – "Dr Chalmers wondered if there would not be a Loch Lomond in heaven" – though he's also not above having the occasional swipe at a poet or a thinker he feels has done their subject or their art a disservice. Moncrieff is also wont, here and there, to ramble on about something that has obviously bothered him or is a topic close to his heart, be it the fine distinctions between wit and humour, comedy and satire or the vagaries surrounding the excellence or otherwise of Scotch whiskey! Either way, he seems quite certain that "the altered pronunciation of Scottish family names… seems often to come from English blundering, modestly adopted by their owners." Who in Australia would know that the surname of its longest-serving Prime Minister, Robert Menzies, should have been pronounced *Meengus*? I stand corrected!

165

Perhaps, then, some enterprising Scottish documentary filmmaker will eventually take up *Bonnie Scotland* in the way Portillo took up *Bradshaw's* and take us on another kind of journey to see what's left of Moncrieff and Palmer's Scotland, a century on. Are the supposed – Moncrieff is not so blinded by sentiment as to accept it as fact – "ploughshares valiantly handled by Bailie Nicol Jarvie, nay, even the identical bough from which he swung suspended by his coat tails," still to be seen at the Saltmarket (if that too hasn't long since disappeared), or once "the change-house of Luck M'Alpine" near Aberfoyle still there "to be seen"? *Bonnie Scotland* can still inspire, across space and time, the urge to follow in Moncrieff's footsteps, at least in this soul, living on the other side of the world.

## POSTSCRIPT:

Wouldn't you know it – none of the three Scottish or Scots diaspora journals to which I submitted the piece were interested, although two of them at least did me the courtesy of acknowledging receipt before declining, one asking if I would "donate it" for publication. A pretty canny lot I suppose.

I've been lucky enough to salvage a copy of Moncrieff's book on Surrey in the same series. I won't bother attempting a review. I'll just settle down to enjoying reading it – sometime.

## THE TROUBLE WITH NEUTRALITY

For the contemporary viewer, a seemingly innocuous and largely forgotten little black and white feature film titled *The Halfway House*, released in 1944, which occasionally flickers across television screens on a Saturday afternoon, might seem as inconsequential as the play on which it was based, *The Peaceful Inn* written by Denis Ogden, but, for just a moment during the Second World War, it was vital part of the effort by the British War Office to reassure the hearts and minds of an embattled nation and perhaps bring a neutral neighbour "back into the fold" in order to beat a common enemy, Adolf Hitler and his Third Reich.

According to his diary entry for 31 May 1940, after seeing a performance at the Duke of York's Theatre in London's St Martin's Lane, George Orwell dismissed *The Peaceful Inn* as "the most fearful tripe" despite its featuring acclaimed writer and actor Mary Hayley Bell, who would marry fellow actor John Mills two years later, in its cast. Three months after that diary entry, as the Luftwaffe began raining bombs on London, for producer Michael Balcon, who'd become head of Ealing Studios in 1938, *The Peaceful Inn* seemed the perfect vehicle to present a very particular case he hoped might just make a difference to the Allied war effort.

Directed by Basil Dearden, whose previous film, 1943's *The Bells Go Down*, had been a poignant observation on everyday life in wartime Britain and in particularly a paean in praise of Britain's Auxiliary Fire Service, the screen adaptation "suggested", as the credits make clear, by *The Peaceful Inn*, renamed *The Halfway House*, was cowritten by Angus MacPhail, who, like Balcon had worked with Alfred Hitchcock in the 1930s, along with Welsh playwright Diana Morgan, and it's pretty obvious that the idea was to take a play that Orwell noted hadn't even mentioned the war despite the timing of its premiere and subtly re-purpose it for propaganda purposes, with a particular emphasis on the contentious issue of Ireland's neutrality.

Released in April 1944, the initial impression *The Halfway House* gives to the modern viewer is of the kind of typically gentle, heart-warming affair that would eventually become something of a template for Ealing Studios, as a motley array of characters are thrown together by circumstance and inevitably propelled towards a comforting, even inspiring denouement.

Set in an idyllic, tranquil Welsh countryside, part real, part imagined through the filter of romantic sentimentality, the lives of the locals seem for the most part untroubled by the horrors of the war that is raging across Europe and so much of industrial England, apart perhaps from the necessary imposition of rationing. The characters assembled also seem comfortably stock. There is the intense young conductor who must face his inevitable "final performance" all too soon if he doesn't step away from his career in order to recover from its stresses and strains. There is the couple in the midst of a divorce neither really wants, accompanied by their daughter Joanna, determined to keep them together. There's the court-martialled army officer, fresh out of prison after having been caught stealing from his regiment's funds. There's another couple, older, a merchant seaman and his unlikely French wife, who have lost their naval son to a U-boat attack for which the Captain somehow feels responsible, and finds himself therefore at odds with his grieving wife. There is the unsavoury black market profiteer – very topical – taking some "time out" in the countryside despite the "success" of his "business interests". And then there is the real focus of the film – a young couple, Margaret and Terence, soon to wed if only they can get over the thorny issue of the young man's career ambitions.

Each of them is heading for The Halfway House, an inn some three hundred years old, where, on arrival, they're greeted by the softly-spoken innkeeper, Rhys, and his winsome daughter Gwyneth. "Quite a lot of people who don't know where they're going arrive here," Rhys, who literally seems to appear from nowhere, assures the army officer. "Time stands still here in the valley," he tells the profiteer, "or so they say." "Pleasant things happen here you know," Gwyneth tells the eager young Joanna a little later in the film. "Wishes come true."

So the stage is set. We all know there's something "otherworldly" about the place and the "signs" confirming our suspicions come thick and fast – the Frenchwoman, played by opera singer and actor Françoise Rosay in her first English feature film, notices that the innkeeper, understatedly played by the fine Welsh character actor Mervyn Johns, bringing her a consoling cup of tea, has no reflection as he leaves her room. The disgraced army officer, Fortescue, played by the usually debonair Guy Middleton, notes that Gwyneth, played by Johns' real life, not quite 20, pre-platinum blonde daughter Glynis, casts no shadow. The calendar on the wall, like the date noted against the last signature in the inn's guests' book, reads 21 June 1942, exactly a year before these guests have arrived. The newspapers in the lounge room are also all similarly dated.

The guests become even more unsettled at dinner when the innkeeper describes in detail the night of the bombing of The Halfway House, despite the apparent lack of any evidence of damage – yet Rhys insists there have been no repairs. Perhaps inevitably, a little later and not a little ironically since the guests are already unknowingly in the presence of ghosts, a séance is suggested by the Frenchwoman, Mrs Meadows, desperate to contact her son, and while it inevitably fails, subverted, in her mind at least by her despairing husband, the truth about The Halfway House is soon revealed and the film ends with everyone reconciled either to their fate or with each other, those who had pursued the more nefarious side of things renouncing their old ways, others finally understanding that their previously held positions, on life, on love, on the War, were wrong, all of them "seeing the light" as it were – the obvious "feel-good" ending. Looking back as they drive away, back into their lives, they see The Halfway House as it actually is – a bombed-out ruin. For all the obvious holes in the plotline, *The Halfway*

*House*, while no masterpiece like, say, *Mrs Miniver*, is a likeable enough little confection, a pleasant hour or so in whose company to while away a lazy rainy afternoon.

Yet that of course wasn't the point. Remember, the film was released in 1944, and despite America having by now joined the fight, the threat of Nazi Germany and its potential to yet defeat the Allies in the titanic battle that was the Second World War remained – for the United Kingdom, and War Prime Minister Winston Churchill – all too real. So, for all the whimsy, the pathos and the gentle romance, it is the core figures within the group – Terence, the young man soon to wed, Mrs Meadows the Frenchwoman and Rhys the innkeeper – through whom the essential message is presented, who provide the *point* of the film.

Terence, played by Irish actor Pat McGrath who, as it happens, was born in 1916, the year of the Easter Uprising, is an Irish diplomat, and while the Nazis have laid waste to all before them, Ireland has opted for neutrality, a position the young diplomat doggedly defends. In fact he's just been offered a plum position – or so it seems to him – as part of the Irish legation… in Berlin. "And why not?" he says to his fiancée, played by Philippa Hiatt. "Ireland's not at war with Germany. My job's my job." Ah, but there's the rub as they say. His fiancée has a job too, in the British Armed Services, and she'll "never be as Irish as that," she tells him when he points out that she'll be Irish after they're married and quits her job to go with him. "When you get back from Berlin" is when she'll marry him she tells him defiantly, walking off in a huff, "or on the day Ireland declares war on Germany."

"From the moment this war began," declared the Irish Prime Minister Eamon de Valera in a speech delivered 12 December 1941, "there was, for this State, only one policy possible – Neutrality. Our circumstances, our history, the incompleteness of our national freedom, through the partition of our country, made any other policy impracticable. Any other policy would have divided our people, and for a divided nation

170

to fling itself into this war would have been suicide." As it happens, "neutral" Norway had been attacked by Germany 9 April, 1940, capitulating to German forces a month later.

The freedom of the still relatively newly-minted Eire had of course been bitterly hard won, and was, as de Valera noted, still not really complete as the Second World War had begun. Despite having gained independence from the United Kingdom in 1922, initially as the Irish Free State, Eire was still technically a British Dominion and therefore was still obliged to recognise King George VI as its official Head of State. De Valera's stand was based on the idea that Eire, the Gaelic name for Ireland taken in order to distinguished it from the six northern counties that remained, contentiously, within the United Kingdom, was a *republic*, a status the nation would not officially achieve until 1949. Yet for all de Valera's "grandstanding" on the issue of neutrality, on the quiet Eire was doing far more to support the Allies than was generally known at the time. It was Irish weather stations, for instance, that supplied the data that allowed the Allies to mount D-Day on 6 June, 1944 with some confidence. Yet for Britain there were still misgivings about just where Eire really stood in the fight against Nazi Germany. After all, "neutral" Spain was known to be riddled with German spies. De Valera's position was also complicated by the Irish Republican Army, whose more militant members were all for taking advantage of the war to push Britain out of Northern Ireland.

"If only England could use the Irish bases," Mrs Meadows suggests during dinner, as the dangers to the vital Allied merchant and naval convoys are discussed, the subject brought up by the conductor, David Davies, played by Esmond Knight, who had seen Captain Meadows' (Tom Walls) ship hit during one such convoy in which he was returning from a European tour. Knight himself had become a naval gunnery officer soon after the UK's entry into the war and been badly wounded in May 1941 while on active duty as a sub-lieutenant aboard HMS Prince of Wales during a battle with the German battleship Bismarck off the coast of Denmark. Despite being blinded by shrapnel and losing an eye, Knight had determinedly resumed his acting career. Just a month before the battle of the Denmark Strait, one of Britain's most effective and memorable propaganda feature films, *This England*, in which Knight played a vicar's son, had been released. He was still partially blind in his remaining eye as he took on the role of Davies in *The Halfway House* and would soon be totally blind.

"If England used our bases," our young Irish diplomat Terence ardently replies to Mrs Meadows, "Germany would see it as a breach of neutrality, and she'd be justified. Germany has as much right to a neutral base as England." She then quietly puts him in his place: "I am French. Some of my countrymen also decided that anything's better than war. Now they see what real Frenchmen have always known – that one doesn't get peace by refusing to fight, because there is no peace for those who are dominated and despised. What's the use of living without freedom and dignity? When they are threatened, there is only one thing to do – *fight*."

"Perhaps compromise is the answer sir," Rhys suggests to Terence after he has another row with his fiancée. "The English have a genius for it." "You, a Welshman can say that?" Terence replies. "We've kept ourselves alone. If one small conquered people can do that, surely another can." That simple word, conquered, was a pretty bold adjective to use in a script that was essentially about pulling together the *United* Kingdom. The gentle subtlety of its delivery is testament to Mervyn Johns' poignant characterisation. As it happens, he'd also played a part in Dearden's previous film, *The Bells Go Down*.

It's then that his character, Rhys the innkeeper, delivers the coup de grâs, in that unmistakeable, unhurried Welsh lilt: "No nation is conquered sir if it keeps its soul and its language as we've done. The English are our friends and our neighbours. We live at peace with them. Their enemies are our enemies, and their war is our war. I'm proud of being a Welshman sir, but I wouldn't put the betterment of Wales before the betterment of humanity." Terence turns on him – "As we're doing?" Rhys smiles and asks if he'll help put away the chairs.

As the clock strikes the hour at which, a year before, The Halfway Hotel had been destroyed by German incendiary bombs, its guests discover themselves somehow placed out of their own time and forced to experience the full horror of that bombing firsthand. Rhys, the innkeeper presents the profiteer, Oakley, played by Alfred Drayton, with his comeuppance in another stirring riposte as the sound of guns and bombs puts the fear of God in him. Terence, meanwhile, protecting his fiancée as the flames seem to engulf them, turns to the sky and rages against the German bombers. Here, then, is one more Irishman who has understood the folly of neutrality in the battle to save not just the United Kingdom but the rights of *all* humanity against the scourge of Nazism. Stirring stuff indeed! One way or another, each of the guests realise their duty – to love, to family, to country.

"The film elusively obtains its effects," wrote *The Times*' reviewer on its release in its 17 April, 1944 issue, "when it appears to be least striving after them, and an occasional *frisson* is achieved by acute touches of direction which light up not only depths of human tension and unhappiness, but also unobtrusively reckon with their cause – the war."

Orwell's opinion of Ogden's original play was probably quite right, and in adapting *The Peaceful Inn* for the screen MacPhail and Morgan certainly added some necessary substance to it, inspired in fact by the deaths of an innkeeper and his daughter in the village of Cwmbach, just outside of Treorchy by a German air raid that had killed 27 people. Nonetheless, the writers seem to have managed to salvage something of the heart of the original play while infusing it with the one thing Britain needed so very much at that moment in time – hope. Did the film make any real difference? That's unlikely, but in the corridors of the War Office, anything was worth a shot.

Eire remained neutral throughout the war, at least officially, though some 70,000 Irishmen crossed the Irish Sea and volunteered to fight as part of the British Army, a figure significantly bolstered by Irishmen who were already living in Britain at the outbreak of war. Eire's neutrality was itself sorely tested when, on Easter Tuesday, April 15, 1941 Luftwaffe bombers attacked the Northern Ireland capital Belfast, killing some 900 people, De Valera sending more than a dozen fire brigades across the border in order to help extinguish the fires. De Valera followed that with a formal protest to Berlin and in a speech delivered at Castlebar, County Mayo five days later, pointed out that, "In the past, and probably in the present too, a number of them do not see eye to eye with us politically, but they are our people – we are one and the same people." Hitler called a halt to any further bombing of Belfast after a third blitz through the night of 5 May not because of De Valera's reaction but the possibility that it might provoke Irish Americans into pressing for the United States to enter the war on the side of the British. Eire ceased to be a British dominion in April 1949.

By the time *The Halfway House* hit the cinema screens of course, Hitler's fears of America entering the war had already been realised, on 11 December 1941, eight months after the Belfast bombings, and within 53 days of the film's release, the Allies had landed on the beaches of Normandy and the beginning of the end of Hitler's Thousand Year Reich was finally in sight. To contemporary ears at least, the message within the film might seem to have been delivered with rather too thick a trowel of cloying pedantry, but why not? After all, there was a war to be won. Then again, if you think about it, hasn't the point of a stay at The Halfway House – of the heart, of the mind – always been to take a little time out of the stresses of life to reconsider the choices before you?

## POSTSCRIPT:

Another little essay that couldn't find a home. Glynis Johns passed away January 4, 2024 in Los Angeles at the age of 100. Mervyn Johns was 93 when he died in London in 1992.

# A LIFE OF SORTS IN SEVEN BOOKS

I've never understood the fascination with lists – the Top Ten books/records/films, 1000 movies/books/albums you must see/read/hear before you die and so on. There was a time publishers seemed to be pumping out books of lists as if there was nothing else worth publishing, and, of course, when in doubt, commercial television will line up all manner of "faces" to comment wittily or otherwise on the Top Ten Funniest Cat/Dog/Humans videos – cheap entertainment for the lowest common denominator and biggest advertising dollar (and let's not forget the ultimate crossover money spinners, "The World's Funniest Advertisements"!).

Who decides? On what authority is this record/book/film better/essential in comparison with another? In the 25 years I worked at a weekly entertainment paper, unlike my colleagues, staff and freelance contributors alike (and this is no slur on any of them), I never once compiled a "Best Song/Album/Concert/Whatever" list for the end-of-year edition since, as far as I was concerned, I hadn't heard every record released, attended every concert that had passed through town, seen every film, read every book and so on, on what basis could I honestly say this or that was the *best* other than on my limited sampling of each across the year. So instead I'd write a socio-political overview of the non-musical events of the year as best I could on the off chance that there might be a handful of readers out there who might wonder what had happened while they were at those concerts or watching those movies or reading those books.

Anyway, all this is by way of finding myself challenged, via Facebook, to present exactly that which I have so studiously avoided all these years – a list! The challenge appeared one morning courtesy one of the first friends I made when I moved to Sydney at the end of the 1970s, one Ian Chambers, now living in New Zealand, with whom I reconnected, as I have with so many old friends, courtesy Facebook, an unexpected side effect of signing up to the social media platform in order to try and connect with my daughters, who both live down in Victoria.

"I was nominated," Ian's post informed all who cared to read it, "by Steve Wood to post the cover of seven books I love, one book per day for seven days, no explanations, no reviews, just covers. Each day, to #promoteliteracy I will invite a friend to take up the challenge. On my third day I nominate Michael Smith."

Once I'd allowed my horror at the idea to subside, I actually started to think about how I might go about addressing such a challenge. I knew I was damned if I was going to present some sort of spurious "Top Seven" list. I may be (at the time) 67 but I'm still a long way from having read enough to play that sort of game. Yet the idea wouldn't leave me alone. I eventually accepted that I had to find a way of presenting some sort of list if only to get a decent night's sleep. So…

**Book One, Day One**: Okay, I'm having a crack at this "seven books in seven days" lark in which young Ian Chambers suggested I might participate. Of course I've loved so many books and for so many reasons I had no real idea which way I should go. Of one thing I was certain however. There was no way I could just plonk a series of book covers here (on my Facebook page) without some sort of short explanatory note. In fact, trying to create at least *some* sort of theme – autobiographical in the case of this selection – was the only way I could even attempt to narrow the field down a bit, to make some sort of sense of the exercise. So, here goes. Selection 1 – Joyce Cary's *The Horse's Mouth*. I was supposed to read this as part of the English class in my final year at Elizabeth High School (South Australia, Year of 1969), but by the time we got around to it, I'd started losing my focus courtesy my growing passion for the guitar, which I played with an arrogant ineptness at every opportunity, coupled with an emerging sense of the poetry within me, which was equally inept – thankfully I eventually figured out that the short story was potentially my

176

real literary direction. So, while I stumbled through F. Scott Fitzgerald's *The Great Gatsby*, which I re-read in 1976 as part of an additional unit – American Literature – for my already completed BA and understood far better the second time around, *The Horse's Mouth* had to wait until my first year at Adelaide Uni – and I loved it. Here was a raggle- taggle of a man utterly consumed by his art, to the point where his vision ultimately overwhelmed the reality that finished him and the book. I can still see, in my mind, the image of the whale's belly Gully Jimson is still painting as it surges out of the wall, suddenly becoming three-dimensional, as the wrecking ball on the other side of that wall strikes. I imagine the book and Jimson resonated with me because of my own consuming passion for music, having thankfully set bad poetry aside. It took another two years to find the *right* musical instrument to finally express that passion properly.

**Book Two, Day Two**: Our dad gave us our love of reading, teaching us to read and write before we got to school, a teacher stuck in a labourer's life. Perhaps that was one of the reasons D.H. Lawrence resonated so strongly with me. We didn't have a lot of books at home, though we kids eventually sorted that out. Either way, my first year at Adelaide University was a revelation. I really *was* starting from scratch in discovering my literary heritage, which I suppose explains why while many of my fellow students might have been dreaming thoughts of Kerouac and Bukowski, I was being totally amazed by everyone from Chaucer to Thomas Hardy – literally a whole new world for me. But it was Lawrence who captured my imagination – *Sons and Lovers*, *The Rainbow* and *Women in Love* in particular. I'd read a short story at school, *The Odour of Chrysanthemums* – but it was another, *The Man Who Died*, that has stayed with me all these years. Perhaps it was the idea that a man can suffer the very worst life can throw at him and yet with love, care and determination, can be "reborn" into whatever next chapter of his life he chooses to enter. Of course, it's easy to suggest that Lawrence "lost it" in the second half of the story, but that was always his problem, so determined, as he was, to make a point that he all too often sacrificed the beauty of his original idea. I'm often guilty of that by my penchant for writing sentences 150 to 200 words long, as if a thought won't allow me to stop for breath. So, my second nominee book is Lawrence's *The Man Who Died*, though I read it in a collection titled *Love Among The Haystacks*, which always struck me as a jolly good alternative to getting crucified.

**Book Three, Day Three**: After two years of solid touring – as a bass guitarist, I eventually found myself in a band popular and proficient enough to attract a recording deal – and a year finding my feet in Sydney once the band and I had parted company, it seemed a good time to go back to university and re-focus. I was incredibly lucky to go into an MA at the University of NSW with lecturer/tutor Jim Allen, who was then presenting a course in Edwardian Literature – just the ticket. It was in his class that I was introduced to George Gissing's *New Grub Street* and boy did that resonate! Here was a story of struggling writers, some inspired and passionate, some just journeymen trying to make a living, all struggling to get their work published. And here was I, freelancing madly, sending stuff off to the music magazines of the day – *Juke* and *RAM* – while I was also playing in three bands, hoping that this or that piece tickled the respective editor's interest and that perhaps one of the bands might capture the popular imagination. Not a lot has changed, apart from no bands, no gigs and practically no music magazines! Jim Allen also helped me de-clutter my first real short story, *"The Black"*, which, as it happens, was rejected by *Quadrant* (this is 40 years ago), published in Mitchell College, Bathurst's long since gone literary journal *Inprint* and went on to be anthologised in three different short story collections. So, Book 3 – *New Grub Street*, and my eternal thanks to Jim Allen, to whom I introduced Richard Jefferies' prophetic novella *After London*.

**Book Four, Day Four**: As chaotic and disparate as much of my reading life has been, a significant part of it has been "catching up", reading what perhaps I should have read years before but never found time to because, as John Lennon would have it, I was busy doing other things, like gigging, relationships, writing, television (film and TV script writing still fascinates me). Anyway, it took that MA in Edwardian Literature, only possible for me in those pre-Hawke/Keating days before fees were reintroduced, to finally get me into the extraordinary world of H.G. Wells. For me, the thing about Wells was that he spoke to both sides of me – the scientist/atheist and the hopelessly human/romantic – so I have to nominate two novels in order to cover both sides. Unlike any of the cinematic treatments, *The Time Machine* spoke to me of the inevitability of universal entropy, manifested in Wells' novel in the bleak scene towards the end of the slim volume when the Traveller arrives near the end of Earth's own time – chilling yet unequivocal – a reminder that, as T.S. Elliot would have it, "This is the way the world ends, not with a bang but a whimper", or in Wells' vision, with a dark shape wearily heaving around at the edge of some dark ocean. On the other hand, *Love And Mr Lewisham* introduced a different Wells, living in our world and struggling with the things with which we all struggle, trying to survive in a world that will never live up to our ideals. Reading *Tono Bungay*, the last of his "social romances", later that year it became obvious to me just how deeply disillusioned Wells had become with the power of the novel to change anything, and I pondered the possibility of doing my PhD on the deconstruction of the portrait of the artist across Wells' "social romances". I might get around to it one day. Meanwhile, my day's nominations are *The Time Machine* and *Love and Mr Lewisham*.

**Book Five, Day Five**: The problem with issues that cloud the mind is that they don't always manifest in obvious symptoms. If there are no "ticks" or "visions" or "voices", how can anyone tell that things inside your head are spiralling out of control? For me there'd been subtle signs – feelings – at particular points in my late teens and through my twenties, but I'd carried on, as you do – keep busy, fill the void or whatever. In the end however, let's just say that I discovered, in the most catastrophic fashion, that for some time I had been prone to increasingly severe depressive episodes not as a consequence of any neurological chemical imbalance, but in response to what can best be described as "environmental" or exogenous factors (though this diagnostic term has long since fallen out of favour), trigger moments recalling early experiences of stress and powerlessness, stemming from a time before words when no matter what I did, the centre of the universe seemed so unhappy, which of course must have been my fault. Thankfully I got through it all. Once you've been guided through a severe episode like that and recognise the trigger points, you're better able to deal with recurrences of similar triggering experiences – and had done so a good 16 years before I read Stephanie Luke's remarkable memoir of her own battle with what was once defined as schizophrenia, a book titled *Harm*, published by South Australia's Wakefield Press in 2000.

**Book Six, Day Six**: Having two ethnicities is a truly wonderful thing, bringing with it as it does insights into the cultures of each and an understanding of "the Other", the Xenos, that then serves to broaden your understanding and appreciation of all the other ethnicities you might meet as you travel through life. Of course there can be pitfalls too, particularly when one ethnicity tries to dominate over another. When I was sent and read a copy of the 1992 Australian/Vogal Literary Award-winning novel by Fotini Epanomitis, *The Mule's Foal*, I had to laugh at all the blather about its being a remarkable example of "magic realism". I knew it wasn't magic realism at all – it's exactly how older Greeks from rural parts see the world. For all the patina of Orthodox Christianity, there have been generations out in the villages who still accept there were older gods, that the plants and animals, even the stones hold secrets, that superstitions are based on realities we just don't see. It's not magic realism – it's life as it has been for centuries in those villages, even if it's a life that is slowly disappearing. So, Fotini presents us with the foibles of a community that are as real to some people as anything you see on *Neighbours* or *Home and Away*.

**Book Seven, Day Seven**: Every family has its stories of this or that relative who might have done this or that, their "moment in the sun" about which they might rabbit on to anyone who will listen. Perhaps it's a moment that holds pride of place in the family. For some, that "moment" might be the family joke – "There there granddad, yes, of course you were..." In *Ancient Highway*, published in 2008, American author Bret Lott looked at a particular moment in a man's life that mattered profoundly to him but had become something of a family joke, and I have to admit that when, towards the end of the book, his family finally discovered that granddad's moment was in fact real, I shed a quiet tear, sitting in a corner of the train home, trying not to be observed by the other commuters. It's a book with which I never expected to relate, but it resonated deeply. And now I too am a granddad.

So there go, a sort of life in seven/eight books with a couple on the side. Perhaps some of you might go and read those books you've not yet encountered yourselves. After all, isn't that the idea behind this whole #promoteliteracy exercise?

## POSTSCRIPT:

Obviously I looked at two of the books covered here in more detail elsewhere in this volume. Hopefully their inclusion here merely adds a little more to their lustre and piques enough interest for you to seek them out yourself. Did the original Facebook post version do that? Probably not.

## PRE-FAB BRITAIN, POP & GANGSTERS

Chatting to Jake Arnott about his novel, *The Long Firm* (Hodder Headline)

Born in Detmold in Germany in 1942, at the age of seven Heinz Burt arrived in England with his widowed mother in 1949. As a teenager, like so many other kids in the UK, across Europe and, of course, right down to the Antipodes, he fell in love with all things American '50s pop culture, and rock'n'roll and American pioneer rocker Eddie Cochran in particular. Burt was soon playing in a local band in the Hampshire town of Eastleigh where he grew up and in 1961 became a member of the session band, The Tornados, that producer and songwriter Joe Meek put together to record his songs as performed by the singers he signed to his record label. The Tornados also backed singer Billy Fury, but it was an instrumental tune Meek had written titled *Telstar* that put the band at the top of both the British and American charts in September 1962. Telstar reached #2 in Australia. So for a few months The Tornados rivalled The Shadows as the top international instrumental band.

Meanwhile the homosexual Meek had plans to launch the handsome blonde Burt as a pop star in his own, the fact that Heinz couldn't sing a mere technicality since Meek could call in any one of the other recording artists he'd signed to cover the vocals – all very well until the artist now known as Heinz was obliged to perform the records in person. None of Heinz's singles made any impact and of course then The Beatles hit and that was that. Burt introducing his girlfriend to Meek finished off any chance of an imagined "relationship", a fantasy Meek never consummated. It was a shotgun owned by Burt that he'd left at Meek's studio with which, in 1967, the producer shot his landlady and then himself. Burt, whose health had been declining for some years as a consequence of motor neurone disease, died April 7, 2000, at the age of 57 following a stroke. For all the failure of any significant musical solo career, Heinz became something of a cult figure within the mists of British pop culture.

All this is by way of introducing one of the background characters in a novel by British novelist Jake Arnott, born the year Meek put together The Tornados and the author of *The Long Firm*, published in 1999. Both Meek and Heinz appear in the first part of the novel, which swirls around the machinations of one Harry Stark, an enigmatic underworld figure in the pre-Fab '60s, before The Beatles changed the musical landscape and made bands like The Tornados redundant, and charts his rise and fall in the seamy end of London Town as chronicled by five different characters from the late 1950s through to the late '70s.

"The character," Arnott explains of Stark and the genesis of the novel, "sort of took me into that world really. I initially thought the book would be set in the Sixties but once I started researching the period, there was so much going on, and it's really Britain's decade I think. For America I think it's the Fifties. It's a time that, stylistically, we still haven't recovered from, and, in fact, very recently, all kinds of retro – I mean, Oasis for God's sake, they're a Beatles tribute band essentially – Cool Britannia, with New Labour [under Prime Minister Tony Blair] is just like a rerun of [Prime Minister Harold] Wilson courting the 'Swinging Sixties' stuff.

"So that's what really took me in, and the more you look at it, the more extraordinary that time was. Also I think because it has been written about a lot but often the emphasis is on the late Sixties. A lot of people writing at that time had been to university and of course their experiences are very different, and looking back actually at the 'Great Student Uprisings' of the world, for the most part they weren't that revolutionary, but the British were probably the least significant of all. All they were doing was protesting about someone else's war somewhere else.

"So I thought there are all sorts of other things there, and people get forgotten about and, as you say, [the phenomenon of] Heinz was just extraordinary, and Joe Meek, he was a gift really. I knew of him of course and I came across stuff about him, and of course, because he was gay, he fitted neatly into Harry's demi-world. And 'The Suitcase Murder' was a real case, and that whole period, although there was pop culture in the Fifties which was largely an American thing really, it really took off in Britain. But then you get this kind of strange seediness about British popular culture, British showbusiness, British film industry – it's all a bit trashy and seedy and I love that. And I suppose it's true the whole world over. You can think about America as being on a much more complex and bigger scale, but you've only got to go to Las Vegas and see how trashy they are as well."

Had Joe Meek lived, he probably would have revelled in the fact that, in the '70s, Las Vegas became the core of the careers of Elvis Presley, Englebert Humperdinck and a young Welshman into whose pant he'd tried to get into named Tom Jones. Back in 1963, as Tommy Scott, Jones had sought out Meek, by then a renowned record producer, to record his band The Senators and quickly discovered there was an ulterior motive behind Meek's request he wear the tightest of white trousers for a publicity shoot!

"I was determined not to have The Beatles anywhere in the novel," Arnott admits. "Every time you see a girl in a mini-skirt, out comes *She Loves You* or something. Obviously The Beatles were phenomenal, but for me, what's more interesting is what went before them, people like Brian Epstein [who ran a record store before he "discovered" The Beatles] and [entrepreneur] Larry Parnes, this kind of strange demi-monde of Soho hustlers, homosexuals, band managers, starlets and gangsters – it still goes on. In a sense now, popular culture is corporate, global capitalism, but then it was kind of organised crime of some sort, with record fixing [payola] and so on. I wouldn't trust someone who described themselves as a band manager at all! Back then it was appalling what went on."

As I've mentioned, Stark's story is told by five different characters – a young "rent boy" (Stark is gay), a dodgy MP, a would-be "partner" in crime, a B-movie starlet and, amusingly, a criminologist who gets more than he bargained for in his attempt to understand the criminal mind.

"What seemed to emerge for me was this sort of sine wave of all these different points and I felt Harry was this kind of equaliser all the way through, that he brings everything back down to basic principles. And actually, things like that did happen. Everybody seemed to be rubbing up against each other in this sort of boom time – minor celebrities would be hanging out with gangsters who'd be hanging out with gay MPs and closeted Tories and even academia started to move in on the act."

Of course, all that came out in July 1961 when the affair between 19 year old aspiring starlet and "model" Christine Keeler and British Secretary of State for War, John Profumo, nearly brought down the Conservative government of Harold Macmillan. The "lovers" had been brought together by the bisexual "osteopath" Stephen Ward, who also introduced Keeler to Soviet Naval attaché Yevgeny Ivanov, which brought in the added possibility that British State Secrets might have been "spilled" between the sheets as it were.

"I actually gave a copy to the British Society of Criminology," adds Arnott, "because this criminologist got in touch with me after he'd read the book, and it was fascinating, that whole world, because criminology is still such an important discipline because it's how we understand the kind of extremes of society, how we tend to lock everything up in terms of what is right and wrong, who is guilty and not guilty."

## POSTSCRIPT:

The original version of this piece was written for *The Drum Media* to coincide with Arnott's visit to that year's Sydney' Writers' Festival. I'm not sure if it ran, but the book itself is in some ways the perfect confluence of some of my abiding interests – novels, pop culture, British socio-political history. I've tried to bring that same broad brush into my series of histories of Australian pop and rock, *What's Been Did (And What's Been Hid)*.

The BBC dramatised *The Long Firm* in a five-part television series starring Derek Jacobi that went to air in July 2004.

# AND A LITTLE OF OBSESSIONS BEYOND

## LAND, RIGHTS AND LEARNING

There's an essay by Leonie Sandercock in a collection titled *A Nation Apart: Essays in Honour of Andrew Fabinyi* (Longman Cheshire, 1983), in which Ms Sandercock calls for a reassessment of traditional teaching techniques "mixed with other kinds of experience, with work, with political struggle and debate, community service and play... education must aim to provide an understanding of the relationship between science and technology, politics and social change." (p. 27) A similar call is made by David Scott in his essay, *Childhood's End*, which was published in the August issue of *Australian Society*, while Neil Hooley points out that the things that interest a child in a learning situation is something that will "enable children to exercise some degree of control over what happens in their lives." (*Australian Society*, March 1983, p. 24)

But can a child really comprehend an abstract notion like politics? Or more to the point, a social issue such as land rights? After all, what do we mean by the concept of the ownership of land, and who decides who owns it? Can a child raised in the comforts of a safe, middle-class suburban home really appreciate the feelings of fear, insecurity and hunger experienced by a refugee or an orphan struggling for survival in a shanty town?

Jill Morris, in her article about the quality of children's television programming in Australia and overseas, *Life On The Box*, again published in *Australian Society* (December 3, 1982), seems to indicate that at least one committee of adults, the Federation of Australian Commercial Telecasters (FACTS), believes that children cannot grasp these sorts of concepts, and in fact just aren't interested, at least according to their investigations.

Those investigations may not have taken into account an innovative program in life experience education that has been developed and tried over a number of terms by a remarkable educationist from the Riverina College of Advanced Education,

191

Mr Tony Hepworth. His premise is simple enough. Most schools already employ a certain amount of role play acting in their teaching methods, mainly among the younger children. What Hepworth has done is to extend the play acting into Years 7 and 8, and allow children of ten and eleven to experience for themselves the realities of living off the land, or living in a shanty town, or working for "the Landowner", or whatever. He calls his program *Compared To Us*, which is also the name of a kind of newspaper he asks his students to write at the end of a term of experiencing whichever social condition they've been set, in which they describe for themselves what they felt while going through these experiences. The resulting "newspaper" is then presented for discussion within the class. Hepworth feels that the experience leads to a greater understanding through the children's expressing those experiences of the various social contexts into which they've been placed from a *personal* point of view, and that the ways they then present those experiences show they understand far more than most adults often believe they're capable of, and certainly far more than they do from merely reading about them.

*Compared To Us* is also the name of an unassuming little documentary about Hepworth's program made by Craig Monahan, who, when I spoke to him about it, was working for multicultural TV station 0/28 (now SBS) at the suggestion of UNESCO, who felt that, in 1982, the program would be a perfect exercise for young filmmakers in their final year of study at the Australian Radio, Film & Television School (AFTRS) in Ryde in Sydney's north-western suburbs. The 25-minute documentary covers a single term of Hepworth's program which, in this case, centred on the concept of land ownership and land rights. The program documented was run in a small primary school in Wagga Wagga with Year 7 children, and began with an introduction to the fact that the land had originally been "owned" by the local Aboriginal people.

"When we first got down there," Monaghan explains, "we thought it would be really interesting because the children would be telling us ideas that they'd first heard around the dinner table. Now, the first question that we asked them was 'What do you know about Aboriginals?' and to our amazement, most of the kids said positive things, except for one kid, Wayne, who the class and the teacher in particular thought was the dunce of the class. He thought they were *dirty* – dirty, with a smile on his face – and the girls all around him were saying 'They are *not*! Don't *say* such a thing,' in horror, and we realised that maybe they'd been briefed a little bit before we got there. I've left that in the film.

"But I feel Wayne is the one who gets more out of the program than any of the children. He's the one that understands that the Aboriginal can, say, get a knife and cut a little bowl out of a piece of a tree and use it to eat food out of, and he got the whole essence of what was being explored to such an extent that he could see the practical necessity of this sort of thing rather than merely intellectualising about it. So Wayne got more out of it than anybody else in that sense, because he wasn't very good with words and so couldn't put his mind into his mouth. But he could see much further than the rest of them."

So the first part of the program presented in the documentary involved taking the children out of the school and into their local environment with a member of the area's traditional "owners" – the area around Wagga Wagga was originally populated by the Wiradjuri people – and let him show the children how his people had utilised that land, from games that taught hunting techniques through recognising food sources and so on. This part of the lesson seemed easy enough for the children to comprehend since, for instance, the practical aspects of throwing a spear at a grass "star" thrown ahead as a target related to their own games. It didn't necessarily explain why the Aboriginals did not *still* own the land.

The second part involved trying to explain the refugee and the concept of dispossession. First the teacher showed the children various places in the world that had a high proportion of refugees living in them and explained the kinds of conditions under which they were living. The practical side of this lesson involved going out into the school yard and, with materials that they found, and only that material, within the school grounds, making a shanty town of their own, an idea to which the children proceeded to apply themselves with gusto.

At first it's all a game of course, but the children settled into their roles quite easily and were soon exhibiting a certain pride in their construction abilities. The twist came when another group of children, of which the first group were totally unaware, were sent in by the teacher to destroy the shanties, no questions asked. At first the shanty group thought it was just another game, but then it became obvious that the second group were serious and the first group became defensive of their "homes", a real bitterness appearing on both sides.

"Instead of reading theories," Monahan explains, "the children are *being* refugees, living in a shanty town owning nothing. They learn cooperation to build these shanties to give themselves shelter. When the other children come to tear down the shanties, the shanty children act as a group to try and protect them, and the teacher then steps in to explain that, of course, the whole thing was an exercise and the children sent to tear down the shanties were *told* to do it, and he asks the children what their feelings were at having this done to them. Who did they think these people were who had come to tear down their homes?

"Now, there's been no prompting, no conditioning by the education system or anything like that, and yet these kids turn around and say 'land owners', 'the military', the police', 'people who didn't want us on the land because *they* wanted it for themselves' – so *sharp*!"

It's likely of course that this was a reflection of ideas the children were familiar with from their own experiences at home, but nonetheless not only could the children "name their oppressors", such as they might be, but could also question the rights of those people to do what they had done, even though they realised that they themselves had no real right to be on that

194

particular piece of land, at least no "legal" rights. These children were asking why they couldn't have stayed on the land since there was so much of it and they couldn't see that the land owner was really doing anything with it himself. Remember, these ideas are coming spontaneously, even if channelled, from ten and eleven year old school children.

As I've mentioned the culmination of the exercise is the making of the newspaper, and we see the children in committee discussing what should and should not go into it, each contribution coming from the participating members of the class, from drawings, essays and poems to lists of what they felt were life's essentials as they tried to express what they'd learned from the experience. It's one of those lists of the ten most important things necessary for survival that gives the film its surprising final punch. As we watch the children discussing the completed newspaper in class with their teacher, he asks them why Love and Care should come before Education in that list, which also included food, clothing, sanitation and electricity.

"The teacher asked Wayne why he thought this should be," says Monahan, "and Wayne stumbled around for almost five minutes before he managed to blurt out an answer. He said, 'You can live without an education, but you can't live without love and care.' So true. None of the other children could have said that. They may have understood it but in the end it was Wayne, the class dunce, who had a clear picture of what was going on and could 'explain' it in his own terms. Which says a lot for the teacher's own preconceptions about what makes a bright student."

"Human needs are complex," writes Leonie Sandercock in that essay referenced at the beginning of this piece, "but paramount among them are the needs for meaningful work, absorbing play and *the need to love and be loved*." (Ibid., p. 18, my emphasis)

## POSTSCRIPT:

Well, here I suppose I'm trying to be a "grownup" again, writing beyond the confines of the music journalism that was providing the core of my meagre income stream, even though my introduction to Craig Monahan that led into the piece was through music video, Monahan being at the time the producer/director of SBS music program *Rock Around The World*. As to its worth after 40 years of development and assessment within the field of educational practice, I'll have to defer to those readers like my sister Selina McKenzie who are practitioners of the science. An abridged version of this piece was published by the *Journal of the Commonwealth Department of Education, Education Now*, for which I was actually paid! Unlike the publisher of the full text version!!

Craig Monahan has gone on to write, direct and produce several feature films including 1998's *The Interview*, 2004's *Peaches* and 2014's *Healing*.

## TRIBES AND BANDS

A review of Neil Murray's *Sing For Me, Countryman* (Sceptre)

"The desert blacks," Alison Anderson, a commissioner with the Aboriginal Development Commission who was living in the remote desert community of Papunya, 240-odd kilometres northwest of Alice Springs in the Northern Territory, pointed out to journalist Andrew McMillan, "don't want to be involved with or tainted by 'the radical city blacks'." (*Strict Rules*, Hodder & Stoughton, 1988)

Singer-songwriter Neil Murray has good reason to feel a little disinclined to be involved with "the radical city blacks" himself. As the white guitarist with the otherwise all-Aboriginal Warumpi Band in the mid-1970s, he had already experienced the suspicions of those city blacks who saw him as exploiting the band in order to gain recognition as a musician. The volatile potential of that suspicion literally exploded in his face backstage at an ANC anti-apartheid benefit concert in Sydney at which the Warumpi Band performed. According to the account of the ensuing altercation as recorded by McMillan, Gary Foley, then Director of the Aboriginal Arts Board, took exception to a comment of frustration directed at him by Murray and Murray ended up with a broken nose.

In *Sing For Me, Countryman*, a thinly-disguised autobiographical novel, the central character, a white musician named Paul Munro, faces a more brutal response to his irritated comment to black activist turned bureaucrat Len Bower. The irony for both the fictional and actual recipients of this aggressive reverse racism is that the Warumpi Band – and the fictional Mandara Band – unlike, say, Yothu Yindi, had never been a "political" band. It had only ever been a "good time rock'n'roll band" that happened to "evolve" around Murray/Munro during his time working in that central desert community of Papunya, the fictional Mandara.

Just why Murray has chosen to present *Sing For Me, Countryman* as fiction rather than write a straightforward autobiographical memoir may be more personal than to merely create enough of an illusion of fictional "distance" to avoid being further criticised by those "radical city blacks". Either way it's an intriguing and at the same time thoroughly irritating book. In fact it's two books, though the second is, obviously, to a great extent contingent on the first. The irritation comes not from the subject matter but from the almost constant slipping from past to present tense, sometimes within a single paragraph (I can talk!), which suggests that the editor, like the proof-reader, was asleep through considerable periods of the production of the book. The fact that *Sing For Me, Countryman* is two books rather than one is perhaps an inevitable result of the episodic nature of the life being recounted.

The facts of Murray's life, and therefore the journey his fictional character hero takes, have been reported extensively in the nation's popular and music press, and are also an essential element of the story Andrew McMillan tells in *Strict Rules*, which is his account of the Blackfella/Whitefella tour of the remote Aboriginal settlements of the Northern Territory undertaken by Midnight Oil (renamed Hidden Gold in Murray's novel) and the Warumpi Band in the winter of 1986. Murray, born in rural Victoria, moved up to Papunya in the early 1970s, initially driving the local's store's truck around the out-stations that sprang up after the various tribal groups that had been brought together by the Department of Aboriginal Affairs into Papunya decided, for the sake of their survival, to go "bush" once more. Murray then taught English in those out-stations for a couple of years before someone asked him about the guitar and amplifier he'd brought out to Papunya with him.

What makes *Sing For Me, Countryman* two books is the fact that in the first half, Murray, through his character Paul Munro, is trying to explain why he decided to trek off into the central desert in the first place, while the second half is a fairly straightforward account of the rise and fall of the Mandara Band. And it's the first half of the book which is the more intriguing, for all the tumultuousness of life on the road with the

198

Warumpi/Mandara Band.

"In some ways… I guess the other guys in the band are really politically naïve, in terms of the overall Australian thing," McMillan quotes Murray in *Strict Rules*. It's a far more naïve Paul Munro who, apparently besotted by some stereotypical idea of the "Noble Savage", quits tertiary studies in Adelaide to hop on the Ghan and heads for the central desert. As desperate as Munro seems to be to "become" a real part of the community into which he then stumbles, he never overcomes the cultural baggage with which he arrived, and it is this "baggage" that ultimately leads to his attempt to make of his erratic fellow musicians a professional recording unit. For all the "bush knowledge" he attains, and the eventual acceptance of Munro by the community, he cannot commit himself to initiation or give up his ambition to "achieve something", which must forever separate him from that community.

Munro finds it difficult to discard his preconceptions, despite the very different realities that confront him in the outback communities, though even *he* finds it difficult to cope with the petrol-sniffing children (and fair enough). After a while, however, he opts to accommodate the car theft and the vandalism, but the alcoholism becomes a real problem only when it affects the performance of the band. Even so, that very "Western" image of the untainted "Noble Savage" stubbornly persists. Ultimately of course, Munro can no more "connect" with these "untainted" tribal Aborigines than he can with his visiting parents. The out-station blacks understand far more quickly Munro's real malaise; the fact that he has no connection with his own "tribe". What chance, then, of connection with any part of the Land.

If the second half of the book tells us anything about Munro, it is that for all that he has shared with the members of his band and the rest of the settlement and out-station blacks, he still hasn't understood that his values and ambitions can never be theirs. He is continually frustrated by the apparent indifference to tour schedules and professionalism his band mates exhibit. Only when the parents of the two brothers in the band die does Munro concede there is adequate reason to behave erratically with the career of the band.

Unlike most of the other Aboriginal bands that have come to the fore over the past decade – Coloured Stone, The Sunrize Band, Yothu Yindi – the members of the Warumpi Band, and therefore the fictional Mandara Band, were always far more intimately connected/committed to their community and their football team-playing than to the idea of music as a profession. Much as they loved to play, it was only ever fun. It was never more important than staying by family and community. In the end, the artificial tribe Munro (and therefore Murray) created, that nurtured him through his periods of self-doubt, was doomed to crumble, as are all such "tribes/bands", as meaningless as the sedentary life we paternalistic whites have been imposing on the hunter-gatherer societies that have been living perfectly attuned to this country for more than 50,000 years. Munro finally accepts the inevitable – the demise of the band – and after six months of "hiding away", "playing" at being a native, he returns to the Big Smoke to pursue a career as a musician on white terms.

McMillan, in *Strict Rules*, also chooses to paint himself out of the story he tells, dubbing himself only as The Hitchhiker. As Midnight Oil, the Warumpis and the attendant media circus quit an evening by Uluru, the Hitchhiker recalls "he'd been through this country before and he'd seen little hope." For all the shortcomings of style, and the political incorrectness of his casual affairs with Aboriginal women, the story Paul Munro tells in *Sing For Me, Countryman* is of a robust, ebullient people positively bursting with hope, rooted in their land, their dreaming, and accommodating only that part of white civilisation that suits their needs. For that alone, *Sing For Me, Countryman* is a more than worthwhile addition to the national literary canon.

# POSTSCRIPT:

"So basically I got there in 1980," Murray recalled his arriving in Papunya for me in 2022, "and I hadn't been there a week and I think the word got out that there was this new Whitefella with a guitar, and so Sammy Butcher just turned up where I was staying and said, 'You've got a guitar.' I said, 'Yeah.' 'Can I have a look at it?' I showed him the guitar and I could tell, straightaway, he could play beautifully. So we ended up jamming that afternoon with a bit of borrowed gear, and he said, 'I've got a little bit of gear – half a PA and whatnot.' We scrounged up some more gear and just started, you know, playin'. It wasn't until later that year that GR turned up. He was actually at Yuendumu at that stage when I first went to Papunya. He was sort of playin' with a band there called The Poor Boys." GR was George Rrurrambu Burarrwanga, originally from Elcho Island, up in Australia's Top End off the coast of the Territory's Arnhem Land, who became the singer with the Warumpi Band. Their full story is in *Volume V* of my history of Australian rock and pop, *What's Been Did (And What's Been Hid)*, which I'm afraid is a few years yet off completion – sorry.

But I will add… "It wasn't until '86," Murray continues, "that Midnight Oil approached us and said 'We're going to do this tour of communities in the Territory and we want you to be part of it.' I remember I was back working with the Aboriginal Artists Agency helping them get ready for the South Pacific Arts Festival and he said" – this was Gary Morris, the Oils' manager – "'Take down these dates.'" Murray again laughs at the recollection. "It sounded like a big crusade, you know. He was goin' on, 'This is gonna advance the Aboriginal cause by twenty-five years' and all this stuff! And I thought he was fully full of it, but we were keen to just get on the road 'cause we'd had a big disappointment just prior to that. Probably the biggest disappointment of our career was we blew out a tour with Dire Straits. We were gonna support them at the Entertainment Centre for about six nights or whatever they had. I won't go into all the details of why that happened but I thought we were finished, so then when the Oils rang up and asked us to play with them on the Territory tour, everyone was really keen again, so that gave us a resurrection."

The seminal month-long Blackfella/Whitefella tour through July took the Oils and the Warumpis out through the Indigenous communities of Mutitjulu, Docker River, Kintore, Papunya and Yuendumu in the Western Desert, back to Alice and up to Maningrida, Galiwinku, Yirrkala, Umbakumba, Numbulwar, Barunga, Wadeye and Nguiu in the subtropical Top End. All the shows were free, with the Department for Aboriginal Affairs covering the fees and costs of the Warumpis while the Oils covered their own costs. For the tour, Hilary Jabaldjari Wirri, from out-station Haasts Bluff, was on bass – mostly. The tour took its title from a Warumpis song, *Blackfella/Whitefella*, which was released as a single in October 1986. Described as Australia's seminal reconciliation song, it summed up what the Warumpis were all about, Blackfellas and Whitefellas together working towards a better future through cooperation, collaboration and the power of music to bring everyone together.

I met Andrew McMillan a couple of times in the early 1980s when both he and I were freelance contributors to the Sydney-based fortnightly *RAM* – Rock Australia Magazine. He was far more attuned to the journalistic style of the day than I and quickly moved up that particular greasy pole only to turn his back on it all to "go bush". He passed away in late January 2012 after a long illness, aged just 54.

Neil Murray republished *Sing For Me, Countryman* himself in January 2004.

# ANIMAL CRACKERS

*A review of Last Chance to See,* by Douglas Adams with Mark
Carwardine (Pan Books, 1992)

This is quite simply a cracking good read. Douglas
Adams, best known for his *Hitchhiker's Guide to the Galaxy*
quartet, has taken the form of the old traveller's tale, based it
around the idea of discovering a few of the planet's most
endangered animals and written the whole thing in his inimitable
sense of twisted logic and humour to create a book that is at
once a quiet plea for the preservation of all the species of our
increasingly degraded planet and a harrowing account of the
pitfalls faced by the traveller prepared to go off the beaten track.

The idea for the book sprang from a chance meeting of
the self-confessed zoological ignoramus and the eminently
qualified zoologist Mark Carwardine on the island of
Madagascar in search of a long-unseen and possibly already
extinct lemur, the Aye Aye, by the British newspaper *The
Observer*, with the idea of coming up with some interesting
copy and graphics for its *Sunday Supplement*. The extraordinary
experience of not only the quagmire of Madagascar's
bureaucracy but actually *finding* a creature not seen in years
prompted the pair to team up again at some point to perhaps
seek out some other creatures faced with extinction like, say, the
Komodo dragon. Three years after the Madagascar trip, that's
precisely what they did, and a couple of BBC radio crew – and
now we – were invited along for what turned out to be the
journey of their lives.

We're shuttled across to Zaire in Africa to meet the
Mountain Gorilla and the Northern White Rhino, then to New
Zealand for a flightless parrot called a Kākāpō, across to China
for the Baiji, or Yangtze River Dolphin and finally to the Indian
Ocean islands of Mauritius and the rarest bird in the world, the
Echo Parakeet, just some of the animals the pair attempt to
rediscover. Along the way we meet a host of oddball characters,
from reptile experts in Melbourne who hate their speciality to

African guides who pretend to be ex-commandos to make the experience more exciting for the tourists they're guiding.

Why, the authors themselves ask, theoretically through the course of the book, should anyone care about whether or not any of us ever get to see a Kākāpō or a Yangtze river dolphin in the wild ourselves? Perhaps the best answer I can present is not one given by either Adams or Carwardine, which has nothing to do with the ecological plea made by them at the end of the book, but by journalist/broadcaster David Dale who, when he launched his own book, *The Obsessive Traveller*, at a literary luncheon, complained that "nowadays we have made a science out of obliterating every race and trait of the individual. Or, as I prefer to put it, ensuring that millions of people can journey in comfort and safety, without being exposed to alarming new ideas."

At least while the habitats exist that allow an Aye Aye or a Kākāpō to survive, there is a chance to experience a world that isn't all fast food takeaways and video/gaming machines. If you never ever thought that concepts like biodiversity or environmental degradation or species extinction mattered in your world then imagine only ever having the choice of one band to see for the rest of time and *then* think about it. Meanwhile, as Adams and Carwardine have so accessibly pointed out in *Last Chance to See*, there are a passionate few dedicated people trying their damned best to ensure that, whether you're interested or not, there will be other realities available to future generations. Personally I might skip the Komodo dragon experience, but I will treasure this book.

## POSTSCRIPT:

This was my second published book review – my first was of Noel McGrath's *Australian Encyclopaedia of Rock, 1978-79* (Outback Press), published in the ABC's *24 Hours* magazine, November 1979, p. 80, which I have to admit was my sneaky way, as a poverty-stricken freelance writer and musician, to get a free copy of a book that included a couple of paragraphs (and happy snap) of the band that had recently sacked me – and get paid for reading it.

I imagine the only reason the music magazine that published it did so was because it was Douglas Adams, as big a pop culture figure as could want back in the '80s – hence the comment about only having the choice of one band to listen to forever – pretty naïve considering that's pretty much what happens with most people, who generally end up choosing to listen to one or two bands.

As most readers will be aware Adams sadly passed away unexpectedly aged just 49 in May 2001. In 2009, his friend Steven Fry decided to retrace Adams' journey with Carwardine to see just how many of the animals discussed in the original book were still alive. The accompanying BBC TV series and book skipped a couple of species – the Rodrigues fruit bat and the Yangtze River Dolphin because both were "in all probability extinct".

## WISDOM OF THE ELDERS – A TIMELY REMINDER OF THE HUMANITY OF PRIMITIVE SOCIETIES

The last place you would have expected to find a kind of confirmation of the values Canadian climate activist Dr David Suzuki and his co-author Peter Knudtson, a Vancouver-based specialist in animal behaviour and ecology, are attempting to legitimise so meticulously in their book *Wisdom Of The Elders*, published in Australia by Allen & Unwin, would be the American music industry bible *Billboard*, but there it was, in the editorial pages of the May 9, 1992 issue, in an essay by the magazine's then editor in chief Timothy White. The intention of the essay, titled *Native American Song, Then & Now*, was to give context to the work of one John Trudell, a Santee Sioux, who had made a musical career of his social activism in the area of pressing for Native American Rights. White comments on the perplexity with which those diverse groups of Native Americans were viewing the then impending 500th anniversary of the landing by Christopher Columbus in the Bahamas, a landfall that would bring cataclysmic consequences for them all and particularly for the islands' indigenous population, which was essentially wiped out either through disease or enslavement.

White then quotes from a book by Jack Weatherford titled *Native Roots – How The Indians Enriched America*, published in 1991: "In the 400 years since the European settlers began coming to North America they have not found a single American plant suitable for domestication that the Indians had not cultivated." White then makes the point that "even our Founding Fathers' concept for governing the wilderness settlements was shaped by the Iroquois Confederacy Great Law instituted in the 15th century by the legendary Hiawatha and Daganawidah."

With *Wisdom Of The Elders*, Knudtson and Suzuki have attempted to bring together, correlated with a broad spectrum of contemporary scientific thought, the myths and legends of a number of native aboriginal peoples from several continents to show just how vast the knowledge base about our world and its environment and ecology in these products of so-called "primitive" peoples is. The basic thesis, acknowledged as originally conceived by French anthropologist Claude Levi-Strauss, is that it is to our peril that this vast treasury of knowledge, buried in these various folklores, that they should be so lightly dismissed in the face of our perceived "superior" contemporary science-based knowledge. It is that misleading "superior ethnocentricity" their book hopes to begin, however tentatively, to address, and it attempts to do so by as scrupulous a scientific methodology as the authors can muster, because it is the "tyranny" of Western scientific culture that has allowed us to so easily dismiss this accumulated "wisdom of the Elders", dazzling us with its extraordinary achievement while obfuscating the fact that all present scientific knowledge is based on a network of theories that appear most likely to explain the various phenomena we observe around us *at this point in time*.

As Professor Randall Albury of the University of NSW's History & Philosophy of Science Department points out, in an essay published in the *Sydney Morning Herald*, "Now that scientists are looking to the past as a source of ideas for solving modern problems, they are beginning more and more often to find what they are looking for." (*Modern Scientific Researchers Find That Everything Old Is New Again*, 23 April, 1992, p. 15) While it is in the field of recorded and therefore essentially Western science Albury is suggesting that today's scientists are discovering insights from the past, Knudtson and Suzuki could contend the case, with *Wisdom Of The Elders*, for those parameters to be broadened far beyond the beginnings of recorded human knowledge itself to include the accumulated experience of thousands of generation that has been passed down to us as myths and oral traditions by the world's Indigenous/First Nations peoples. In fact, their contention is that if we are to find a balance with our planet, its environment and those fellow creatures that have thus far survived the depredations of we humans, the answers to many of the questions about how this might be achieved are already there, buried in the various mnemonics employed by those generations in transmitting that knowledge through those myths and traditions.

The only real impediment then, apart from having to overcome the intransigence of politicians and business interests to any ideas that might prevent their continuing the pillaging of the planet's commodities for their own gain, is that ethnocentricity in scientific perception, so masterfully dismissed by Levi-Strauss, quoted in the opening chapter of *Wisdom Of The Elders*: "I see no reason why mankind should have waited until recent times to produce minds of the calibre of a Plato or an Einstein. Already over two or three hundred thousand years, there were probably men [I know – he should have included women and beyond, the Author] of similar capacity, who were of course applying their intelligence to the solution of the same problems as those more recent thinkers." (Quoted from an essay titled *The Concept Of Primitivism* included in *Man The Hunter*, edited by Richard B Lee and Irven de Vore, Aldine Publishing, 1968, p. 351)

Speaking to David Suzuki before he headed off to Rio to attend the 1992 Earth Summit, for which he admitted he held no real hopes, he added a number of other scientists to the list of those whose ideas helped shape the book, not least the work of Harvard biologist E.O. Wilson, who developed the idea of socio-biology, and internal-medicine-turned-atmospheric-scientist James Lovelock, whose most influential contribution has been the concept of Gaia, in which he describes the synergistic relationship between life and inorganic matter in maintaining the conditions for life on Earth. "I think we're helped by the fact that we quote a lot of scientists," Suzuki admits, "including Albert Einstein, so that it is obvious to the readers that what we are presenting as the wisdom of the elders is not just aboriginal elders but that of many of our leaders and scientists, who

209

themselves are saying that science by itself is too restricted and that we need to broaden it out. So there is, I think, a lot of support coming from scientists for this 'new' way of looking at the world. I think, as well, certainly in Canada, that there has been a *tremendous* shift in interest in native people, so I'm always telling people that ten years ago, if I said 'Indian' in Canada, the *immediate* response would have been the image of a drunk on skid row. Today there are several individual leaders who have gained a respected national prominence that has shifted the stereotypes away and changed perceptions radically, so much so that polls now indicate that the vast majority of Canadians are supportive of native land claims and want to see a just settlement. That shift in perception makes it much easier to try to present the ideas with a book like *Wisdom Of The Elders*.

"Some of that shift in perception has been due to the actions of environmentalists, and there are some native peoples that accuse the environmentalists of having used them, which in some ways they have. Environmentalists have seen that many of the struggles of native peoples to save their lands are environmental issues and have joined those peoples in their struggles, and some have exploited those natives by getting them to rekindle some sort of interest in an area about which they have done nothing and prompted a land claim in order to save it.

"I'm very interested in Australia because I suspect that Australia is still back twenty years ago with respect to its native peoples as compared to Canada. I saw one thing about the relationship here that even made *our* news, a documentary about your police and the suburb of Redfern."

Now, all this harking back to what might seem at first glance like naïve belief systems belonging to unsophisticated primitive tribal groups could easily be dismissed as romantic sentimentalism with an undercoat of Western post-colonial guilt, or even an inevitable outgrowth of that dubious area of the contemporary search for meaning, "New Age philosophy", were it not for the credentials of the authors. Quite apart from his high public profile as an environmental activist and speaker, David

Suzuki is a Professor of genetics at the University of British Columbia, while Peter Knudtson, as mentioned, is a widely published and respected anthropologist. Each has drawn as much from their own life experiences working with and understanding native peoples as they have from the body of recorded scientific research on these peoples and their respective belief systems.

"The knowledge base of these so-called savages is extraordinary," Suzuki contends, "I mean, I went down and lived on the Amazon with these 'stone-age' people and there wasn't a plant I asked them about that they couldn't name – unless they were faking it!"

This last comment shows just how conscious Suzuki is to the possibility of being duped by "Stone-age" people, something that has become the bane of anthropologists since the revelations of just that called into question the studies of coming of age in Samoa on which the late Margaret Mead built her career. And it shows how carefully Suzuki and Knudtson approached all their research in putting together *Wisdom Of The Elders*. The co-authors even cite an example of native "wisdom" that turned out to have been only tenuously based on the words of the native elder to whom it has popularly been ascribed, which was liberally "embroidered" in the 1970s – The Case of Chief Seattle – whose attributed words, described as an impassioned plea for respect for Native American Rights and their concomitant environmental values and wisdom, seemed a genuine parallel, one hundred or so years later, to those of today.

Inevitably, a book like *Wisdom Of The Elders* can only hope to provide an introduction to what must have been a vast, even daunting body of work available on the subject from the scores of indigenous First Nation peoples around the world from which it is drawn. "Peter in fact did most of the research," Suzuki admits, "and basically we just dabble. We haven't even covered the Maoris of New Zealand for example. Part of it was a convenience of finding experts who knew about particular groups and part of it was to try to get as broad a spread as possible, but it is basically a superficial look at a *vast* literature. Peter got literally hundreds of stories and then it was a matter of choosing the ones that best illustrated the points we were trying to make. But I think there are hundreds of lifetimes if you really want to become an expert and dive into it."

The arguments which the choices within the book are meant to illustrate concentrate on the environmental and ecological, a natural extension of the focus of many of Suzuki's previous essays and books, among them *It's A Matter Of Survival* or *Inventing The Future*.

"Al Gore," said Suzuki, recalling former Vice President in the 1993-2001 Clinton administration, Democratic nominee in the 2000 Presidential elections and a leading advocate on environmental policy change, "pointed out to me – politicians only care about the priorities of people that vote. What about all the future generations to be born? They don't vote. You look at the policies Australia carries out – we don't give a shit about future generations! We don't even *consider* them in the decisions we make today. They are made almost exclusively for political, economic and social reasons, so we've effectively disenfranchised all future generations just to serve this present one. Politics is simply incapable of dealing with these issues."

As I mentioned earlier, when I spoke to Suzuki, he was on his way to the United Nations Conference on Environment and Development – the Earth Summit – that was being held in Rio de Janeiro, Brazil, over the fortnight June 3 through 14, 1992, where he was to present what he dubbed the *Declaration of Interdependence* in the hope that the fracturing non-governmental organisations and various environmental lobby groups attending the "alternative" Summit being held would find it something of a rallying point around which to find common cause. A number of native aboriginal peoples from around the world were also attending the Summit in what they described an Earth Parliament. The likelihood of their collective voice being heard above the din of calls for "sustainable development" based on "economic rationalism" in the face of potential "world economic recession" and a Climate Convention made toothless by the political imperatives of, among others, then US President George W. Bush, was, to say the least negligible.

"Both scientists and politicians have failed," wrote Jeremy Leggett in a piece in the May 2, 1992 issue of *New Scientist*. "The scientists of the IPCC (Intergovernmental Panel on Climate Change) have undersold the worst possibilities outlined in their analysis of global warming. And policy makers have misunderstood fundamentals of scientific method." In the face of all this, as the world turned its focus on the negotiations in Rio, the former Commonwealth Secretary-General Sonny Ramphal voiced his own vague hope: "Nobody, surely, can have a veto on human survival."

## POSTSCRIPT:

I was incredibly lucky to get to interview David Suzuki several times between 1990, when the editor of the Sydney-based free weekly music, arts and entertainment magazine *On The Street* very generously put him on the cover and gave me a two-page centre spread, and 1997 when our last interview had to be foreshortened by news of the imminent arrival of my second daughter – she ended up running a fortnight overdue.

The final paragraph was originally part of an opinion piece I wrote for *The Drum Media* around the same time as the essay on *Wisdom Of The Elders* that, in the event, wasn't published.

Nineteen ninety-seven also saw me review an extraordinary book titled *Laboratory Earth: The Planetary Gamble We Can't Afford To Lose*, written by a chap named Stephen H. Schneider, a specialist in the new interdisciplinary field of Earth Systems science. Originally a mechanical engineer, while a postdoctoral fellow at NASA's Goddard Institute for Space Studies, Schneider co-authored a study published in the July 1971 issue of *Science* on the role of greenhouse gases and suspended particulate material on climate in which he concluded that the impact of those gases and particles could tip the world into an ice age, only to later realise that the simple model on which his conclusions had been based underestimated the impact of carbon dioxide on the atmosphere by a factor of up to three. Recalculating that impact, he published a retraction of his earlier findings the following year, horrified by the possibility that he might have been the cause of irreparable damage with regards to the whole climate change discussion. Over the next 38 years until his untimely death in London in July 2010 at the age of 65, Schneider became committed to the cause of educating the world to the realities of and, more importantly, the science *behind* global warming, sharing, as a member of the UN Panel on Climate Change, the 2007 Nobel Peace Prize with Al Gore.

Schneider founded and edited a journal titled *Climate Change*, first published in 1977, as well as becoming Professor of Environmental Biology and Global Change at Stanford University, a Co-Director at the Center for Environment Science and Policy of the Freeman Spogli Institute for International Studies, and a Senior Fellow in the Stanford Woods Institute for the Environment and as a consultant had the ear of the incumbents of the White House from Nixon to Obama. In 2006, he also served as an Adelaide Thinker in Residence advising the South Australian Government of the then State Premier, Mike Rann, on climate change and renewable energy policies, helping that state move from zero towards 31% of its electricity generation being based on renewable energy.

In *Laboratory Earth*, published at the beginning of the year that saw the Kyoto Climate Change Summit prove as ineffectual at achieving any sort of international consensus as Rio and the others that had preceded it, Schneider states quite simply that we cannot take the risk of allowing political and business interests to use our planet as, by his definition, a laboratory with which to decide who is right. As he suggests at the beginning of this immensely important little book, "When the laboratory is the Earth, we need to anticipate the outcome of our global-scale experiments *before* we perform them." (My emphasis) Adopted in December 1997, the Kyoto Protocol took until February 2005 for it to *finally* come into force, though only 192 countries have ratified it. It took another 11 years for the Paris Agreement in November 2016. The science and the increase in severe weather-related events, from floods to fires, makes it clear that "limiting temperature increase to 1.5°C above pre-industrial levels" is already unlikely to be achieved before the Statement's proposed deadline of 2025. In fact, current estimates see the temperature passing 2°C by 2050. I won't be around, but my daughters should be and my granddaughter definitely will be.

In *Laboratory Earth*, Schneider made it clear that "the prospect of climatic surprises is chilling enough to lend considerable urgency to the need to speed up our understanding, slow down the rates at which we are forcing nature to change, or better (in my value system), to do both." That was in 1997. My review was never published.

Way back in 1966, the head of America's Atomic Energy Commission, Glenn Seaborg, a research scientist who taught at the University of California (UC) Berkeley who had shared the 1951 Nobel Prize in Chemistry, addressed a commencement audience at (UC) San Diego and, as quoted by Rachel Maddow in her extraordinary book, *Blowout* (Crown, 2019), made this point: "At the rate we are currently adding carbon dioxide to our atmosphere (six billion tons a year), within the next few decades the heat balance of that atmosphere could be altered enough to produce marked changes in the climate – changes which we might have no means of controlling even if by that time we have made great advances in our programs of weather modification. I, for one, would prefer to continue to travel towards the equator for my warmer weather rather than run the risk of melting the polar ice and having some of our coastal areas disappear beneath a rising ocean." (p. 14-5). Let me repeat the date of that comment – *1966*!

**STOP PRESS**: Produced jointly by the World Meteorological Organisation and the European Union's Copernicus Climate Change Service, *The State of the Climate in Europe 2022* report, released in June 2023, noted that Europe has been warming twice as much as the global average since the 1980s, and that in 2022, Europe was approximately *2.3°C* above the pre-industrial (1850-1900) average used as a baseline for the Paris Agreement on climate change.

Global sea surface temperatures are the highest on record, the ice in Antarctica is melting at around 150 billion tons a year, while Greenland is losing around 270 billion tons a year. For goodness sake, July 2023 and the island of *Rhodes* is on fire! By November, the evidence was in – 2023 was the hottest year on record. Can't wait for 2024!! Of course, for readers who might accidentally discover some rare tattered copy of this collection sometime in the future, it's all academic.

"Are we willing to accept another wasted decade of greenwashing as the planet burns?" Dr Joëlle Gergis asked in her deeply personal and powerful essay, *Highway to Hell: Climate Change and Australia's Future*, her contribution to the *Quarterly Essay* series, #94, published in June 2024, as her discussion oscillated between optimism and pessimism.

In his 2020 book, *A Life on Our Planet: My Witness Statement and a Vision for the Future*, David Attenborough wrote: "The natural world is fading. The evidence is all around. It has happened during my lifetime. I have seen it with my own eyes. It will lead to our destruction." Like Dr Gergis, and Dr David Suzuki, who pointed out that the 1990s was "the Turnaround Decade" to no avail, at the of 94 when he published the book, Attenborough still had hope: "Yet there is still time to switch off the reactor. There *is* a good alternative."

I knew there was a good reason to build a house in the NSW Blue Mountains, 100 kilometres from the coast and 1017 metres above sea level. Then again, I've basically swapped sea level inundation for higher bushfire threats. Either way, time, I think, to reconsider that beachside retirement property.

## THE HARM IN YOUR MIND
An interview with author Stephanie Luke for *The Drum Media*.

In October 1999, as part of National Mental Health Week, I interviewed the Chairman of the Marketing & Development Committee of the Neuroscience Institute of Schizophrenia and Allied Disorders (NISAD), Alan Turnbridge about a condition once called Dementia Praecox, literally "the Madness of Youth", but known today as Schizophrenia. He made one particular point: "People with schizophrenia can rarely speak coherently for themselves."

Adelaide-based writer Stephanie Luke is the exception, someone who has experienced what Turnbridge described as "not a 'split mind' at all. It's disordered thought," and come out the other side to not only speak coherently but with a quiet eloquence and subtle lyricism that makes her first novel, *Harm*, more than a necessary insight into a condition so little understood but announces an important new voice in Australian literature. The fact that *Harm* is in a sense written from "within" the experience of a "psychotic episode" is certainly something new to the Australian literary canon.

"The fact that there wasn't a lot around was in part the reason I got into writing," Stephanie admits. "There are a couple of books on these issues written by an author in Colorado that worked for me, but that was it. There are other books that are the aftermath, that are like apologies for what went before."

Stephanie presents not only her own experience through the central character, Anna, but another sort of potentially more destructive sort of psychotic episode as experienced by another character, Jacob, who transforms from something of a potential "saint" figure, for Anna at least, in actions that might imply a certain monastic aestheticism, into a destructive "sinner" with a very different sort of chilling potential: "Did you hear about the murder in Bowden?"

"That was actually a reference to something he was planning to do," Stephanie explains. "That's a suggestion of the ambiguity within the lives of these people between reality and fantasy, generally leaving you hanging."

It's intriguing to be reminded that a young woman like Anna, in another age, might have been perceived in equal parts as being possessed by demons or in touch with angels, as happened, for instance, with Jeanne la Pucelle – Joan the Maiden – as she described herself, or Joan of Arc as we've known her since she was burned at the stake in May 1431, aged just nineteen. The "voices" she heard ultimately helped deliver France from the British.

These days, what you seem to be left with is questions as to whether the person sitting before a doctor discussing "voices" is "playing a role" or is actually experiencing a psychotic episode. In the case of the character Anna, after she has left the institution in Adelaide to which her partner, Sarah, and Jacob have taken her once her psychosis has gone beyond the point where there is any guarantee her behaviour will not place her in potentially serious danger, she starts seeing a new doctor and, after deciding he is not the sympathetic soul she initially imagined, decides to merely "sit and answer his questions prettily and put him at ease."

"I think she had incredible sadness," Stephanie qualifies Anna's response, "that the doctor has eyes that suggested he would be interested, but then played his role and she retreated. My own memory of these experiences is that it's a way of expressing yourself because almost every other avenue of expression has closed down, so that you get into a deeper and deeper recess so that the only way to get out is explosion. Perhaps now I would say no to things earlier. It's always interesting when I come back to Sydney, within ten minutes I'm back in exactly the same position I was when I left, chatting to my parents or old boyfriends, and you think, 'How did you deal with it?'"

Of course, once Anna tips over the boundary between not being able to deal with the relationships around her and the "voices" apparently directing her actions and behaviour, we see just how permeable is that boundary and how difficult it is for those watching what's happening to recognise that a friend, a lover, a sister or brother has crossed that boundary and might be slipping into a psychotic episode. The way Stephanie has structured *Harm*, you get Anna presenting her experiences alternating with Sarah and Jacob presenting their, initially very contrasting experiences of Anna during those episodes. While Anna experiences "signs and symbols", Sarah perceives anger and vindictiveness.

"Then for Anna there is the worry, almost terror that it will be taken away," adds Stephanie. "She's approaching everything that feels right and comfortable which has its own integrity or rules that she can understand. That's the beauty of it. It's just that even the voices that she has relied on so strongly start to give you mixed messages and you can't tell what games *they're* playing, to a kind of *disregard* for whether you're alive or dead. Then you realise the only person keeping you alive is yourself. So I suppose in a way, the fact of not having anyone around to provide any support, you're forced to get to that point, recognise it, make that decision and turn around, where people I know keep going back into it, keep getting rescued, keep getting into hospital or on drugs, which is Jacob's situation. Then again, I don't want to suggest some pat answer to let them go to the end of whatever they want to do, because they might end up killing themselves."

As I pointed out in the piece I wrote back in October 1999, *Singing Away The Madness Of Youth*, "the suicide rate for those suffering the symptoms of schizophrenia is three to five times the national average, which directly translates to some 76,500 or so Australians alive right now who are in all probability likely to take their own lives." Perhaps *Harm* will help some of these people and those who know and love them find another way out. It's an important book either way.

219

## THE HARM INSIDE YOUR MIND
A review of *Harm* (Wakefield Press, 2000)

Sydney-born, Adelaide based Stephanie Luke is a young woman who has experienced what is probably best described as late-onset schizophrenia. She was lucky. She has come out the other side and has written about her experience in a novel that is intensely personal rather than buried in analytical jargon.

More than 160,000 Australians endure this much-maligned and misunderstood condition, and that number is increasing annually by around two thousand souls male, female and whatever gender identity each feels most comfortable with. The number is probably higher, since no one knows precisely how many of the young people who are committing suicide in such alarming – and increasing – numbers have actually been tipped over the edge by an undiagnosed case of schizophrenia.

Subtitled *A Memoir of Dark, Glorious Days*, in her introduction to *Harm* Stephanie describes the central character Anna as "the centre of me, someone who has the ability to break out of this body and tell a story of visions with all their psychotic fictions and terrible truths." That said the book is no mere exercise in "faction". Stephanie brings all her imaginative powers to bear in the creation of a small but significant "supporting cast" of characters providing readers insights not only in terms of their impact on and their perception of Anna, mentally and physically, but also individual internal lives of their own, whether "normal", like Anna's girlfriend Sarah and sister Lucy, or the ultimately even *more* "damaged" Jacob, a gay work friend who transforms, as the story progresses, from something of a potential boyfriend/lover into mentor/saint, for Anna at least, into, finally, a chilling "sinner".

Jacob comes closest to fulfilling the schizophrenic's potential for suicide as he slips further into his own "psychotic episode", though ultimately his rage is externalised rather than internalised. Despite moments of despair where Anna herself internally screams pleas for self-immolation of one kind or another, she recognises that, thankfully, she is incapable of killing herself. Two peripheral characters in the novel do actually take that ultimate way out, and in the case of one, Lisa, who overdoses on sleeping pills, the suicide manifests in her mind as one more "crime" of which the increasingly paranoid Anna believes she is guilty. Suddenly, even watching the news on television becomes dangerous as, notes Sarah, Anna starts to see that "all human tragedy was directly attributable to her."

The problem for Anna becomes how to "interpret the signs correctly'. She knows the voices are pointing her towards her destiny, but they can be so perversely obscure. She hears clues on the radio, sees signs in car tail-lights and license plates, but all too often they seem to lead to dead ends, some benign, others potentially dangerous. At one point Anna takes herself to the beach to listen for the messages in a spoken-word performance being broadcast on Radio Triple Jay by one of her favourite contemporary artists, the splenetic American post-punk singer-songwriter Henry Rollins. Her ultimate reaction to his "messages" however is a stark reminder that the audience of artistic expression may not always be capable of surviving the "confrontation". Rollins' words mortify her: "In a few seconds my world has collapsed with the revelation that I am a whingeing, whining, indulgent, pathetic woman of nearly thirty… [too] scared to move in case I make more mistakes… thanks Henry. What do I do now?" Others experiencing Anna's internal tumult might have picked up a gun, or a bottle of pills. At the other extreme, one journey "in pursuit" of an "obvious sign" ends with Anna allowing herself to be defiled in the grossest possible way. Yet what can she do? At one point, she says to herself, "I have to stop having doubts about the universe."

There's a certain irony too in reading Anna's faith in her voices. Today, it's all too easy to dismiss, as Anna believes Rollins has "told her", mental anguish as "attention-seeking" adolescent tantrums. Anna's sister initially sees things that way, and her girlfriend Sarah isn't initially sure whether this is just

Anna's way of breaking up their relationship. The problem is distinguishing where a person has crossed that boundary between what we assume is reality and what may be madness. *Harm*, again, is an all too timely reminder of just how difficult it is for those on the outside to recognise that a friend, a lover, whoever, has crossed that boundary. Anna's determination to "cure" herself is only finally overcome when she proves to Sarah, Jacob and Lucy that she really is at the point of doing herself harm, and when she accedes to their requests to help, she actually does seem to find some sort of peace in an "open door" mental institution. Even after the worst of the crisis has passed and Anna has submitted to taking medication to stabilise her moods however, her response to others continues to be fraught and guarded.

Perhaps *Harm* can help teach a few of us a little more about the realities of this condition and allow us to develop some of the necessary understanding and compassion needed to help those who find themselves, like Anna, assailed by "a thousand chattering sounds bearing in on her" and unsure if this really is "God whispering", to help get them through the experience without causing themselves and those who love them too much harm.

## POSTSCRIPT:

Apart from a couple of short stories and some poetry, Stephanie Luke seems to have only worked on one other novel to date, this one partially set in Hanoi, Vietnam.

My own experience with mental illness was thankfully fairly benign in comparison to that experienced by Stephanie. After another relationship breakdown I started seeing a psychotherapist on the off chance there was any possibility of tipping into reactive depression once more. I pointed out my propensity towards feelings of invisibility. "What?" she replied. "You're the most visible person I've ever seen!" At that time my hair was still an ebullient entity unto itself atop my head. I didn't need a psychotherapist.

On the other hand guitarist Mark Lacey, with whom I played back in 1973-4, first in Jimmy Barnes' first band Tarcus and then, for a year, our own, Slim Pickings, wasn't so lucky. I discovered years later that through the rest of the decade and beyond, Mark suffered from bouts of severe depression, though he continued to play and ever more brilliantly. Perhaps he stopped taking his medication but it seems one day he decided to take a walk, straight into the oncoming traffic.

**FRED SMITH: *THE DUST OF URUZGAN***
Allen & Unwin, 2016

As I was reading Canberra-based singer-songwriter Fred Smith's remarkable memoir, *The Dust of Uruzgan* (Allen & Unwin), of his 18 months working as a diplomatic advisor at Australia's military base in Tarin Kowt in Afghanistan's Uruzgan province 2009-10, reports were coming in about a Taliban advance on the town from which Australia departed in November 2013, after a 12-year mission of 12 years that saw 41 Australian Defence Force personnel killed and 261 seriously wounded.

I first got to know Smith when he was touring his 2002 album, *Bagarap Empires*, based on his time in Bougainville in the late 1990s working as a UN Peace Monitor. "Bougainville was much happier circumstances," he admitted to me during the first round of touring for his 2011 album, *Dust of Uruzgan*, based, as is the book under review, on his "tour of duty" there for the Department of Foreign Affairs & Trade (DFAT), "because we were in the upswing of a peace process that was working whereas Afghanistan, you know you're participating in a war, rockets coming in occasionally and getting out on patrol always aware of IEDs (Improvised Explosive Devices), armed escorts and occasionally boys get killed and maimed, and you feel the grief of that amongst the people you're working with."

Smith has, as he describes it in his book, "managed to maintain both careers through a sophisticated process of indecision"; those two careers being singer-songwriter and, to give it in full, diplomatic officer in the Civil Military & Stabilisation Section of the Humanitarian Division of DFAT. For all his self-effacing comments regards his "indecisiveness", Smith has proven, over an eight-album career as an independent artist and on the evidence of his ability to do "his day job" with personable equanimity, remarkably adept. The triumph of his book is that he's able to explain so much – about Australia's military commitment to a war in which many of us, including himself, felt we had no right to be involved; about the process of songwriting; about the incredible complexity of the "politics of personality and tribal influence" at the heart of life in Afghanistan, and at the same time the unstinting generosity of everyone involved, from the Australian, Dutch and American troops to the interpreters, the various aid workers to the common Afghans – with an easygoing deftness of style and narrative flow that provides the most human of insights into every part of the story – from the tragedies of soldiers killed to the ways a song can evolve, from the hilarity of certain Dutch "customs" to the heartache of parents facing having sons return home in coffins.

And for Smith, turning what he was experiencing into songs was the obvious way to try and understand those experiences and to get through it all, as he told me: "We'd get together on a Saturday night and have these sort of I suppose you'd call them dance parties, where I'd thrash along on guitar and they (the Afghans) play the (lute-like) rubab and the (seven-string) tambur and a bunch of interpreters would reel around the room." In the book he recalls a comment by an Afghan after one of those "dance parties": "There is a Persian saying: Music – it is a ladder for the soul!" But we already know that, don't we.

Anyone who's seen Smith in concert knows he has a wickedly dry and subversive sense of humour, and that helps leaven some of the stories in the book, mostly at his own expense. When, for instance, shortly after arriving at Tarin Kowt, "Sleep-deprived, and breathless at my own prescience and eloquence," he sends a draft email to various members of DFAT "recommending a range of countermeasures" against an apparent epidemic of the curious Dutch propensity to "swaffelen", it's suggested in the friendliest of term that, funny as it may be, "it might not be a good idea to distribute this sort of thing too widely. The embassy sent a short sharp email: 'Save this for the memoirs.'" Not only does the whole swaffelen phenomenon make for a very funny chapter in that memoir but also a hilarious song on the album of the same name.

*The Dust of Uruzgan* is also the title of perhaps the most

searingly moving song written by any Australian about the experience Australians at war, and unlike *Only 19* and *Khe Sahn*, it's written by someone who, while not on active duty, was actually there. So important did Fred's work in Tarin

Kowt become that he returned for a second stint in 2012-13 to help close the Australian base, and as well as this book, a second album, *Home*, was born.

****

Smith is a junior diplomatic officer in the Civil Military & Stabilisation Section of the Humanitarian Division of the Australian Department of Foreign Affairs & Trade (DFAT). His father Richard Smith, now retired, was a former senior public servant and diplomat who, among other things, was appointed Australia's Special Envoy for Afghanistan and Pakistan in April 2009. In the late 1990s, the younger Smith had worked as a UN Peace Monitor in Bougainville. In July 2009, he became the first civilian to be posted to Afghanistan's Uruzgan province, serving an 18-month tour working out of the Multinational Base in Tarin Kowt as part of the second Mentoring and Reconstruction Task Force.

Smith is also a singer-songwriter, and it was through that "other career" that he was able to bridge the cultural divide between himself and the tribal leaders he was obliged to work with in order to achieve the aims of the Provisional Reconstruction Team (PRT) during that tour. Inevitably, he wrote songs about what he saw and experienced, most movingly in the song that gave the album he made on his return to Australia its title and, subsequently, this book, which rounds out his experience of that first 18-month tour with his second six-month tour in 2013 to help facilitate the Transfer of Authority of the base in Tarin Kowt to Afghanistan's Defence Forces.

While the tone Smith takes in the book is more reflective of the singer-songwriter/entertainer, the chapters headings the titles of the songs featured on *The Dust of Uruzgan* CD and the one that followed, *Home*, the diplomat is also very much in view as he explains how Australian troops came to be in Afghanistan, something of the challenges those troops faced and what might have been achieved during their tenure there. It's also a very human and sometimes deeply personal insight into what Australia lost to the dust of Uruzgan and beyond, all leavened with his insights into the political and tribal dimensions of Australia's work in Afghanistan and, of course, Uruzgan in particular, as well as his typical wit, irony and self-deprecation. Apart from whatever might have been achieved militarily during Australia's time in Uruzgan province, at the time of publication there were now 200 schools, 38 of them specifically for girls, six times the number there had been when they'd arrived in 2006, and there were 32 health clinics. More than 200 kilometres of roads had been repaired, and bridges had been built. By 2015, across Afghanistan, some eight million children were attending school where only 900,000 had attended in 2001.

As he points out, "Soldiers at the forward operating bases in Ghilzai, Noorzai, Barakzai and Achekzai country worked closely with tribal leaders like Malim Sadiq and Malim Habibullah to protect their people. The PRT, meanwhile, went out of its way to ensure that leaders of those tribes got a share of the projects." As well, "Most of the ADF's time and energy in Uruzgan was invested squarely in the Fourth Brigade of the Afghan National Army... We worked on building the institutional capacity of the ANA Fourth Brigade, but in Afghanistan, 'big man culture' prevails; personalities dominate over institutions... It's called a patronage system."

For all the necessary geopolitics underpinning it, *The Dust of Uruzgan* is an accessible, often self-deprecating and occasionally funny entry point for anyone interested in the complexities of the efforts of the Western Alliance, and Australia in particular, to bring some sort of order to the chaos that is Afghan politics.

## POSTSCRIPT:

The first page of this review of Smith's book was written for music bi-monthly *Rhythms*, while the second page is a second review originally aimed at US political bi-monthly *Foreign Affairs*, which declined it, so I thought I'd send it to *Quadrant*, which did run it.

What follows is my review of Smith's second "Afghanistan" book.

## FRED SMITH: *THE SPARROWS OF KABUL*
Puncher & Wattman, August 2023

"At the Airport's North Gate, a little girl about a year older than my daughter pops out of the crowd of thousands of desperate people, carrying an orange plastic bag … tears streaming down her cheeks, her bottom lip trembling, …" So begins this second book, *The Sparrows of Kabul*, from Iain "Fred" Smith based on his on-the-ground observations as a junior diplomatic officer in the Civil Military & Stabilisation Section of the Humanitarian Division of the Australian Department of Foreign Affairs & Trade (DFAT). An additional paragraph on the cover says it all: "A deeply personal tale of Australia's mission to evacuate people from Kabul International Airport."

The events in Afghanistan of the last weeks of August 2021 in the wake of the unexpectedly rapid collapse of the 300,000-strong Afghan Army as the Taliban marched into Kabul, the chaos at Hamid Karzai/Kabul International Airport (KIA) as hundreds of thousands of people tried to escape that unrelenting march, images of desperate people falling from the wheel arches of American airplanes taking off from KIA, of people bleeding and bodies butchered by ISIS-A suicide bombs, seem so long ago as the voracious avalanche of the 24-hour news cycle has moved onto ever more horrendous disasters, man-made and natural, all vying for our attention.

Yet those images, seared into the collective consciousness, of desperate humanity clambering for the all-too few places available on flights out of KIA over those final couple of weeks must not be forgotten. Why should Australia care what happens in Afghanistan or to the Afghans? Smith made the point plainly and simply in his 2016 book, *The Dust of Uruzgan*, based on his experiences as the first civilian to be posted to Afghanistan's Uruzgan province, serving an 18-month tour (July 2009 – January 2011) working out of the Multinational Base in Tarin Kowt as part of the second Mentoring and Reconstruction Task Force, "The problems that brew in these 'failed states' become our problems – terrorism and narcotics to start with, as well as mass migration. Syria, Iraq and Afghanistan are currently the leading sources of refugees to Europe, and there are over seventeen million people displaced by conflicts in Africa looking for somewhere to live." That was six years ago, so you can probably double that figure now. And how pleased were the Taliban to announce that 2022 yielded one of the country's biggest opium crops to date.

Smith – "Farid from DFAT" as he became known among locals – is the son of Richard Smith, now retired, who himself is a former senior public servant and diplomat who, among other things, served as Australia's Ambassador to China between 1996 and 2000, Australia's Ambassador to Indonesia between 2001 and 2002, Secretary of the Department of Defence between 2002 and 2006, and, in April 2009 was appointed Australia's Special Envoy for Afghanistan and Pakistan.

The younger Smith undertook a second six-month "tour of duty" in 2013 to help facilitate the Transfer of Authority of the base in Tarin Kowt to Afghanistan's Defence Forces, and his experiences subsequently became the core of an album titled *The Dust of Uruzgan* – Smith is also a folk-based singer-songwriter, his "other career" through which he'd been able to bridge the cultural divide between himself and the tribal leaders with whom he was obliged to work in order to achieve the aims of the Provisional Reconstruction Team (PRT) – and led to a series of 80 performances around Australia based on the album and the stories behind the songs in what he describes as a 12-year project/obsession. Among the things achieved by the ADF and AusAID on his watch included funding the building of the Malalai Girls School which, 2011, boasted some 1000 students. That, of course, was immediately closed by the Taliban.

Then, as Smith explained it to me, "When the music industry collapsed in March 2020, I went to Kabul to work at the Embassy for a year and a bit. This was good until it wasn't – things didn't end well as you're no doubt aware."

Early in 2020, DFAT had advertised a development job at the Australian Embassy in Kabul, work that Smith admits "did not come naturally", being "a diplomat from the political side of DFAT" rather someone who "actually needed to know something – tedious stuff like contracting, risk matrices and gender-sensitive programming…" As it turned out, after arriving in May Smith gradually got the hang of things, but everything changed with the signing, in February 2021, of the Doha Peace Agreement, the culmination of a deal that had been initiated by the Trump administration with the Taliban. As Chief Foreign Correspondent for *The Sunday Times* Christina Lamb noted in the July/August 2021 issue of *Foreign Affairs*, "By the autumn of 2018, with midterms approaching, Trump raged to his generals that their strategy had been 'a total failure' and he wanted out."

So, despite the fact that, just before he was to return to Afghanistan, Australia's Embassy in Kabul was closing, in July Smith accepted the development job in what was to be Australia's "virtual Interim Mission to Afghanistan" in Abu Dhabi. By August 17, he was back at KIA trying to help get Australian visa holders and their families out of what was quickly becoming hell on earth.

Smith assures us that *The Sparrows of Kabul* will not be "a scandalous expose of skulduggery and folly in Canberra policy processes," since in the work of public servants of all stripes "there will always be a malodorous melting pot of conflicting agendas, political interference and good sense in the face of practical dilemmas." This book then is, as noted, simply his experience of those two weeks that followed the fall of Kabul to the Taliban as he experienced it over four days in KIA and then in the evacuee camps at Al Minhad Air Base in Dubai. Nonetheless, the book is also his personal attempt to give the efforts of DFAT a human face, as against the standard presentation of its work through "disembodied press releases with dot points listing achievements suggesting the mission ran perfectly," that he admits "will not be read and in any case will not be received as plausible." And again, "People respond to people, they respond to stories, they respond to candour, they respond to vulnerability and they just want to know they are not being lied to."

Elsewhere in the book Smith reminds us that "Australians need to understand that a scrupulous, well-resourced public sector – federal, state, local, Defence, nurses, Judiciary, chalkies, firies, cops, ambos etc. – is what keeps us from chaos. Australians need to appreciate good government, boring and expensive though it is, since, in a chaotic world; it's what saves our country from descending into tragedy like Afghanistan."

As you'd expect, there's some quietly fine writing in the telling of his tale. Within an hour of arriving at KAI as part of Australia's four-man team processing would-be evacuees, Smith has to tell an Afghan interpreter who has worked for both Australia and the US that, since his parents don't have the requisite visas they must stay behind. The interpreter chooses to remain with his parents but they eventually convince him he must go and he returns "with tears streaming down his face as two Turkish soldiers with linguistic sympathies to the parents led them shuffling into the warm Kabul night with a quiet dignity that took our breath away."

In his essay, *The Last Days of Intervention*, published in the November/December 2021 number of *Foreign Affairs*, former British Secretary of State for International Development Rory Stewart suggested that the international interventions in both Afghanistan and Iraq were "unstable hybrids of humanitarianism and counterinsurgency that soon became even more unstable hybrids of state building and counterinsurgency". (p. 61) A little later in that same essay, he notes that in 2009, US General Stanley McChrystal "maintained that no amount of US military power could stabilise Afghanistan 'as long as pervasive corruption and preying upon the people continue to characterise governance.'" (p. 67) In *The Dust of Uruzgan*, Smith reminded us that "In Afghanistan, 'big man culture' prevails; personalities dominate over institutions ... If we'd been prepared to stick around another couple of hundred years, perhaps we might have been able to make a dent in that. In the meantime, we could only do what we could do, with what we had."

For Smith, one of the overriding reasons for writing *The Sparrows of Kabul* was to tell the truth of what he witnessed at first hand, even though, as he admits, in the midst of the chaos, "Eighty per cent of the DFAT operation (was) running off my telephone." The bulk of his 20-hour work days was based on WhatsApp messages – from DFAT, from colleagues, from desperate Afghans who had worked for Australia's Embassy or the ADF as translators and so on – constant, pleading, hopeful, despairing – requests that brought enough successes to prevent Smith's own sense of despair in the face of it all kicking in. The reality on the ground, sadly, was that "expats and visa holders had expectations for what we could do for them that far exceeded what we could do."

"The narrative," he opines, "on the evacuation has been dominated by advocates who didn't get their people out. I understand and respect their motivations... I would do the same if I were them." And he has to admit that "What dismayed our LE (Locally Engaged staff) was that we didn't, or more accurately couldn't do more. Their point of reference was the Afghan government system in which things happen through personal influence – you have a mate or cousin in the right position or bribe the right official in the right place and you get the results you want. It works in the short term and very efficiently, but of course in the long term it erodes the credibility of the system, breeding resentment among those excluded until eventually the system collapses. And that, alas, is about 50 per cent of the reason the Afghan government disintegrated in August 2021."

At least US President Biden had pushed back the original withdrawal date of 1 May, 2021 demanded by Trump under the Doha Peace Agreement four months to August 31, but that meant that all Australian personnel – military and diplomatic – along with however many Afghan Australian-visa holders as possible had to be out of KIA and Afghanistan by August 24 in order to allow America's Marines and their associated personnel enough time to get themselves out by the 31st.

In the face of all subsequent reports painting the efforts of DFAT and the US as catastrophic failures, Smith underlines the fact that, "In the last two weeks of August, we got 4100 people out, 3300 of whom have come to Australia. That was the fifth highest number of any Western country, and not bad given we were the 12th largest contributor to the ISAF (International Security Assistance Force) mission over its twenty years." And that is an achievement worth writing about.

On reading his son's manuscript Smith's father felt "moved to write a fourth piece of post-retirement extracurricular prose," as the younger Smith describes it, his father having been a reticent commentator on all things Australian diplomacy over the years, but, in an email to his son, finally accepted that he'd "had a go at getting Afghanistan off my chest." That "extracurricular prose" analysis, *Afghanistan: America's Dilemma was Australia's too*, is included as an Addendum to *The Sparrows of Kabul* and is a worthy piece of pragmatic analysis that succinctly counterbalances the more personal observations of his son.

In *The Dust of Uruzgan*, Smith noted that former UK

Ambassador Sir Sherard Cowper-Coles, in his book *Cables from Kabul*, had lamented "the lack of a coherent political strategy throughout the international community's mission in Afghanistan." Smith goes on to state that, "After returning from Kabul in 2010, Cowper-Coles became the UK special envoy for Afghanistan, working with my dad and counterparts from other coalition countries for three years to try to create a shared strategy for promoting a viable political accord in Afghanistan, central to which had to be some dialogue with the Taliban. In the end they failed, thwarted by the multiple tyrannies of complexity involved."

For all the effort on the part of a lot of good people, in the end, as we now know all too well, the fall of Afghanistan to the Taliban was inevitable. Of course, everything the Taliban assured the negotiators at those peace talks that they wouldn't do they did, particularly the reimposition of strict Sharia restrictions on the lives of women and girls.

As for the sparrows of Smith's book's title, they get a rambling 244-line piece of prose poetry all to themselves, unconstrained by either diplomatic niceties or poetic conventions as the human tragedy of those final weeks of life in Kabul before the Taliban takeover unfolds below their fluttering wings, the flocks of "little brown birds" going about their lives regardless. Smith recites the piece as the concluding track on his twelfth CD, also titled *The Sparrows of Kabul*, which he has been touring since its release in July 2022. He was obliged to delay the publication of this book until his superiors at DFAT were satisfied that it didn't breach any protocols or national/international sensitivities inherent in its content. That's bureaucracy for you.

## POSTSCRIPT:

In much the same way Smith initially found it difficult to secure a publisher, who then ensured any potential diplomatic sensitivities would not become problematic for him in his "day job", finding a journal to publish my review took more than a year and three rejections before it found a home. (See Acknowledgements) I'd much rather it had secured publication in *Australian Foreign Affairs*, America's *Foreign Affairs* or *Overland* but there you go – life as a freelance writer.

## AN AUSTRALIAN IN AMERICA: THE VIEW 60 YEARS ON
Revisiting Allan Ashbolt's *An American Experience*

Allan Ashbolt was 38 when, as the ABC's first North American correspondent, he arrived in New York City with his wife and children in May 1958. They lived there until July 1961 and the original edition of *An American Experience*, published by Alpha Books in May 1966, was based on his observations of the country over those three years. My edition, salvaged from the "toss out" bins of my local Op Shop, is the revised and updated edition published in 1969, and therefore includes some of his thoughts on post-1961 events like the assassinations of President Kennedy and his brother Robert on one hand and those of Martin Luther King Jr and Malcolm X on the other, as well as the emergence of the various youth protest movements, women's liberation and Black Power among other things.

The cover flyleaf notes begin, "The major question posed by this book is whether the United States of America is living up to the very high values enunciated by its Founding Fathers." The major question I might pose in reading Ashbolt's account of an America now more than half a century along whatever path has been determined by its leaders and its population since the book's publication is how much of what Ashbolt observed of America's socio-political stance has remained the same and how much has changed, apart of course from the natural, obvious and, in some ways, inevitable social, economic and technological changes that have affected us all in the intervening years. Of course, no one could have predicted the tectonic chaos instigated by the 45th President, which one can only hope will eventually be seen historically as an unfortunate aberration, but it's interesting to read a comment from an unnamed contemporary American reviewer of the book also included in that flyleaf note: "We don't mind our own writers being so critical of us; but we can't take it from others." That said, Ashbolt makes it clear in his Preface to the

1969 edition, "I went to the United States more in search of good than of ill, looking hopefully for signs that the principles embodied in the Declaration of Independence and the Bill of Rights were being fulfilled nearly every day in almost every way." As he goes on to admit however, "I was, quite frankly, disillusioned – and that reaction may help explain the tone of the book." It would be interesting to know how he might have felt sixty years on. I think disillusionment might reflect the least of his feelings, for all the tremendous advances, the incredible literary, musical and artistic achievements as well as the mindboggling scientific and technological achievements, undeniably making for a far better and perhaps safer world than someone at a time living with the knowledge that the future could so easily be wiped out by a nuclear holocaust courtesy the then still simmering Cold War might have expected. After his return to Australia, Ashbolt got to experience firsthand the social turmoil created by and the political hypocrisy of Australia's and America's involvement in the Vietnam War. That too informed this revised edition.

Born in Melbourne in 1921, Ashbolt had seen active service in the Allied Imperial Force during WWII and, after a period working as an actor and theatre director during which he co-founded the Mercury Theatre with fellow actor Peter Finch and entrepreneur John Kay, in 1954 he was hired by the ABC as a producer. A couple of years after his return from the US, Ashbolt became executive producer of a pioneering new program titled *Four Corners*. As well as being a respected broadcaster and producer, Ashbolt was also a book reviewer for *The Sydney Morning Herald*, wrote critically about film and theatre, and was a contributor to *New Statesman* magazine in the UK.

"He was a symbol of the courageous independent, slightly left-wing broadcaster and for many of us he was a great hero," fellow ABC broadcaster Phillip Adams wrote on Ashbolt's passing. David Bowman's obituary in *The Sydney Morning Herald* June 15, 2005 noted that writer Sandra Hall had

described Ashbolt as "the ABC's conscience-in-residence."
Bowman also reminded us of Ashbolt's decision to commission
one Dr Peter Russo to comment on the Cuban Missile Crisis of
October 1962, "and Russo dared to mention American lies
alongside Russian lies. The Americans complained.
Commonwealth police raided Ashbolt's office by night. They
broke open a cabinet and, to satisfy the prime minister, Bob
Menzies, seized Russo's script, of which copies had been on
open sale for a month, price seven pence. The ABC chairman,
Dr James Darling, was summoned to Canberra, where the
Postmaster-General conveyed the government's concern at this
heresy. And for some time afterwards, Russo's voice was not
heard." Ashbolt was "twice banished" from *Four Corners*. He
was eventually "prompted" to retire from the ABC after some 25
years' service.

Sixty years on, how little has changed on that front. In
July 2017, the ABC broadcast a program titled *The Afghan Files*
compiled by investigative journalists Dan Oakes and Sam Clark,
which was based on leaked Department of Defence documents
that exposed clandestine operations in Afghanistan undertaken
by Australia's elite Special Forces between 2009 and 2013 that
included evidence of the killing of unarmed men and children
that were quite obviously war crimes. June 6, 2019 saw the
Sydney offices of the ABC raided by the Australian Federal
Police (AFP), just a day after they had raided the home of News
Corp journalist Annika Smethurst, who had had the temerity to
write a story discussing the then current government debate on
whether the powers of the Australian Signals Directorate should
be expanded to allow monitoring the conversations of ordinary
Australians. At the ABC, the armed AFP officers took
possession of more than 9200 documents and emails relating to
the work Oakes and Clark had done. A year on, Australia's High
Court ruled the warrant used to justify the AFP search of
Smethurst's home invalid and the charges against her were
dropped. The Federal Court of Australia ruled however that the
raid on the ABC was legal. The Liberal government tightened

Australia's security laws in 2018 to make it a criminal offence for journalists to receive classified information from military or intelligence sources. Nonetheless, the government was obliged to establish an Office of the Special Investigator to prosecute Special Ops war crimes in Afghanistan after the tabling of a damning report it had commissioned on the issue by Major-General Paul Brereton. But I digress…

Of Allan Ashbolt, "His personal politics and his actions," notes David Bowman, "owed much to an impregnable belief in four freedoms: of speech, inquiry, association and publication. Brought up, as he put it, in the Methodist religion, the Anzac mystique, the culture of British imperialism, and the middle-class ethic of self-improvement, he made a slow passage from the status quo to democratic socialism and eventually, in early 1966, to a protest meeting against the Vietnam war. In a wild scene, Ashbolt the peaceful humanist leapt on stage as if possessed and seized in a headlock the leader of the Australian Nazi party, who had collared (Australian publisher) Francis James's microphone. It was an instant transformation into radical activist. Outraged by 'the indecent and inhumane spectacle of the mightiest, most awesome military state in history trying to pulverise and obliterate a tiny band of Asian peasants,' he marched in front with Jim Cairns, he demonstrated, he addressed conferences and fired crowds up to 9000 strong, and became a Cold War target for the forces of B.A. Santamaria." It was during this period that Ashbolt published *An American Experience*. In 1974, he published a second book: *An Australian Experience: Words from the Vietnam Years.*

As much as it might have been something of a personal memoir, albeit written as a journalist and therefore thoughtfully weighted with quietly studied observation, Ashbolt also hoped that *An American Experience* would be seen as "an attempt to evaluate current trends in American thought and behaviour." While he was no Alistair Cook, I certainly feel he succeeded in that attempt, framed, as it is, in what he defines as "documentary authenticity". He can certainly turn a neat phrase, such as when he notes, for instance, the annual frenzy among New York City's worthies, from social workers to editorial writers, prompted by the inexorable rise in juvenile crime and arrests: "Then the anguished analysis starts in serious magazines, and learned phrases wander up and down the page in search of a thesis." There's a quiet elegance in his writing rarely found in contemporary works, particularly when he feels he must disagree with some aspect of the standard wisdom of the day, gently suggesting for instance, in his original 1966 Preface, in considering Arthur Schlesinger Jr's 'cyclical theory' of American political thought that "I must confess to lacking Mr. Schlesinger's faith in the natural benevolence of pragmatism." And he freely admits that *An American Experience* "is something of a polemical scolding".

So, what was the America of 1959-61 like, as seen through the eyes, understanding and research of a middle-aged white Australian five and then eight years after his time there. Uncannily – sadly? – all too familiar it seems. On the state of the health system for instance, Ashbolt quotes a then recent estimate by one Donald Gould published in *New Statesman* August 4, 1967: "The price of illness and injury in the United States has reached a frightening level. The rich can manage, the poor can get treatment of a kind, but the great mass of the middle income earners in between are left with an appalling problem, and serious sickness can reduce a prosperous family to poverty." For all the advances in technology, the glamour and dedication presented in pretty much every medical drama coming out of the States in the intervening 60 years, and the sterling efforts of a couple of Democrat Presidents, the House of Representatives and the Senate have ensured that nothing much has changed on that front. At the first Democratic presidential primary debate of 2019, the former Representative for Maryland's sixth district, John Delaney, reiterated one of the main arguments *against* the concept of "Medicare for All", as presented by fellow then Democrat presidential aspirants Bernie Sanders and Elizabeth Warren: "Hospitals say that Medicare for All would mean serious revenue cuts for them." Note that the emphasis here is on *revenue* rather than patient care, which one would have thought was the premise on which hospitals exist in the first place, but there you go, in the end it's always about the money isn't it? What's interesting to note, however is the fact that, according to Robert Berenson, a health policy analyst at the Washington DC-based think tank, the Urban Institute, "many hospitals that rely on private insurance could cut elsewhere first. They have high staffing ratios, generous salaries, engage in capital expansion and have billions in reserves from 'retained earnings'. The reserves alone would forestall bankruptcy for some time." Billions in reserves? Patients without those necessary "reserves" continue to face exactly the same problems Donald Gould enunciated back in 1967. Meanwhile, the 45th White House incumbent railed against that "horrible Obamacare", the removal of which was one of his major electoral planks, that removal consistently undermined by those damned "socialists", the Democrats, aided and abetted by that "traitorous" Republican, Senator John McCain, against whom he continued to occasionally hurl abuse long after his death. No wonder McCain's daughter voted for his second impeachment, despite being a Republican.

In that same 1969 Preface, in making his position in *An American Experience* clearer, Ashbolt defers to American novelist and playwright Paul Goodman, quoting a few paragraphs from his 1966 Massey Lectures for the Canadian Broadcasting Corporation. I'll just pull one quote from those paragraphs, simply because it seems pertinent considering the current state of the Union. As part of one of "three plausible predictions" Goodman makes of where America seemed to be heading at the time, he writes, "American democracy will vanish into an establishment of promoters, mandarins and technicians, though maintaining for a while an image of democracy as in the days of Augustus and Tiberius. And all this is probably the best possible outcome, given the complexities of high technology, urbanisation, mass education and overpopulation." Remember, this was written in 1966.

As with the majority of commentators seeking to understand what it is that makes Americans and the United States who and what they are, as a starting point Ashbolt turns to Alexis de Tocqueville's *Democracy in America*, originally published in 1835, noting that, as a consequence of his experience of the French Revolution, "Tocqueville was of course afraid of the tyranny of the majority. Fundamentally he favoured government by a privileged elite – which is exactly what Alexander Hamilton had advocated and what has eventually developed in the USA." As far as social historian Craig McGregor is concerned, Australia has ended up in the same place by another route. "There is no such thing as a classless society," he announced, rightly of course, in the 2001 revised edition of his *Class in Australia*. "The attempt to run away from class does credit to the heart of Australians… It disguises the way in which a small class elite sets out to run the country for its own benefit and largely succeeds in doing so." (p. 1) "Often," Ashbolt continues, "when Tocqueville praises American democracy he is actually praising its neo-aristocratic elements, like the separation of society into status groups which preserve the principle of inequality." One wonders what Tocqueville might have made of Australia had he focused his observational skills on this other emerging nation, that latter description qualified of course by the fact that Australia, unlike the America of which he was writing, was still a British colony. Still, what would he have made of our Squattocracy?

Ashbolt presciently goes on to suggest, as he asks question after question in considering what to make of what he had come to know of America, that "the central drama of American life is to be found, no longer as it was in Tocqueville's time, in the contrast between democracy and aristocracy, but in the contrast between appearance and reality, between hope and fulfilment, between eighteenth century promise and twentieth century performance." Sixty years and a new century on, appearance certainly seems to have won the race against reality for far too many Americans.

Ashbolt also notes that the "theory" underpinning the "chosen-race concept" to which so many groups within America seem to adhere "is a defence mechanism against the divisiveness of American life." The "melting pot" perception of Americanisation was still held as an inviolable truth. The irony is obvious as he goes on to discuss the emergence of "restrictive residential districts", then America's "polite" answer to the idea of community-led "ghettoisation". Again, sixty years on, that "defence mechanism" continues to assert itself right across America as previously "white" suburbs become "black" or "Hispanic" not because the "whites" have been driven out but because they weren't prepared to remain in suburbs where more and more "non-whites" have moved in. I'm reminded of a quote Australian social historian Frank Crowley drew from an essay by Hugh Stretton in the December 1971 issue of *Australian Quarterly*: "It has been shown how southern European communities are in general more residentially and occupationally concentrated in Australia's large cities than those from north-west Europe, and thus less assimilated." (Cited in *Tough Times: Australia in the Seventies*, William Heinemann Australia, 1986, p. 31) As a half-Greek, I was saved this possibility by my parents moving the family, on our arrival in August 1964, into Elizabeth in South Australia, a white Anglo-Saxon "ghetto" some 18 kilometres north of Adelaide, courtesy my father being a Londoner born and bred.

Meanwhile, at least at the time Ashbolt was pondering the whys and wherefores of the American ethos, those at the top of American society quietly got on with running things, embracing "a limited number of people brought in to represent the middle-class masses, so that the masses might be comforted and the spirit of democracy appeased," despite the odd hiccup created by interlopers like Joe McCarthy, the self-styled enemy of perceived covert Communists within the American Body Politick. As the world learned all too clearly, appeasement was not in the vocabulary of the 45th Commander in Chief, whose raison d'être seemed be a commitment to a very different equation – divide and conquer. Not that this was new to American politics. The daughter of one-time presidential hopeful George Wallace, Peggy Wallace Kennedy has noted that "The two greatest motivators at (Dad's) rallies were fear and hate. There was no policy solution, just white middle-class anger." At least, as a life-long "appeaser", the 46th President, Joe Biden, has certainly done his damnedest to redress the damage.

Ashbolt again suggests, taking his lead from an historian named EH Carr, that "most members of the power elite seem to be utterly sincere in their belief that they are acting in the national interest." A pity then that the "self-evident truths" of so many of the current Republican members of the US Senate and Congress seem to blithely personify insincerity and self-preservation rather than the national or public interest, and seem neither capable of nor interested in curbing either trait. Across the nearly 300 pages of An American Experience, Ashbolt covers a lot of ground and takes a few contemporary commentators on a variety of subjects to task along the way. I'll look at a few of his observations if I may:

> The issue of desegregation and the concomitant road to full equality for black Americans, obviously one of the major topics of the period after the US Supreme Court "outlawed" racial segregation in public schools in May 1954, remains a potent symbol, as one of 2019's crop of Democratic presidential nominees and now Vice-President, Californian Senator Kamala Harris made clear when calling out the now President Joe Biden's record on the issue of "busing", which he once described as "an asinine policy" and on which subject he co-authored an anti-busing amendment in 1975. While the lot of a great many African-Americans has obviously improved exponentially over the intervening sixty years, a great many more remain on the lowest

rung of the socio-economic ladder, remain disproportionately represented in the nation's gaols and similarly are disproportionately more likely to die at the hands of the police, despite the rise and best efforts of the "Black Lives Matter" movement, a situation now front and centre in the current battle to win votes as streets continue to see opposing protests and more shootings.

America's love affair with litigation, suggesting that, in Ashbolt's view, "lawyers are the priests of American society, and corporation lawyers are the high priests." No big changes there! It's interesting to note that Ashbolt feels Americans seem to need a fairly regular bit of legal public "blood-letting": "Along with this fondness for the wiles of litigation, there is in American society a subsidiary craze for public revelations of corruption… to re-establish faith in America's moral purity." Whether the concept of moral purity can still be considered part of the wider contemporary American consciousness must remain something of a moot point. After all, despite a deluge of evidence and opinion pieces, the bravery of television series' like The Good Fight and the satirical taunts of Saturday Night Live and Full Frontal with Samantha Bee among many, not a scintilla of "moral purity" seems to have been summoned from even the bowels of the carnivorously litigious Administration that lost office in November 2020. Still, since American courts are essentially adversarial, it all goes back to "entertainment" in a sense, the bread and circuses of Imperial Rome, so the "ruling elite" will get through unscathed, while the interlopers, who never really "belonged", will no doubt "fall on their collective swords" – and sell the book, film and serialisation rights to the highest bidder in the tried and tested "American way". Striking a cautionary note Ashbolt reminds us that, "Americans tend to view corruption in terms of individuals, not as the result of broad social and economic influences. The essence of the popular American belief is: people corrupt society; society seldom corrupts people."

Ashbolt reminds us that in America, according to conservative White Anglo-Saxon Protestant wisdom the problems of crime, corruption and juvenile delinquency can all be lain at the feet of the immigrants. No change there in the intervening 60 years.

Elsewhere, he recounts the anecdote of Nikita Khrushchev who, on his second visit to New York City and, noting the heavy air pollution as the ship he's on is entering the East River, admonishes the harbour health officer, telling him America should do what the Soviet Union does – "change from coal and oil to natural gas as a means of generating power." Ashbolt reports the editorial comment in the following day's edition of The New York Times: "For once Mr Khrushchev was right." A very different kind of "Russian interference"! It's worth noting too that, back in the early 1960s, local authorities along the Eastern Seaboard seemed happy to dump low-level radioactive waste in concrete drums into the Atlantic, despite knowing these drums often burst. That would have been one of the many somethings the Environmental Protection Authority (EPA), founded in 1970, six years after the first edition of An American Experience was published, by a Republican President, Richard Nixon, though not necessarily happily, would have been set up to sort out. And let's not forget that barely two months after the Paris Agreement was signed, the passing of one of the major pillars upon which the Agreement had been based being the commitment, finally, by the United States,

- which had until then refused to sign any of the previous international climate change protocols, to a signature climate change initiative put forward by that very EPA and unveiled by the then President, Barack Obama, on August 3, 2015, dubbed his "Clean Power Plan" and recognised as an important step towards a national consistency in reducing carbon pollution from the country's power plants into law, had been halted by the US Supreme Court until the US Court of Appeals for the DC Circuit was in a position to bring down a decision on the merits of a lawsuit filed by *29* US states, coal-fired power industries and, on the periphery, the automobile, oil and other fossil fuel-based industry groups with an obvious interest in preventing its implementation. At least President Joe Biden has recommitted the US to the Paris Agreement from which his predecessor had withdrawn the country, and rescinded most of the more than 100 pieces of environmental vandalism – sorry, legislation – Trump had bulldozed through during his administration, and has committed to zero carbon emissions by 2050. For all that international commitment however, on the other side of the planet, as Australian science journal *Cosmos*' then Editor-in-chief Elizabeth Finkel pointed out in her *Editor's Note* in the February/March 2016 issue: "China and India alone plan to build more than 1,600 new coal-fired power plants by 2030." So it's wasn't all Trump – or our own coal-loving former Liberal Prime Minister – or the previous President of Brazil, who fired the director of his nation's space agency INPE, Ricardo Galvao, for revealing the acceleration of deforestation of the Amazon's rainforests soon after he became president in January 2019.

- America is obviously no longer the automobile economy it once was, certainly when *An American*

- *Experience* was published where, as Ashbolt notes, "the most accurate prosperity index is to be found in Detroit, not in the New York Stock Exchange, not in the Labour Department's estimate of joblessness." Sixty years on though, the lobbyists who ensured that, as far as Ashbolt was concerned, their then masters – "the automobile industry, the steel industry, the oil industry, the chemical industry" – got what they wanted are still there, even if some of those industries are not, a new set of lobbyists quietly running the country for the benefit of their various employers and associated pressure groups. It's funny; I'd assumed that *they* were The Swamp to which Trump was constantly and derisively referring – silly me.

- It's good to be reminded that it was only in 1958 that Congress, for the first time in US history, voted for *Federal* money to be allocated for education. Ashbolt notes that *The New York Herald-Tribune* suggested the grant was made "in recognition of Soviet scientific advances." This was soon after the successful launch of Sputnik I. In contrast – and again remember this is the way it was sixty years ago – he writes, of his own children of school age: "In New York City especially, the strains are such that about the most you can ask of any sort of education, public or private, is that your child comes home in the afternoon, alive." Sixty years on, after Columbine, Sandy Hook and Stoneman Douglas High School, to name just a few of the far too many mass shootings over the past couple of decades, those words resonate even more poignantly for *all* of America. Ashbolt quotes one Dr Robert Hutchins, once president of the University of Chicago: "All we can say of American education is that it's a colossal housing project designed to keep young people out of worse places until they can go to work." Obviously a blanket

- statement like that must be tempered with the knowledge that schools and colleges are all run differently in every suburb, town, city and state, and the quality of education inevitably varies. "If," Ashbolt qualifies, "American education is a colossal housing project, care would appear to have been taken to preserve a good many individual designs." It certainly wasn't all hoodlums/delinquents as portrayed in *Blackboard Jungle*, the then contemporary 1956 feature film based on the Evan Hunter novel that ironically "launched" rock'n'roll via Bill Haley & The Comets' version of *Rock Around the Clock* – ironic in that the delinquents in the film were championing not rock'n'roll at all but rather the jazz of Sinatra against their teacher William Holden's be-bop records, and doubly ironic in that the lyrics of *Rock Around the Clock*, used over the opening and closing credits of the film, were written by one Max Freedman, who, in 1954 when he co-wrote it, was a 63 year old veteran of America's "Tin Pan Alley", hardly the obvious role model of "teen rebellion". Either way, one would hope things have improved vastly in the intervening years, even if we all know, too, that American education is nothing like it's portrayed in the torrent of anodyne teen movies and television shows the American entertainment industry produces each year ostensibly based on school and college life. Thankfully, most American children not only survive but blossom during their education, like most children the world over, when given the opportunity of a decent education, even if it's often a little too Americentric.

- An aside if I may, US business journalist Elizabeth MacBride pointed out in *Forbes* magazine, "Gun stores had revenue of about $US11 billion, IBIS World said in its 2018 report. Gun and ammunition manufacturers had

250

- revenue of $US17 billion, but the majority of that revenue comes from the defense side of the equation: arms sales to the U.S. and foreign governments." (*America's Gun Business Is $US28B. The Gun Violence Business Is Bigger*, 25/11/18) IBIS World is a US-based international business information and market research company. "Children under six should show a natural interest in Blastwell firearms, but should not be allowed to fire a gun, except in special circumstances." So read, Ashbolt notes, a directive from a sponsor's advertising agency with regards to how writers of a TV Western should present the shoot-outs between the cowboys in white hats and those in black. Need I say more?

- "There is a difference between the fake past," writes Ashbolt, pondering the preponderance of "historical sites" that dot America, "with its public-relations atmosphere of nostalgia, and the genuine past, which essentially is still alive." As became all too obvious over the four years of the Trump presidency, the lines between fake past, present and future and genuine past, present and future have become so blurred beyond recognition in America that any truth seems capable of being dismissed, any lie ratified as truth, reality/unreality so contiguous in the general consciousness. There was a time, it seems, when America could be said to have been guilty of "fact-worship". Ashbolt cites an essay by literary critic Dwight McDonald in a collection titled *Against the American Grain*, published in 1963, as presenting America as just that. It certainly seems that, for a few too many Americans, "fact-worship" has long been out of fashion and even forgotten. Still, as Ashbolt goes on to say, noting the cancellation of a proposed second visit to the US, apparently for security reasons, "Mr Khrushchev was sensible in asking to see Disneyland,

- for it would tell him more about the American social character than dinner at the White House. It is a microcosm of America's wishful historical thinking." Had Khrushchev visited during Trump's presidency, both experiences would have essentially reflected a similar kind of commodified unreality – history as mass entertainment, Independence Day parades to match Bastille Day celebrations. "There is about these people," Ashbolt asserts elsewhere of Americans, "a tremendous exhibitionism, an almost brazen outgoingness that demands satisfaction through either watching or participating in big public performances." A generalisation of course, but in the Internet/Facebook/Snapchat/Instagram/TicToc age, *everything* is on show, *anyone* can be a star, a celebrity, and a hell of a lot of Americans seem committed to becoming just that, whatever that means. Either way, pre-COVID, American YouTube "stars" of surprisingly diverse stripes and with no discernable concert experience were mounting international tours based on the number of "Likes", "Views" and "Streams" accrued, substantive evidence of their particular claims within the "popular cultural" landscape of their "audiences".

- "The central historical division in the Supreme Court," Ashbolt could assert in 1966 and again in the 1969 edition of *An American Experience*, "has not been between liberals and conservatives, nor between Democrats and Republicans; it has been between those justices for whom the basic human right was protection of private property and those justices for whom it was protection of individual liberty." Was anyone thinking along these lines as the Senate Judiciary Committee pondered the "merits" of Brett Kavanaugh to take up the seat on the Supreme Court vacated by the retiring Justice Anthony Kennedy? Or Amy Coney Barrett to fill

252

- the vacancy created by the death of Justice Ruth Bader Ginsburg? Cementing a conservative majority on the bench for the Republicans, one can only suppose the hope was that the balance would now be tipped towards those Supreme Court justices for whom the protection of private property is paramount. In the event, of course, that same Supreme Court wasn't prepared to defy the American Constitution and overturn the 2020 Presidential election results in order for Trump to retain the Presidency.

- Elsewhere, Ashbolt reminds us that, to America's conservatives, "a liberal is either a bungling amateur, a wishy-washy humanist, a hopeless dupe or a traitor to his class." Not much of a change there, even if what constituted a Democratic platform and what a Republican has changed completely in the intervening sixty years. Ashbolt adds that, "When somebody like Nixon jumps on the liberal bandwagon, it is time to about turn, fall out and take stock." What no one could have known then was that Nixon was playing the "Liberal" card with such consummate duplicity in order to ensure his conservative agenda would be implemented, representing his position as merely the will, of course, of "the Silent Majority", as he named them in a 1969 speech. Bruce J Schulman points out in his 2001 book, *The Seventies: The Great Shift in American Culture, Society and Politics*, that "Nixon's indirect, underhanded strategy with regard to welfare, environmental protection, housing and the arts represented more than a career politician's cunning or a pathological liar's need to be devious. Every one of these manoeuvres advanced Nixon's larger political objective: his ambition to transform American politics by creating a new majority coalition in the United States." (The Free Press, p. 35) "The dilemma of the

253

- liberals," Ashbolt surmises, "is… over Communism. They spend a good deal of their time and energy trying to avoid the Communist tag." Sixty years on, their more virulent critics are *still* smearing liberals and Democrats alike as Communist/Socialists.

- Some random Ashbolt quotes: "The primary motive of the government seems to be, whatever happens, to keep national strength at its maximum." "In times of crisis, the passion for national unity plays a dominating part in US politics, precisely because at other times there is no clear sense of unity." "The American people have always wanted freedom and wanted strength, but the structure of American society has tended only to give freedom to the strong and strength to the free."

- Then there was the issue of American supremacy, egged on by a perceived battle to the death with a USSR that seemed determined to challenge that supremacy. "Among those Americans who acknowledged that a world outside America existed," Ashbolt observes, "there was in the late 1950s an almost psychotic anxiety that America should everywhere be regarded as the top nation." Acknowledging that America had been empire-building in a manner unlike previous empire-building nations, "What the Americans have done," Ashbolt felt, "is to modernise the procedures of colonisation. Instead of raising a flag, they raise a business." Sixty years on, America's biggest "issue" seems to be that other nations have learned the lesson and begun "raising businesses" themselves not only in parts of the world where once American business reigned supreme, but also in America itself, which has become the target of all manner of international corporate "takeovers", and in particular by China, which, as Trump might have ruefully noted, isn't "encumbered" by this whole

- Democracy/Bill of Rights/Free Speech business that seemed so problematic to the "world's best dealmaker" and must therefore be seen as acting without the moral compass ostensibly guiding America in *its* obviously far more benign (and profitable) empire-building. Think about Trump's arguments with NATO and the EU and then let Ashbolt remind us that "When De Gaulle started to cut the subtle ties binding France to America, many Americans asked angrily if it was a reasonable return for the dollars that had been poured into France since 1945." After all, wasn't all that effort, the wars fought, the lives lost, the money invested about making the world a better place? "For they expected other countries to emulate America. They take the measure of a country's progress to be its likeness to America's." So in an ideal world, we all kick back, sip a Coke, munch on a McBurger and watch American TV, freely, happily, accepting all as simply the obvious universal beneficence wrought of the "chosen" nation's Manifest Destiny. Today of course, we can add Google, Facebook, Netflix and the rest of America's digital manifestations to that list of American beneficence, threatened, clearly, indisputably, by nefarious Russian hackers on one hand and Communist Party apparatchiks working within Huawei on the other. Of course, for all the railing against China, Trump was happy to have all his election paraphernalia, from caps to banners, made in China, for sound economic reasons – that that paraphernalia would have cost him far more if made in America.

- Observing the rise and rise of the "celebrity", their journalistic cohort and the public relations industry, Ashbolt notes that "They often work, too, in a twilight world of corruption, building perverts, gamblers and crooks into folk-heroes. For in these days of pseudo-

255

-    events and publicity-mongering, heroism is measured
     not by a man's achievements but by the space he rates in
     the mass media." That, then and now, can at least be
     leavened by the fact that, as he goes on to say a little
     later in that particular chapter, "It is hardly necessary to
     say that there are some fine newspapers in America,
     some brilliant and humane editors, some first-rate
     reporters. The best of American journalism is easily the
     best in the Western world." He could not know that two
     determined young journalists would become the
     instruments to bring down a President – Nixon – or that
     today, a media monopoly owned by an Australian would
     have so virulently endorsed and propped up the least
     capable President ever to occupy the White House.

Of course *An American Experience* isn't all prognostications
on the shortcomings and limitations of the nation's institutions.
There are soliloquies on a variety of aspects of America – the
culture, the literature, the theatre, the landscape, the roads less
travelled – he suggests leaving the "superhighways" and
checking out the real America on its back roads. Ashbolt's look
at the year as experienced by its inhabitants, albeit primarily
those of the Eastern Seaboard, in a delightful chapter titled *The
Silly And Sorrowful Seasons*, is positively lyrical, with not a
little of the Walt Whitmans in its rolling lists. Then again, noting
the American obsession with the road trip, "They are almost
constantly peering through a camera lens, and obviously their
journey is only a prelude to re-living it in photographs later on."
He lived long enough to see the whole world determined to
experience pretty much everything, from food to concerts,
landscapes to each other, vicariously, digitally, via screens large
and small, since actually living in the moment seems to have
become terribly passé.

Obviously much has of course changed in the years since
the publication of *An American Experience*, in America and the
rest of the world, and not least courtesy of the now near

universal access to so much and so many courtesy the digital revolution – quaint how Ashbolt credits the first state-of-the-art general-purpose electronic digital computer designed in the US, Univac, with the potential capability to self-generate half-hour TV show scenarios, replacing overworked scriptwriters unable to keep up with local and global demand. At this distance and thankfully, the futile "air-raid drill" people were then obliged to practice in the event of a nuclear attack seems as quaint as it was chilling, a generation growing up under the constant spectre of potential thermonuclear annihilation. Ashbolt notes that, "by 1960-61... US investment in military hardware amounted to $US20 billion a year. One-third of America's scientists and engineers were directly engaged in military effort. One-half of the funds spent for scientific research and development were used on military projects." The US Department of Defence budget for the fiscal year 2019 was $US693 billion. In 1960, arms production accounted for 12 per cent – $US40 billion of the US GDP (Gross Domestic Product). In September 2017, *The New York Times* noted arms production was roughly ten per cent of the $2.2 trillion of US factory output, "sold mainly to the Defence Department". (Louis Uchitelle, 22 September 2017) "The tie-up," Ashbolt adds, "between industry and the Pentagon was so close that arms production, controlled and financed by the government but labelled free enterprise, had by 1961 become almost an economic function in its own right, regardless of military needs." Talk about a military-industrial complex indeed. Now it's also a function of the number of *jobs* a sitting President can help "create".

Ashbolt's observations on the various major political players of the day, from Eisenhower, Nixon, Kennedy and Adlai Stevenson among others on the American side to his chapters on Khrushchev and his two US visits and Cuba's Fidel Castro on the other, remain interesting and insightful. Most of the statistics on everything from automobile and aviation accidents to pollution levels to the various manufacturing and production levels of all kinds of goods and so on quoted for activities *within*

America are of course now only of historical interest. But it's well to be reminded again that way back in 1958, manufacturers were well aware, for instance, of the fact that automobiles were a major contributor to atmospheric pollution. Some things remain – and have always been – true: "the GNP says nothing about coping with unemployment, nothing about lifting low wages, nothing about preserving and developing natural resources." Then, it was all about mass production and conspicuous consumption, good old American social pragmatism. Now? You know the answer. "Success," as Ashbolt again notes, "has become the great American goal." So again, no great change there.

In the end, the thing to remember about America, as the polymath Ashbolt makes clear right at the beginning of his book, is that there really isn't one America at all. For all the homogenisation courtesy the various mass media, the corporations and the automobile, there are many Americas. The '60s saw the re-emergence of the hyphenated American – the Polish-Americans and Irish-Americans, the Hispanic-/Mexican-/Puerto Rican-Americans, even the unhyphenated Native Americans, and of course, the one "ethnic" group that was never going to easily "melt", in the old "melting pot" sense of whatever it was that Americans once thought they were, the African Americans, simply because of the colour of their skin. At least, sixty years on, by rights African Americans no longer have to fight the battles their pre-civil rights reforms brothers and sisters did, can work, prosper and become successful in any field they choose – as long as they've been born into the right kind of family in the right kind of neighbourhood and don't come up against some bull-nosed officer of the law with a happy trigger finger and defective body-cam. Then there's the inevitable proliferation of sub-sets within the population as groups splinter into ever smaller "special interest" groups, from Pentecostal to Amish, from Rastafarian to Muslim, Jew to Mormon, Republicans, Democrats, "Yankees", "Confederates", New Agers and Doomsday Preppers, neo-Nazis and those who identify under the LGBTQI rainbow, among far too many to mention. Perhaps what we saw January 6, 2021 was the opening volleys of some sort of final titanic battle launched by a certain tawdry, nay nihilistic kind of "White" America to enshrine *its* right to rule, unilaterally, over *all* other Americas. Despite the Senate's refusal to affirm Trump's second impeachment, the storming of the Capitol building in Washington DC was incontrovertibly launched by a thousand Presidential tweets. That's something Ashbolt could never have foreseen.

Again Ashbolt reminds us that the two major forces tugging at the heart of America are, recalling the insights of commentator Michael Harrington, in his 1963 book *The Other America*, "the high-minded humanism and humanitarianism of the Declaration of Independence against the arrogant sense of economic proprietorship and privilege that informed the Constitution." He recognises, of course, that the reality is qualified by infinitely subtle shades of grey, but it's the conflict between these two forces that decides where America stands at any moment in its evolution. Either way, given the opportunity, it's worth travelling in Ashbolt's company for a few hours to see how things were, how far we've all come and how we might better understand where America might be going. Perhaps the most troubling aspect of the book is that the questions he raises in its closing pages remain the same. "The answers are vital to all of us," he finishes, "because America has taken the democratic adventure further in hope and hypocrisy than any other Western country."

Ashbolt passed away on June 9, 2005, at the age of 83 after a long illness, having lived long enough to see that Cold War end, the Berlin Wall fall and the Twin Towers collapse. He died as the 43rd President, Republican George W. Bush, celebrated the first six months of his second term in office and America and its Coalition of the Willing were in Afghanistan and Iraq fighting for our freedom. One way or another America's and Australia's freedoms remain under threat.

## POSTSCRIPT:

On page 29 of a modest yet quietly remarkable little collection of essays titled *A Thousand Shards of Glass* by Greek (Cretan?) American writer and photographer Michael Katakis, published in 2014, is this intriguing yet disturbingly apposite sentence: "The trouble we have in America is not intolerance but the tolerance of the intolerant and intolerable by the enlightened." Even more disquieting is a sentence that precedes it: "Some believers think that President Obama is not an American, while others think Donald Trump matters."

As we all know, Trump was then able to convince enough Americans that he actually cared about them to win the 2016 Presidential election and, worryingly, may still manage to con his way back into the Presidency in 2024.

It was during his Presidency that I found Ashbolt's book and decided it was important enough to have a crack at reacquainting at least some of Australia of its existence by writing about it. Sadly, though *Overland* were very positive in their rejection note and invited me to send them anything else I thought might be worth their reading, I've had nothing – yet. The Ashbolt essay has found no home and is published here for the first time.

# WHEN GINGER MET LOLITA

I could start this little observation with a nice comfortable cliché like "it was a more innocent time", but of course it was no more innocent as the world is now or was a thousand years ago. It was a time when the whole world was at war and the world certainly needed a little innocence and gentle laughter. Perhaps the difference between then and now is that we've lost so many more layers of innocence in the years between.

Screen and theatre actor Ginger Rogers was working on the feature film *Roxie Hart* when the Japanese bombed Pearl Harbour December 7, 1941, finally forcing America to act and joining the Allies in their battle against fascism and totalitarianism. Even writing that last word is problematic. After all, among those allied against fascism was a totalitarian of the worst order, one Joseph Stalin. Nevertheless, America was at war and Hollywood was inevitably going to become a part of the effort to win that war.

Screenwriter Samuel "Billy" Wilder had every reason to feel the need to be a part of that effort. Born into a Jewish family in the penultimate decade of the Austro-Hungarian Empire, he'd grown up in Krakow and Vienna and like so many had become infatuated by the cinema and the products of Hollywood in particular from an early age. In 1927, aged 21, he left Vienna for Berlin to work as a journalist but soon moved into scriptwriting and by 1933 could boast screenwriting credits on 13 features – his credit on his 14th, *Was Frauen träumen (What Women Dream)*, was removed from the final cut before it screened, as it happens, on Hitler's birthday. The rise of the Nazis signalled a prudent departure, first to Paris, where Wilder directed his first feature film, *Mauvaise Graine (Bad Seed)*, and then to board a ship bound for New York City, where his brother was already living. Wilder arrived in Hollywood aged 27 and within five years had re-established himself as a screenwriter, his first major success his collaboration on the script for Greta Garbo's first foray into comedy, 1939's *Ninotchka*.

As it happens, his co-writer on the film was Charles Brackett, with whom he would collaborate right up until 1950. Brackett had served with the Allied Expeditionary Force in WWI and been awarded a French Medal of Honour. Going into writing on his return from the war, among other things he was *The New Yorker*'s drama critic for four years and published five novels before beginning his next career, as a screenwriter. He'd even been president of the Screen Writers Guild in 1938. As he watched Europe descend once again into war, Brackett was all too aware of how important keeping up the morale of the troops and those waiting at home would become.

The producer of *Ninotchka* was Arthur Hornblow Jr. An aspiring playwright, in 1927, he'd been hired by Sam Goldwyn to work at Paramount Pictures as a production supervisor and was soon producing what Hollywood seemed to do best in the 1930s, light, frothy films within that witty little genre dubbed screwball comedies.

It was while Ginger Rogers was on the *Roxie Hart* set that she was approached by Hornblow and Brackett about a film in which they hoped she would take the starring role. It was titled *The Major and the Minor*. "I loved the story the moment I heard it," she tells us in her 1991 autobiography, *Ginger: My Story*, "I told Charlie and Arthur that I had had similar experiences as a child on the Interstate circuit: when Mother and I didn't have enough money to ride the train at full fare, I used my stuffed-doll Freakus as a ploy and a pillow. The story they were telling me was, in a sense, the story of my life."

Hornblow put Wilder's name forward as his choice for director. As he had yet to direct a film in Hollywood, there was no way of knowing if he was up to the task, but Ms Rogers agreed to meet him. They met, got on just fine and Wilder got to make his directorial debut on a feature film that would star Ginger Rogers and Welsh actor Ray Milland. She was already a star, 31 years old and *The Major and the Minor* would be her 47th movie.

Now, the premise of the film is pretty much as Rogers sketches out in her recollection of that meeting. Her role is that of Susan Applegate, who works in New York City as a scalp massager. While working on a client, Albert Osborne, played by the wonderful character actor – and sublimely comic writer in his own right – Robert Benchley, delivers a line that for some years afterwards became part of the American lexicon within certain kinds of conversations – "Why don't you slip out of that wet coat and into a dry martini?" Naturally offended, Applegate promptly decides to quit the Big Apple and head home to her mother back in quiet, leafy Middle America – Stevenson, Iowa. Her problem? She hasn't the full fare – so she poses as a child, Susu, in order to travel half fare.

Spotted smoking by a suspicious conductor, she takes refuge in the carriage of a Major Philip Kirby, played by Milland, who somehow doesn't see through either her flimsy story or her barely credible disguise as 12 year old "Susu" – it turns out he has an issue with his eyesight that is preventing him from active service – and agrees to let her share his compartment until the train reaches his stop. Accepting her story about fear of the conductor, he offers her his lower bunk. There is never a hint of impropriety between Susu and Kirby throughout the film. Kirby teaches at a military academy, though he's keen to get an overseas posting and see some real action, something his scheming fiancé is keen to ensure doesn't happen. As luck and a tried and tested plot twist would have it, the train is delayed by a flood and the fiancé and Kirby's commanding officer drive out to rescue him and inadvertently discover "Susu" in his compartment.

It's all too obvious where this is all leading, of course, but the light, witty script carries the viewer along as all the usual elements that made Hollywood screwball comedy such great escapist fare during those years, the upshot being that "Susu" is obliged to continue her ruse, accepting an invitation to join them back to the college until the train lines are repaired and she can continue her journey home. Susu inevitably becomes the object of desire for the full complement of cadets at Kirby's academy. There's a lovely moment during the inevitable graduates' ball when Susu looks across at the girls from a neighbouring school attending the evening all sitting in a row opposite all sporting the current "craze" in hairstyles, the Veronica Lake, each girl with one side of her face partially obscured by a resplendent sweep of hair. Just five years before, the "pageboy bob" that stylist Louise Mehle had designed for Rogers had similarly swept the nation's secretarial pools. As it happens, it was Hornblow who had given aspiring young actress Constance Ockelman her new name – Veronica Lake.

The other inevitability of *The Major and the Minor*, of course, and the one the audiences expected, was that Kirby and Susu would finish the film happily in love and that Kirby could go off to war knowing someone was "back home" waiting for him, as patriotic a conclusion as anyone in 1942 could have hoped for. Within a year, Ginger too became an actual war bride, marrying Private First Class John Calvin Briggs II in January 1943.

*The Major and the Minor* was a critical and commercial success and established Wilder as a significant directorial force, going on to win Oscars for 1945's *The Lost Weekend*, for which its star, Ray Milland, also won an Oscar, and 1950's *Sunset Boulevard*. As Rogers admits of *The Major and the Minor* in her autobiography, "I believe I had more fun playing this role than any other, with one exception... Kitty Foyle. A lot of my enjoyment had to do with Billy."

As the September 17, 1942 *New York Times* review by Bosley Crowther noted, "Never once does either (Milland or Rogers) permit the suggestion of a leer to creep in."

And here's where all that preamble about more innocent times and the loss of so many layers of innocence comes into this narrative. I'll let one of Ms Rogers' biographers make the point: "What, of course," writes Sheriden Morley in his 1995 book, *Shall We Dance: The Life of Ginger Rogers*, "Wilder was making, just twenty years ahead of time, was his very own

Lolita; but so subtly was it disguised, so slavishly did it follow the Hollywood-comedy conventions of the time, that the code was never cracked."

Raised a practising Christian Scientist, Ginger would have been utterly mortified if for one moment she thought that she'd made a film that even remotely suggested a sexual relationship with a minor was anything other than totally abhorrent. It's also quite plain from her own recollections that there was never a moment she thought she was making anything other than a screwball comedy based on mistaken identity, as eternal a plotline as anything from Shakespeare to, well, a good many Hollywood movies before and since.

The problem is that perceptions have changed, and quite rightly of course. Throughout the film, the original audience – and the contemporary one, viewing it on television – is "in on the subterfuge" – we all *know* Susu is not 12! – but contemporary eyes bludgeoned with the all too nasty revelations of decades of institutional abuse – why, even the more "liberated", "rebellious" generation growing up with rock'n'roll found Jerry Lee Lewis marrying his 13 year old cousin hard to accommodate – cannot fail to be aware of the fact that Milland's character becomes more than a little smitten by the "child" Susu, just as Hubert Hubert does with Lolita, the difference of course that Lolita *is* a child. No matter that the real intent of Nabokov's novel – a scathing *allegorical* indictment of the America that the Russian émigré had come to know – it has been lost in the scramble to extract every ounce of possible salaciousness from the text.

Then again there's the issue of Morley's suggestion of Wilder working to a very dubious subtext. Wilder was directing a film co-written with Bracken, which must therefore implicate Bracken in on that "code that was never cracked". But their script for *The Major and the Minor* had actually been taken from a successful play titled *Connie Goes Home*, written back in 1922 by American playwright Edward Childs Carpenter, for which Paramount owned the screen rights. Does that then mean

Carpenter too was somehow a co-conspirator to this "unbroken code"?

There's no going back to any mythical more innocent time of course. It's far better that iniquities, abuses and injustices are exposed and that those against whom those iniquities, abuses and injustices were meted out receive the justice that is their right. It's just a pity that, as a consequence, that universal loss of innocence must impose a subtle sense of discomfort that diminishes something made long ago to bring a smile to a population facing forces that quite possibly could have spelt the end of the free world as it was known, long before *Lolita*.

## POSTSCRIPT:

While this film is hardly the pinnacle of Ms Rogers' cinematic career – in fact it's pretty trite fluff, though disarmingly fun fluff – the point of the piece is the "dangers" of revisionism…

A *Quadrant* reader made it very clear that "Arthur Hornblow Jnr. was NOT the producer of *Ninotchka*; it was Lubitsch (and another, uncredited). Hornblow didn't come along until later in Wilder's career. I have this on the authority of *On Sunset Boulevard: The Life and Times of Billy Wilder* by Ed Sikov, NY, Hyperion, 1998." I defer to her superior knowledge.

## Y1K TO Y2K: A Thousand Years in a Thousand Words (or Thereabouts)

Good evening and welcome to the 11th century, which I must admit is a tad confusing since the jury is still out on whether it begins in 1000 AD (or is that BCE, Before the Common Era) or 1001 AD/BCE. There seems to be some problem about the idea of a starting point since no one seems keen on the idea of a Year 0 between 1 BC and 1 AD. Definitely a problem for the Arabs who, having swept across northern Africa, seem to have collected an awful lot of books, mostly in Greek and mostly about maths, that had somehow survived the burning of the Great Library of Alexandria. Adding to their confusion is the fact that according to *their* calendar, it's the year 378, and none of that BC/AD nonsense thank you very much.

Anyway, in news just to hand, it looks like a 1-0 win to the Normans in their first away match of the season, after the English captain copped a blinder at the Hastings pitch, though the decision to take not only the Cup but the Crown as well seems down to a contentious technicality based on the ground rules set by former English captain Edward the Confessor. Still, the cheer squad is already hard at it sewing the winning team's colours into the Bayeaux Tapestry and the self-titled William the Conqueror is not about to allow a rematch.

In other news from around the world, it looks like trouble for Pope Gregory VII, who has gone and got himself on the wrong side of the French king (typical), who has sacked him and installed their Antipope (?) Clement III. Ah those continentals, what? Keep Britain Saxon I say. And in late breaking news, it seems the first load of illegal immigrants has hit the beaches of the last uninhabited piece of Pacific real estate with the Maoris reaching what we'll be calling New Zealand in another 600 years or so. Word from the neighbouring and significantly larger island, which itself will be illegally dubbed Terra Nullius by a future visiting English team, suggests that, since they're currently celebrating Y57,000K with another year-long corroboree, the Aborigines are just pleased to be keeping Bondi Beach to themselves. Ah, roo meat one day, witchetty grubs the next. What a life!

Fast forward to the 13th century (just 'cause I can) and the Saxons and Normans are still not happy about the rules governing their Sceptred Isle and while that Nottingham celebrity drag artiste Robin Hood might have been telling us all along to watch our backs when that nancy King John is around, it's taken a meeting of the Union of Miscellaneous Dukes, Earls & Sundry Lords (Norman Bench) to pull the bugger down a peg or two with a stop work meeting at a very nice pub near Runnymede-on-Thames. The MDESLU managed to get a firm commitment on improved conditions for the, uh hum, Ruling Classes under the Magna Carta – lots of stuff about forests, not a sausage about shrubberies! – though there is still some contention from the Monty Python League as to the legitimacy of undemocratically elected autocratic dictators claiming some dubious hogwash about the Divine Right of Kings.

On the financial front, the bottom has fallen out of the Kentuckawehanna Fried Moa business in New Zealand due to lack of forward planning on the off chance the giant flightless bird might prove to be a limited commodity. Neither the franchise nor the bird look likely to see the 14th century.

Meanwhile, in an item just in from the 16th century, more problems with those bloody Italians, one Pope Gregory XIII having somehow managed to misplace a reported ten days. There are bound to be questions over in Greenwich where the Miscellaneous GMT Observational Trades & Apothecaries Union shop stewards are less than happy about the loss of overtime and holiday pay, not to mention those people born during the ten days in October that had been summarily dissed.

It seems the for the moment Terra Australis has had its first major problem with boat people with the unexpected arrival of a number of Dutch tourists on the cruise ship Batavia alleging they were shipwrecked off the northwest coast of the country, honest guvner. The local authorities had been considering whether to invite them to a cracker barbie at what was eventually to become Port Hedland but, in typical Eurocentric fashion, the survivors seem to have been more intent on butchering each other that tossing another roo tail on the barbie. In an official statement from the Mitjinster of the Pitjinjirri, he commented that, "She'll be right mate," and hopes that's the last he'll be seeing of European feeding customs for a while.

In the latest travel news, it looks like the Italians are definitely winning the Place Race, with Marco Polo having recently repatriated spaghetti, while a chancer named Christopher Columbus has managed to get the Spanish Delegation of the IOC to sponsor his Atlantic Challenge in order to be the first to bring smallpox, measles, syphilis and olive oil to the underprivileged natives of the recently renamed West Indies. The neighbouring continents have no idea what horrors they're in for. A spokesman for the Europeans has suggested that if the Black Death was good enough for the Belgians, it's good enough for the rest of the world.

There have been a couple of other late entries in the Place Race, with the Spanish overruling Italy's claim to Columbus and therefore claiming all real estate south of that big bit above Mexico, while the late British entry, Sir Walter Raleigh has retrospectively been beheaded for his contribution to the advancement of mouth, throat and lung cancer as well as heart disease courtesy of his kicking off the tobacco import trade.

Throughout this whole business, the Chinese have very wisely recognised that, since they had already created the perfect society with the development of Tao and Confusion philosophy a good millennium before the Brits, Froggies, Ities and other assorted Europeans got their act together, why would they bother going anywhere beyond Taiwan for their summer holidays?

Having undermined the roving troubadour and news commentator trade with the invention of the printing press,

Europe now seems determined to stamp out the illegal trade in broomsticks, black cats and Halloween party hats with the introduction of the Spanish Inquisition, which no one expected and which has instituted a work-to-rule and the banning of witches for burning to only those who are not blonde, blue-eyed and contracted to the Papal State or Foxtel.

There's been another report of boat people, this time arriving on the east coast of the newly renamed Terra Nullius, a decision which has caused consternation among the locals who have known they've been in this vast place for a good 60,000 years or so and by chance just happened to all be on the other side of the country for a big footie match and missed the chance to suggest Captain James Cook go play boats in someone else's bathtub. It looks likely the "William the Conqueror" defence will be used to retain the "best beaches I've seen this side of Bognor" for future British back packers, convicts and the "Friends of Princess Robin Hood (if you know what I mean Ducky) Society".

Meanwhile the latest Pope seems rather pissed off at the news from Galapagos that a certain uppity Brit named Charles Darwin reckons he's got the numbers wrong and Gregorian calendar or no Gregorian calendar, it took a darn sight longer to make Adam than an afternoon messing about with Playdough.

Having obviously lost all track of time in this particular bulletin and overstepping the 1000-word mark, we'll just turn to the weather and it looks like April showers for Sydney every weekend from May to Mid-February as the Greenhouse Effect kicks in nicely. And in another piece of late news, the British Prime Minister has finally managed to break the Norman monopoly in the House of Lords, bought Park Lane and Mayfair back off the Arabs and put hotels on them.

So it's goodnight from me and it's over to the IOC, Y2K and the Grand Order of Soothsayers, Sorcerers and Suspicious-Looking Characters with 666 tattooed on their foreheads to see if the coming century will prove either the Mayans, the Pope, Darwin or Rupert Murdoch was right.

Have a wonderful Christmas, New Year and false start to the next Millennium which, of course, starts in 2001 AD/BCE (or 58,0001 for our Indigenous readers… oh, and of course 1420 for any Muslim readers). Good night. (Roll credits and… cut. That's a wrap.)

## POSTSCRIPT:

First of all my profound apologies to anyone and everyone I might have offended in this bit of flummery meant merely as a little light-hearted bit of fun. Just blame the Normans!

I should add that this whole confusing business of dates courtesy Pope Gregory, was actually a lot more of a bother for the Brits than just deciding to lose ten days. First of all, the Pope was a dagoe, which was bad enough in late 16th century England, but was a bloody Catholic dagoe and godly Protestant England wasn't about to fall over to any old edict coming out of his Papal Office or anywhere else south of Southend! So England didn't actually adopt the Gregorian calendar until 1751. So that's when the whole tizzy over Greenwich Mean Time actually took place, and, a mere 18 years later, why Cook was sent off to Tahiti, to observe the Transit of Venus and get this whole time business sorted. Oh, and as a side project on his way home, see if he could discover this mythical place already well and truly discovered 60-odd thousand years earlier by another group of wandering humans… give or take ten days.

# HARRY'S WAR, OUR PEACE

Imagine being born and raised in a country your family has been born and raised in for untold generations and being proud enough of that country and your countrymen to be prepared to serve, to join in any fight against forces antagonistic to that country, and to be prepared to die for that country knowing full well that as far as that country is concerned you don't even exist.

Welcome to the world of Australia's Indigenous peoples, at least up until 1967, which saw a Referendum pass that acknowledged their existence enough to finally at least include them in the Australian Census, and then in November 1972, when the newly-minted Labor Prime Minister Gough Whitlam further recognised those peoples by awarding them the right to vote. This was the world of Harry Saunders who, in 1942, left the Condah Mission, on the traditional lands of the Gunditjmara four hours' drive west of Melbourne, Victoria and enlisted in the Australian Army determined to do his bit to defend his country against the Japanese Imperial Army in the jungles of Papua New Guinea. He never came back.

"You blokes make me sick," says actor Kylie Belling, who plays the part of Maude Green, the wife of another Aboriginal soldier whom Saunders meets on the train heading to the departure point for Australian troops in a short film, *Harry's War*, made by filmmaker Richard Frankland based on the true story of his uncle, Harry Saunders. "You think it'll be one big adventure, that everything will be fine when you come home, that you'll get equal bloody pay, that you won't need a bloody permission slip to leave the Mission." Sadly of course, she was right.

"It's a very important story for Australia," Frankland suggests. "A lot of people see Aboriginal people as a problem in this country, where we've contributed in many, many ways. And of course leads to the point where non-Indigenous Australians have been denied information such as this, which is so pertinent to the growth of this country.

"And it's such a simple tale, and so beautiful, and I don't mean the technical side of my method of storytelling, but just the story itself, a black fella and a white fella becoming mates beyond colour and heritage, and having the courage to step outside their cultural boundaries but at the same time looks at those cultural boundaries and content as wonderful, beautiful things."

As Frankland points out, the core of *Harry's War* is the friendship between Saunders, played by David Ngoombujarra, and Mitch, a white Australian, played by Peter Docker. "The actors threw themselves right into it and they honoured these men, and they were easy men to honour. They were the most highly decorated section of the entire British Commonwealth Forces, ever. They fought their way up the Kokoda twice. They just did amazing things – and one of them wasn't a citizen, was regarded if at all as a second-class citizen by this country. Yet he had the courage when Australia called out for its sons and daughters, like many other Aboriginal people, to go and fight. I just think that's a story that Australia needs to hear time and time again until it sinks in."

In the film, Harry Saunders himself sums up why he joined up, regardless, in a way that is so typically, no, more than that, archetypally Australian, that no one can fail to recognise themselves, whether black, white, yellow or brindle – "You've gotta 'ave a go mate. You've gotta 'ave a bloody good crack at it."

"When I was learning about my Uncle Harry and his mate, I was told all these stories, little stories which I didn't have enough time to put in the film, but they were just fantastic little things that were so Australian, uniquely Australian. The depth of mateship that they shared was phenomenal. It's really strange. You make a film like that and you'd think, sixty years on, that Australia would have reconciled its differences, and yet now we're in a worse bloody position than ever! It's shocking. I've got a lot of Aboriginal mates who, when all this stuff was happening about the Stolen Generations, were terribly, terribly bloody depressed.

"I was in Hollywood recently, won a big award (Frankland became the first Indigenous Australian to win an award at the 2000 Hollywood Black Film Festival) and coming home, we hit Auckland about four in the morning and I thought, 'I don't want to go back there! I don't want to come back to this shit fight where I have to justify my depth of being a contributor to this country, of being able to say I'm Gunditjmara and I'm bloody proud of it.' I knew I had to come back, that I've got an obligation to stand up for my mob as long and as hard as I can, but I was coming back to a hostile government [led at the time by Liberal Prime Minister John Howard], to someone who, from the second they got into power has been attacking Indigenous Australians in a horribly aggressive manner and who, in my opinion, has contributed to the deaths in custody count."

Frankland's grandfather, Chris Saunders, fought in France during WWII, while his other uncle, Captain Reg Saunders, Harry's brother, became Australia's first commissioned Aboriginal officer. Frankland himself has also served in the Australian Army for three years.

"Attitudes perpetuate legislation and policy," he asserts. "If we look at society as a structure, we can say that there are access points to wealth and power, and that those access points are controlled by the dominant culture. Minorities are made, not born, and that's why my people don't get through those access points to wealth and power, and those things enable symbol and image creation, cultural maintenance, economic growth, cultural development. And Howard contributes to the denial of that. *Harry's War*, in my opinion, is a tool to be used to try and change those attitudes because it is such a pure story, because it takes a snapshot of Australian history and shows the best of what we can possibly be."

It is also a deeply moving cinematic experience.

## POSTSCRIPT:

It took another eight years before a new government, a Labor government, led by Kevin Rudd, to finally stand up in Parliament and formally apologise to the "Stolen Generations" of Australia's Indigenous peoples. Sadly, Indigenous deaths in custody have continued unabated, despite an exhaustive Royal Commission, which handed down 339 recommendations in its 10,000 pages.

The Voice is about respect. It's time. New Zealand never went through this kind of hand-ringing paranoia in accommodating the original Maori inhabitants the Europeans displaced.

## 2007: WHAT IF THE ANIMALS GOT REALLY GRUMPY?
ABC Radio National's host of *The Science Show*, Robyn Williams, discusses future possibilities, and the novel his thoughts prompted him to write.

Environmentalists and scientists have been telling up for at least four decades that if we don't change our ways, we might push the planet so far that we could suffer all manner of cataclysmic weather events as a consequence. Of course, we've all become "Greener" in our consciousness, but have we gone far enough? What if the other inhabitants with whom we share this planet were to decide that we haven't and choose to gang up on us to make the point in no uncertain terms?

That's just what happens in the timely, witty and thoughtful first novel, *2007*, by one of Australia's most respected scientific commentators, Robyn Williams, who has been running the ABC Radio Science Unit since 1972. His novel presents a tale in which the world's dogs and cats and rats and goldfish – and basically every other creature that walks, crawls, flies or swims – gang together in the most surprising way to try to tell the one species that's not been paying attention that they're messing things up for all of us. And since the book is written by an Australian-Englishman – Williams was born in the UK – the man who might just be able to solve the problem isn't some American, like, say, the President, but a lowly, publicity-shy Australian expert in ecosystems tucked away in an isolated research station on a windy promontory somewhere in Tasmania.

As you'd expect, considering his day job, Williams shows himself not only up to speed on all the latest scientific discoveries, from fields as diverse as microbiology and meteorology, but also displays an extraordinary breadth of literary references which he is able to bring to bear in the writing of *2007* to create a reasonably credible tale.

"Most people in my sort of area expect you to be

making a 'science' statement," Williams admits. "There's a 'science problem' and you fix it with 'science things', and it's all *now*. But I wanted to show that it's historic, that it goes back to Lucretius, back to George Orwell; Gilbert White going down various country paths looking at birds and wondering why they behave as they do, and looking at the whole vastness of human culture. It's only when you understand that, some of the history as well as some of the science that you can see how it all links together. And that's to some extent why the animals and the birds and the children are there doing different things, so that you don't imagine that there's an intrepid scientist, played by Dustin Hoffman, with his sidekick, usually blonde, usually leaping out of a helicopter, who are going to fix it all."

There's also a lot of humour in a book with an ostensibly "apocalyptic", at least on an environmental level, theme. Certain prominent political figures are placed in amusingly uncomfortable situations, and then there's the first televised conference the hero of the piece, Dr Julian Griffin, experiences in the US, which is hilarious, as he "spars" with the three eminently more famous environmentalists brought in to question Griffin's deductions, all, oddly enough, named David.

"There are so many things that land up on our screens with people arranged in funny chairs to tell you how to handle the rest of your life or the rest of the available time for human beings, I just thought I'd put various scenarios on tilt! I sent copies of *2007* to two of the (real) Davids – Suzuki and Attenborough (the third of course is Bellamy), but I haven't heard back. They're friends… I hope!"

The genesis of the book is, of course, based in something much more serious, as perceived by a man who, each week, has to present a program that highlights the discoveries being made by eminent – and not so eminent – scientists in all manner of areas and specialities, from climate and the environment to biology and beyond. Then there's this whole concept of Gaia, a hypothesis first presented by English scientist James Lovelock that is grounded in the ecological interdependence of living organisms with the inorganic environments within which they exist.

"The first thing about Gaia is that it suggests that when you're pushing matters environmentally to an extreme, you don't 'defeat' nature, it just flips, so that you get a new kind of stability. That's what its proponent, Jim Lovelock, talks about. And that's what the physicists talk about with climate change, that you might get turbulence as a result of global warming, but then for all we know, instead of things settling down at what would be a very nice, convenient temperature and stability for us, you might get a new stability that's actually an Ice Age. We *can* get Ice Ages from warming, through all sorts of simple feedback mechanisms.

"But I was also interested in a kind of *bigger* Gaia idea, and I say this as an atheist, of a kind of collective subconsciousness amongst animals, so that if you push that idea further to see how various creatures could start acting together, I believe you could start a whole new set of scenarios that I explore in the book, so as to imagine how they could interact without necessarily spelling it out. The only time I spell it out is in the scene depicting the geese flying together. That seems to be a cooperative event within one species that no one could necessarily foretell, but when you deconstruct it, it seems quite simple. Lyn Margolis suggests that cooperation is as much if not more important than competition among animals. So I thought if you took that to a behavioural level, what would happen if the animals did cooperate? Mind you, they still eat each other! There's nothing sentimental about this."

## POSTSCRIPT

Subtitled "a true story waiting to happen", *2007* was published in 2001 by Hodder Headline Australia. Obviously, 2007 is long past and the animals didn't put their collective paws, hooves, flippers or whatever down and try to get we humans to stop thrusting our shared planet into the abyss of environmental catastrophe. But that's the thing about speculative literature – it can only speculate. Those environmental catastrophes have steadily become the norm, yet we still kowtow to the coal, oil and gas companies who make their millions without a thought for the consequences of their activities.

Back in 1993, comparative psychologist David Smith published a novel titled *Freeze Frame* (Penguin), enacted across four continents in exhilarating Ken Follett thriller style, bringing together a cast of players from Greenpeace, the American NBC News, the French Secret Service and a secret cartel of capitalists based in the Amazonian city of Manaus, the latter somehow involved in subverting the idea of establishing Antarctica as an inviolable World Park within which exploitation of its potential mineral and other wealth would be against international law. A ripping yarn without an ounce of preaching presented with a certain balance of viewpoints and yet with enough factual material to get the reader thinking about what is actually at stake. I reviewed it at the time for Melbourne-based music magazine *Juke*.

English novelist and archaeologist Elisabeth Ayrton published a truly extraordinary and intriguing novel titled *Day Eight* (Hutchinson) in 1978 that turns on an idea similar in some ways to that of Williams without the humour, with the central characters experiencing various animals living in the plains, jungles and mountains of Kenya, a country through which she had travelled extensively, suddenly exhibiting very unusual behaviours. Is this a consequence of man's interference with the natural balance of things?

A very, very short list, but I would urge everyone to seek out these books.

## STORIES OF NATIVE AMERICA'S 500 NATIONS
Jack Leustig talks about his documentary series, *500 Nations*.

When Christopher Columbus bumped into what he thought were the Spice Islands (essentially the islands now known as Indonesia) in 1492, thereby "discovering" the North America continent, there are estimated to have been some 20 million people already living there, at least two million of them inhabiting the area that would become the United States of America.

From the ice-bound northern reaches of what became Alaska to the southern border of Guatemala and out into the islands of the Caribbean, named for the ethnic group, Carib, so named by Columbus, actually the Kalinago, that inhabited the island he happened upon, some 500 "nations" existed, some as "primitive" as the hunter-gatherers Captain James Cook would stumble upon 288 years later when he skirted along the east coast of what became Australia, and as complex as anything that had developed in Ancient Egypt. Yet these indigenous societies and cultures were as summarily dismissed by the Europeans who encountered them as were Australia's. In fact, as we know, those Australian indigenous societies were dismissed completely, a state of Terra Nullius being pronounced that "justified" a necessary colonisation by the English.

There are still a vast number of Americans who are totally unaware of the extraordinary richness and diversity of pre-Columbian indigenous cultures, and in part that was one of the reasons why filmmaker Jack Leustig decided he should do something about it. The result was an extraordinary eight-part documentary series titled *500 Nations: The Story of the Native Americans*.

"I'd been working in feature films in Hollywood for some time and was pretty burnt out in 1987," he explains. "So I decided to take a motorcycle trip and spent two months camping in Indian ruins in the American Southwest, and I realised – I was of course writing, and that's what it was about, searching for something – it wasn't originally about Indian people; I was looking for myself of course – but in the process, as I was looking at these amazing ruins and reflected on the fact that I had heard *nothing* about them in my education. I was just infused with the purpose, if I could find the opportunity, of trying to express a story that said something about the people that were here before us."

At the beginning of the 20th century, a remarkable pioneering photographer named Edward S. Curtis set himself the task of documenting what he saw as a traditional body of indigenous cultures that would soon disappear. It was a task that consumed some 30 years of his life and resulted in 20 volumes, 40,000 photographs, 10,000 recordings and even a full-length ethnographic feature film.

"The first thing I did," Leustig continues, "was I put together a research team and we did a single-line document of over a thousand pages in which were outlined the hundreds of stories we gathered. It was from those that we narrowed it down to the twenty or so stories that we featured in the series. I thereby gained some perspective on selecting events that were particularly important as well as telling the stories of heroic individuals that just had to covered, and got it down to what was manageable within an eight-hour film."

Leustig chose, as points of entry, the moments of "first contact" with Europeans, which also allowed him to follow a linear historical timeline from 1492 through to the turn of the 20th century.

"There is so much that one can explore. This is not even the tip of the iceberg. These are just a few flakes of snow. What we hope we've done is tell the larger reality of what happened between cultures."

Across the eight films, the stories are presented through a mix of drawings and paintings from the period, images of artefacts, location shots, computer animations, interviews, voiceovers and a selection of the photographs of Curtis and others. Those stories told include that of Aztec emperor Motecuhzoma, who, when the Spanish conquistador Hernán Cortés came to what is now Mexico, commanded an army of more than 200,000 men armed with steel and gunpowder, was met by people armed with wood and stone; Wahunsonacock, leader of the Powhatan Confederacy of 30 nations, who was betrayed by the colonists of Jamestown; Chief Joseph, leader of the Nez Perce nation of the interior Pacific northwest, and, of course, the Ndendahe Apache leader known as Geronimo. The series begins and ends, however, with the massacre of a peaceful band of Sioux who were camped at a place called Wounded Knee."

"The value of the film for me," Leustig points out, "is that it shows there *is* hope, there is a feeling that in whatever form the culture struggles into the future, the Indian people of North America *will* retain an identity and *will* survive into the future. The words of those people who speak in the film who are bridging themselves with the future I find very moving."

## POSTSCRIPT:

I can't remember if this ever ran in the magazine for which it was written, *The Drum Media*, but I have to admit I never saw the series. I was probably too consumed with a young family, a fulltime job that demanded as much after-work work as my nominated daytime hours – and of course my gigs. But I did get a copy of the accompanying book, *500 Nations: An Illustrated History of North American Indians*, by Alvin M. Josephy Jr, published by Pimlico, which I treasure. Again, this stuff is important – or at least I feel it is. Like every aspiring teacher, all I can do is put it out there.

While there are no accurate figures for the number of indigenous Australians who were living in "Terra Nullius" when Cook sailed passed – estimates vary wildly between 300,000 and 950,000 – there were certainly around 260 distinct language groups, which could be extrapolated as equating to a similar number of tribal groups or "nations". It looks like we in need of a Jack Leustig to document *their* story.

# JOHN TRUDELL: 1947-2015

The news bulletin read: "At 1.30am, February 12, 1979 a fire ripped through the house of Arthur Manning and his family. Manning was a member of the Duck Valley Tribal Council who was actively working for Shoshone-Paiute treaty rights."

They never did find the culprits behind the suspicious fire that claimed the lives of the pregnant wife, three children and mother-in-law of Native American activist John Trudell, out there on the Shoshone-Paiute Tribes Duck Valley Indian Reservation in Nevada. Manning, his father-in-law survived. While nothing was ever proved, Trudell was in no doubt that the US federal government and more specifically the FBI was behind the tragedy, and their aim had been to silence him. Only the day before, he had set fire to a US flag on the steps of the FBI building in Washington DC during a protest over the treatment of Native Americans. The tragedy proved a turning point for Trudell – from that day on, he found himself compelled to express his feelings through poetry.

Born into the Santee Sioux Nation February 15, 1946, and dropping out of school at 17, John Trudell had signed up with the US Navy in 1963 and saw active duty in Vietnam before leaving the service four years later. He soon got involved in Native American activism and having studied radio broadcasting after leaving the Navy, from November 1969 to June 1971 he became spokesperson for the Indians of All Tribes occupation of the decommissioned prison island in San Francisco Bay known as Alcatraz, and then, basing himself in Minneapolis from 1973 to 1979, Trudell served as Chairman of the American Indian Movement (AIM). The loss of his family was naturally a devastating blow, something he never really got over it. It would inform everything that followed in his quietly prolific career.

Trudell was 36 when he finally got around to recording his first album of spoken-word, *Tribal Voice*, to the

285

accompaniment of traditional Native American music, released independently in 1982. By then he'd met singer-songwriter Jackson Browne, himself an activist, who encouraged him to explore the possibilities of putting his poetry to music. Trudell recorded his second album, 1986's *AKA Graffiti Man*, with fellow Native American, guitarist Jesse Ed Davis, a member of the Kiowa nation. The album would be re-recorded and re-issued in 1992. In 1988, Trudell was invited to tour the US as supporting artist on Midnight Oil's *From Diesel and Dust to the Big Mountain* world tour. In 1993, Peter Gabriel invited him to be a part of that year's WOMAD tour.

The album for which Trudell will probably be best remembered however is his 1994 release, *Johnny Damas and Me*. Like all his work, the album is a blend of rock, blues, Native American melodies and rhythms, socio-political/protest lyrics and poetry. "Half of everything is the female spirit and energy," he said of the album at the time. "I wanted to express some of that."

Along the way Trudell also published three books of poetry and a collection of his album lyrics, *Lines From A Mined Mind*. He also set up the Hempstead Project Heart (Hemp Energies Alternative Resource Technologies), an initiative aimed at raising awareness of the many uses of hemp designed to help contribute to a sustainable "green economy" in the US. Trudell even did a bit of acting, appearing in three feature films – Michael Apted's 1992 thriller, *Thunderheart*, alongside Val Kilmer; 1995's *On Deadly Ground*, which starred Steven Seagal, and 1998's *Smoke Signals* – while in 2005, he was himself the subject of a documentary made by filmmaker Heather Rae titled simply *Trudell*, in which a declassified FBI memo included in the 17,000-page dossier the agency had compiled on him was read, noting that "He is extremely eloquent, therefore extremely dangerous." Trudell released his 14th and, as it turned out final album, *Wazi's Dream*, with his band Bad Dogs, only months before he finally succumbed to cancer December 8, 2015, aged 69.

*"Historically speaking, we went from being Indians to pagans to savages to hostiles to militants to activists to Native Americans. It's five hundred years later and they can't see us. We are still invisible."* John Trudell.

## POSTSCRIPT:

I had the privilege of interviewing Trudell, albeit by phone, around the time of his tour supporting Midnight Oil as Graffiti Man. I wish I still had the tape. You never, it might be buried in the library somewhere. Doing the research for the interview and learning of what happened to his wife and children at the hands of the FBI I was shattered. I can't remember if the feature based on the interview ever ran. Again, if it did, it'll be in the stacks of *Drum Media* issues in the library. If I find it, I'll add it to a second edition of this collection if there's enough interest. I only wish I could have done more for his music and his cause. Again, seek out his music for yourself. It's worth the effort.

## ACKNOWLEDGEMENTS

*"The Black"* was originally published in *InPrint*, Vol. 4, No. 2, September 1980, pp. 30-7. Reprinted in *Greek Voices in Australia: A Tradition of Prose, Poetry and Drama*, Edited by George Kanarakis, Australian National University Press, 1987, pp. 493-501 (minus, for some reason, the last five paragraphs) and *The Strength of Tradition: Stories of the Immigrant Presence in Australia, 1970-81*, Edited by RF Holt, University of Queensland Press, 1983, pp. 240-252.

*Avenue of Remembrance, Ballarat* was published in *Access Magazine* No. 9, February/March 1983, p. 5

*Land, Rights and Learning*, originally published in *Access Magazine* No. 15, February/March 1984, p. 27; abridged version published in *Education News*, Vol. 19, No. 3, May 1985, p. 36

*War Games*, originally published in *Brave New Word*, Issue No. 5, pp. 59-64. Reprinted in *A Bundle of Yarns*, Australian short stories compiled by Michael Kavanagh, Oxford University Press, 1986, pp. 83-89

*For The Children* was published in Greek-Australian Monthly Magazine *To Neo*, July 1986, pp. 88-90

*Hellenising* Terra Australia*: the Greek factor in redefining the Australian character*, originally published in *Journal of the Royal Australian Historical Society*, Vol. 73, Part 4, April 1988, pp. 313-320

*Snapshot* was first published in Greek-Australian magazine *The Monthly Chronicle*, October/November 1995, p. 14; reprinted in *The Drum Media*, September 1, 1998, p. 58

*Animal Crackers*, a review of *Last Chance To See*, Douglas

Adams with Mark Carwardine, *Juke* magazine, 4/4/92, p. 22

*Wisdom of the Elders* was originally published in *The Scholastic Times*, June 1992, p. 12

*Rediscovering the Greek Surreal*, A review of *The Mule's Foal*, by Fotini Epanomitis (Allen & Unwin), originally published in *Overland*, No. 132, 1993, pp. 84-5

*Conlon in the Name of Justice*, originally published in *The Drum Media*, March 8, 1994, p. 51

*Tribes And Bands*, a review of Neil Murray's *Sing For Me, Countryman*, originally published in *Overland*, #144, 1996, pp. 88-9

*Footprints*, originally published in *Overland*, No. 149, 1997, p. 24

*The Road to Smithfield Hostel*, a review of *Alien to Citizen: Settling Migrants in Australia, 1945-75*, by Anna-Mari Jordens (Allen & Unwin), originally published in *Overland*, No. 151, 1998, pp. 103-5

*Y1K To Y2K: A Thousand Years in a Thousand Words (or Thereabouts)* published in *The Drum Media*, December 21, 1999, p. 54

*The Wound* review originally published in *The Drum Media*, March 23, 1999. My interview with Zoe Carides appeared on page 59 of the March 16, 1999 issue.

*Harry's War, Our Peace*, originally published in *The Drum Media*, April 18, 2000, p. 67

*The Harm Inside Your Mind*, the Stephanie Luke interview

originally published in *The Drum Media*, October 10, 2000, p. 44, the *Harm* book review originally published in *Overland* #163, Winter 2001, pp. 118-9

*2007: What if the animals got really grumpy?*, originally published in *The Drum Media*, January 29, 2002, p. 58

Reviews of Fred Smith's *The Dust of Uruzgan*, originally published in *Rhythms*, September-October 2016, p. 99 and *Quadrant*, July-August 2017, p. 104, respectively

*Living by the Book: Ramblings of a Bibliophile* was originally published in *Quadrant*, April 2018, pp. 87-8

*When Ginger Met Lolita*, originally published in *Quadrant*, December 2018, pp. 82-4

John Trudell's obituary was first published by *Rhythms* magazine in its additional online website content

Review of Fred Smith's *The Sparrows of Kabul*, under the title *Humanity Amid The Shambles*, was published in *Quadrant*, March 2024, p.80-4

An ancient African proverb states that
"When an old man dies, a library burns to the ground."
So it will be with us all,
but some of us try nonetheless to preserve a few pages of our
all too brief lives that they might help build someone else's
library.

## About the Author

Michael George Smith (or just plain Michael Smith for much of his non-literary career) has been a professional musician since 1970 and a professional writer since 1977, when he was invited to contribute a column on bass playing for a small independent Sydney-based musicians' magazine. As a musician who still plays by ear and with no music theory to fall back on, he somehow still managed to not only fulfil his first assignment and follow it with a further five but, over the next 40-odd years, translated that first stumbling effort into a second career – between gigs – from freelancing to the position of Associate/Contributing Editor for a Sydney-based weekly music, arts and entertainment street paper *The Drum Media/The Music* for 25 years, while also contributing literary book reviews, socio-political essays and the very occasional short story to journals as diverse as *Quadrant, Overland* and even *The Journal of the Royal Australian Historical Society*. He's performed and recorded with a variety of bands in a variety of genres, from glam pop to prog rock to surf instrumental to blues rock, appeared on a few Australian TV shows including *Countdown*, MC'd concerts and festivals, done a handful of spoken-word performances and judged rather too many band competitions for his own good.

He also holds a BA with majors in English/American Literature and Geography, an MA in English Literature from the University of New South Wales and another in Studies of 20th Century American Civilisation from the same university.

Smith lives in Katoomba, NSW, with his partner Jane, a cat and a ridiculous amount and variety of wood products covered in print.

"Each generation defines the normal by what it experiences." David Attenborough, at the age of 94, writing in his 2020 book, *A Life on Our Planet: My Witness Statement and a Vision for the Future* (Witness Books/Penguin).

www.ingramcontent.com/pod-product-compliance
Lightning Source LLC
Chambersburg PA
CBHW070848260626
47170CB00007B/2544